"What my son needs, Ms. Guiness, is none of your concern," Richard said coldly.

"You're wrong, Mr. Keaton. My job is to look after Andrew. And do you know what I see? I see a scared little boy who idolizes his father, and a father who is intent on ignoring his son. If you—"

Richard's eyes narrowed, and he interrupted her, his voice more chilling than ever. "Don't meddle in things you know nothing about."

"How can I know anything, when you tell me nothing?"

The remark hung in the air, filling the library with angry tension. Her cheeks flushed and her chest heaved. Abruptly their gazes locked, and the air between them heated several degrees.

Suddenly he spoke, his voice harsh and thick with some unknown emotion. "If you want to run, Ms. Guiness, you'd better do it now. Or I won't be held responsible for the consequences...."

Dear Reader,

Welcome once again to a month of excitingly romantic reading from Silhouette Intimate Moments. We have all sorts of goodies for you, including the final installment of one miniseries and the first book of another. That final installment is *MacDougall's Darling,* the story of the last of The Men of Midnight, Emilie Richards's latest trilogy. The promised first installment is Alicia Scott's *At the Midnight Hour,* beginning her family-themed miniseries, The Guiness Gang. And don't forget *The Cowboy and the Cossack,* the second book of Merline Lovelace's Code Name: Danger miniseries.

There's another special treat this month, too: *The Bachelor Party,* by Paula Detmer Riggs. For those of you who have been following the Always a Bridesmaid! continuity series from line to line, here is the awaited Intimate Moments chapter. And next month, check out Silhouette Shadows!

Finish off the month with new books by Jo Leigh and Ingrid Weaver. And then come back next month and every month for more romance, Intimate Moments style.

Enjoy!

Yours,

Leslie Wainger
Senior Editor and Editorial Coordinator

Please address questions and book requests to:
Silhouette Reader Service
U.S.: 3010 Walden Ave., P.O. Box 1325, Buffalo, NY 14269
Canadian: P.O. Box 609, Fort Erie, Ont. L2A 5X3

AT THE MIDNIGHT HOUR

ALICIA SCOTT

Silhouette®
INTIMATE™MOMENTS®
Published by Silhouette Books
America's Publisher of Contemporary Romance

SILHOUETTE BOOKS

ISBN 0-373-07658-4

AT THE MIDNIGHT HOUR

Printed in U.S.A.

Books by Alicia Scott

Silhouette Intimate Moments

Walking After Midnight #466
Shadow's Flame #546
Waking Nightmare #586
At the Midnight Hour #658

ALICIA SCOTT

is thrilled that her dream of being published has finally come true. Born in Hawaii but now a resident of Massachusetts, she recently graduated from college and is now working for a management consulting firm.

She has a deep appreciation for different peoples and cultures. And while reading and writing romances is one of her favorite hobbies, she also enjoys traveling and just talking to people—so much so that in her junior year of high school she entered a contest for impromptu speaking and won eighth in the nation!

Lucky enough to have journeyed to exotic locales such as Venezuela, Ecuador and Mexico, she intends on using them all in future books. Alicia brings her natural enthusiasm for life to her stories, and believes that the power of love can conquer *anything* as long as one's faith is strong enough.

To Nancy, for all those long phone calls
that showed me the way.
Special thanks to Rob Baumgartner for his knowledge
of capacitors, and particularly his patience in explaining
them again and again and again.

Prologue

Thick black clouds teamed against the late-night sky, choking out even the brightest star as they rolled and mushroomed in early-fall fury. Thunder boomed in deep bass rage, but the thick stone walls of the hundred-year-old mansion didn't even tremble. They'd stood up to storms before. They'd stood the test of time through far, far worse.

With one last gasp, the sky exploded into a downpour. Rain pounded down, until the twisted cypress trees bent beneath the onslaught and appeared to weep their submission. The mansion's stone walls endured the rain, its windows staring out into the night like the eyes of a condemned man, stoic and unyielding to the last. The walls had been built by Keaton hands and the stories they'd heard had already passed on to legend. The violence they'd seen was already myth.

On these dark nights, no one in the Stamford, Connecticut, community dared look up at the stone house on the hill. No one wanted to see the ivy-choked walls or gnarled towers, especially by the fiery crack of the lightning. No one wanted to know if a light still shone in that one left-hand tower window.

The townspeople whispered that *he* worked there, slaving all night in the mausoleum comfort of his wealth, as if, in his lab, he could find redemption for his crime. As if, in his lab, high up in the tower, he would no longer hear the sound of his name wrung from her lips as the beautiful blond angel who had been his wife plunged to her death from the opposite tower.

Sitting beside the faint remains of a dying fire, the man in question didn't even notice the boom of the thunder that was so close the library window trembled. Long ago, he'd learned to block out most things, including the whispers of the people he'd once called friends. He had little use anymore for their opinions, and he had even less use for the anger of the night. It was the darkness within that consumed him.

Absently, he swirled the glass of brandy in his hands. Then he raised the crystal to his lips for one last burning drink.

Five years. Five long years. And suddenly the child was coming home. Alycia's victory would now be complete.

His face twisted in the dim light, his icy blue eyes harsh and grim. Unable to take it anymore, he rose from the leather chair and began to pace the room with the restlessness of a caged panther.

He hated this house, he thought suddenly. To hell with the fact that he was fourth-generation Keaton and Keatons had always lived in this damn house. To hell with the fact that he'd been raised here all his life, that it was his birthright and his home.

There was nothing homely about this sprawling, overgrown mansion. There were no faint odors of apple pie, no lingering traces of laughter in the halls. Instead, the structure was an overgrown beast, filled with overbearing walnut wood, stifling oil paintings and dark-woven tapestries. Its long halls were choked with the rancid odor of decaying memories, while the vaulted ceilings still rang with the bitter screams of past rage.

And even after all these years, he could still turn a corner in the long, winding corridors and catch the faint scent of her perfume. On the late, late nights, when he was hunched over his computer in his lab, he swore he could still hear the sound of her mocking laughter.

He should have left a long time ago, he thought darkly. Gotten out while he could. But he hadn't. And, he acknowledged brutally, he never would.

Because somewhere in these dark halls, Alycia's secrets still lingered. Somewhere in all the twisted staircases and cavernous rooms, the final answer to all his questions lay waiting. The house itself never told its secrets, but perhaps the answers lay buried in the diary he knew she'd kept with such malicious pleasure. So far, however, in all of the sleepless nights of the past five years, he'd never once found any clues to the questions that haunted him.

Alycia would have been proud.

He turned sharply, his face growing dark and the muscle in his jaw clenching with brutal strength.

He didn't want the child back, he thought harshly. He didn't want the constant reminder, day in, day out, of Alycia and all her tormenting games. Besides, he was a scientist, the tenth sharpest mind in the country. He didn't know anything about children. He was a man comfortable only with electrodes, circuitry and computers. He'd taught himself to read when he was just two years old. He'd memorized the phone book one week when he was three. By the age of four, he'd taken apart the TV and put it back together again.

He wasn't *normal*. He was the fourth generation in a family known for its money rather than its brains, and he had somehow been born a genius. How they'd stared at him for that, they had grown uncomfortable when he'd entered the room.

But they had needed him for his genius later. The plane crash that had abruptly killed his parents when he was just sixteen years old had left a huge estate to manage, complex finances to untangle. Richard was the only one who could do it. After all, he had already been taking care of most of the business matters since he'd turned fourteen. Surely he could take care of everything, and his younger brother, Blaine, as well.

Still, there had been whispers, whispers that had gone on for as long as he could remember: "That kid's not right." "He's just not normal."

They were right, he thought darkly. He wasn't normal, had never been normal.

Just ask Alycia.

He tried to remember now, maybe because he'd had two glasses of brandy, what he'd seen in her in the beginning. It had been seven years ago that they'd met. Seven long years ago.

She had been the blond angel, debuting on the Connecticut social scene. She'd had delicate, porcelain features, with long flaxen hair and the bluest eyes. Even her laugh had been light and musical, so much so that she'd seemed almost not of this world. When she stepped into a room, conversations would die, and men and women alike would stare. She'd been that beautiful.

The minute he'd seen her, he'd wanted her. For three months, he'd virtually forsaken his work. For three months, he'd recited poetry to her and delivered roses. He had pursued her with all the buried passion of a recluse's lonely heart.

He'd won in the end. With his family's name and immense fortune, the Wynstons had been only too happy to pair him up with their only daughter. They had even been willing to overlook his dark features and formidable build, as well as his *unnatural* abilities.

That had been then.

What had Alycia's parents called him at the funeral? *Devil's spawn. Lucifer's own.* They'd hustled Andrew away as soon as the services ended, not wanting the child to be contaminated even one minute more by his father's menacing presence.

They'd taken the boy, telling Richard they would never let the man who had killed their daughter have their only grandchild, as well. And he'd let them take Andrew, because he'd known the truth.

Mr. Wynston had even managed to look him straight in the eye, pointing one gnarled, bony finger. "You may have gotten away with destroying our Alycia, you...you...beast. But you'll never have our grandson as well."

All his life, Richard had only really loved two things. And the first one had destroyed them both.

Even now, however, he could remember the faint impressions of the past—the smell of baby powder, tucking the child in at night and reading sweet stories until Andrew's huge blue eyes fell, heavy with sleep. Playing patty-cake. Playing the silly airplane game to entice him to eat. The late nights, pacing the floorboards back and forth while Andrew screamed in colicky discontent. And finally, at long last, rocking him to peaceful sleep.

Andrew wasn't a baby anymore, damn it. He was six years old. Richard didn't know anything about six-year-olds. It wasn't as if there was any choice in the matter, however. Mr. and Mrs. Wynston had died, each succumbing to a heart attack within two weeks of each other. God knows, on their deathbeds they had probably still cursed his name and found him to blame.

That they had never found enough evidence to have him arrested for their daughter's murder was probably their last regret. They'd had to settle for a public hanging of his innocence, instead. Now, he had only to appear outside to see the thin-lipped faces and hear the stabbing whispers. "Murderer... killer. They would've gotten him if only he wasn't so rich."

He whirled sharply, hating the restlessness that ate at his gut.

"Enough," he roared out loud. He whirled away, grabbed his brandy glass and swallowed the last burning gulp. Then he hurled the one-hundred-fifty-year-old crystal into the fire, and grimaced at the sound of its crashing.

The child was coming home. There was nothing he could do about it. Six-year-old Andrew with his mother's face, his mother's hair, his mother's eyes. In a matter of days, he would be here.

Richard would hire a nanny, and the nanny would watch the child. It would be as simple as that. Richard would still be free to work up in his tower. He could still keep his long hours, still maintain his sleepless nights. He wouldn't have to see the child, wouldn't have to be around him at all.

It would be better. For both of them, it would be better.

But then, abruptly, the anger passed, leaving him alone in the cold library with his bleak ice-blue eyes.

After all these years, he wished the walls of his prison could talk. After all these years, he wished he could get on with his life once and for all. But Alycia had died, and in doing so, she had indeed won the vicious game she'd played with him, with everyone. Now he would never know the answer to the doubts that plagued him so. Now he would never know the truth.

Alycia had fallen from the right-hand tower five years ago. Or rather, she'd been pushed. There were no answers to all the questions everyone had—the police had never concluded their investigation, and had let him go due only to the lack of any concrete evidence against him. They had never even tried to find any other suspects, the jealous husband the easiest man to pursue.

So Alycia had died and everyone thought he'd killed her. It was better to just let it all go.

And so he left the cold comfort of the library, walking to the long, curving staircase that led up to his lab in the left-hand tower. Climbing to the turret, he could hear the sound of the pouring rain, beating upon the slate roof. He could hear the sound of the wind, whipping harshly through the twisted branches of the cypress trees.

But even then, inside the dark recesses of his memory, he could swear he heard her last, dying scream.

Chapter 1

Dusk was already falling by the time the lone cab pulled to at the bottom of the hill. In the back seat a woman ran a tired hand through the tousled mess of her long brown hair. She'd been traveling all day, train station to train station, waiting, boarding, waiting. But now she was here, wherever that was.

All at once she could feel the tightness in her stomach, her nerves were knotting themselves into one ferocious ball. She took a deep breath, and forced herself to look out the window.

She had to look up a long way to see it, the house was perched so far up the hill. There it stood, like a lone sentinel, a dark, watchful eye in a deepening night. Huge, gray, cold. She'd never been a weak woman, four older brothers just didn't allow it. But looking at the house now, she felt the first tremble of genuine fear run along her spine like ice.

She forced herself to take another deep breath. It was too late for second thoughts. The cab had stopped and the driver was already standing in front of her door, holding it open for her.

You wanted a new life, Elizabeth, a little voice inside her whispered. *Now here it is.*

But looking at the hulking house on the hill, she didn't feel so eager anymore—she was feeling very scared and very small town. She wasn't prepared enough, she thought frantically. Classes weren't enough for all of this, regardless of how good the agency. Her whole life had been lived in one little town, where she'd lived in the same house with four brothers. She'd gone to the local high school, the local college. She had even married her childhood friend and high school sweetheart.

Holding his head on her lap, she watched the blood dripping down. Blood was everywhere . . .

"That's thirty-five dollars, ma'am." The cabdriver's words interrupted her thoughts. Feeling somewhat numb, she fumbled for the money in her purse, handing it to the man with slightly trembling hands. He accepted it, then swung her single bag out of the trunk.

To tell the truth, he would be more than a little glad to drive away. The house disturbed him, sitting on the hill like that in the faint light. It just didn't look right. Wasn't that where the guy who'd bumped off his wife lived? Yeah, that's right.

The cabbie looked at the silent girl one last time, feeling torn—she really was an innocent-looking thing, and with all that tumbling hair . . . He scratched his grizzled beard.

"You sure you want to be here?" he asked at last.

It took her a moment to answer. When she did, it was with a tremulous smile that made even his old heart turn.

"Yes, sir," she replied softly, forcing her chin higher, though her cheeks were pale. "I'm the new nanny."

He lingered one last moment. She was a pretty girl, and her voice carried that soft Southern lilt that soothed a man's nerves. Did she know what she was getting herself into? But then, with a last awkward shrug of his big shoulders, he climbed back into his cab. It was none of his business. He shifted the cab into gear and drove away.

Alone now, Elizabeth Guiness looked through the iron gates to the stone-carved mansion on the hill. With a resolute squaring of her shoulders, she picked up her bag and trudged forward. It was time for new beginnings.

She pressed the buzzer on the small intercom next to the gate. There was a brief pause, then a sharp feminine voice barked, "What?"

Momentarily taken aback, she faltered. "Hello? Hello, my name is Elizabeth Guiness, ma'am," she began politely. "I'm the new nanny."

There was a long pause. Then, silently in the darkness, the thick wrought-iron gate slowly rolled back. She hesitated for a moment, but it clearly seemed to be intended as a welcome. So setting her slight uneasiness aside, she raised one foot and planted it squarely forward onto the overgrown driveway that snaked out in front of her. Nothing happened, so, gripping her bags more firmly, she continued forward. Behind her, the gates slid quietly shut.

She kept her eyes resolutely on the house looming ahead. It was almost completely dark now; she could only see the faint outline of a huge main structure with twin towers, and behind them, two long sprawling extensions of the original structure. It was huge, and impressive on the hill. Unfortunately, it also reminded her of a mausoleum.

And it looked very, very dark.

Only two lights offered a dim welcome. There was one downstairs—probably a main room—and one high up in the left tower. Everything else was completely black. She hesitated for a moment, coming to a stop on the driveway. Maybe she'd arrived too late in the evening? Perhaps it would be better to go to some hotel for the night, then present herself first thing in the morning. Unsure now, she turned around to glance back down the hill. The darkness had closed in completely, obliterating the gate and swallowing the rest of the path. In spite of herself, she shivered in the cooling night. No, going back down definitely didn't look too appealing. She would just have to continue.

Adjusting her grip on the bag, she began walking once more. She could just make out the shapes of twisted trees growing on the periphery of the circle of the driveway. Long thin branches extended in front of the dim light of the bottom window. The branches looked like hands clutching at the sky....

She shook away the notion immediately, but not before her uneasiness grew tenfold.

Finally, she came to the top of the small circular driveway. She set down her luggage briefly, taking a moment to wipe the palms of her hands on her overcoat. One more deep breath to steady the nerves. One last hand through her hair, and a brief smoothing of her deep blue skirt. Then, angling her chin in determination, she lifted the heavy brass knocker and let it fall upon the thick wood.

In the distance she could hear the sound echoing through the entranceway. *Echoing?*

The door cracked open.

"*You're* the new nanny?" the same sharp voice from the intercom rang out. This time, however, Elizabeth could see that the voice belonged to a stout, graying maid in a starched black uniform. Her pinched face, peering from around the door, matched her voice.

"Yes," Liz replied, trying to sound as friendly as possible. She stuck out her hand, hoping the other woman wouldn't notice the quiver. "Elizabeth Guiness, pleased to meet you."

But the other woman only frowned at her through narrowed eyes. "Matilda Pram," she said abruptly, her voice flat with the Northern curtness Liz was still becoming accustomed to. "I'm the head housekeeper." Mrs. Pram added extra emphasis to the last two words, clearly defining her high status. Liz nodded, her hand dropping unanswered to her side. Feeling her nervousness grow, she attempted a small, open smile.

It also went unreturned.

Definitely uncomfortable now, she had no other option but to proceed. So, picking up her bag, she stepped inside. The heels of her brown boots rang out clearly on the hardwood floors as she advanced to the middle of the room, bag clutched tightly in her hands. The room was immense, the vaulted ceiling rising high above her, while on either side of her broad staircases swept up to the second floor balconies. Dim light scattered from the drooping crystals of a poorly lit chandelier. It threw the walls into deep shadows haunted by the dark outlines of a huge oil painting.

The sheer size of everything was overwhelming. It was like being in a museum, she thought vaguely, a huge, badly lit museum. Mrs. Pram just stood in the doorway, watching her with unfriendly eyes.

What was she supposed to do now? Where was the section in the agency handbook that dealt with this? Swallowing hard, she looked around once more. Toward the right, she could see a long tunnel-looking passage that must lead to the right-hand side of the house. A similar hallway was on the left. Directly in front of her rose the main wall, which towered up the entire three stories. In the middle sat an immense oil painting of what appeared to be some sort of religious scene. But the colors were dark, just as the entranceway was dark. Everything was dark.

And she was miserable.

Then she became aware of the man standing on the left-hand stairs.

He was at the top, his face lost in the shadows, but she could make out what appeared to be black leather shoes and dark gray slacks.

"Mr. Keaton?" she ventured. Though spoken in a whisper, the name seemed to reverberate through the vaulted ceilings like a roar.

There was no immediate reply, but abruptly, the man began walking down the steps.

"Miss Guiness?" his deep voice responded. He must have known something she didn't for his low baritone barely bounced off the walls.

She nodded, starting to feel the first glimmer of hope. He would have to be more helpful than Mrs. Pram. "Yes, sir," she said. "I'm the new nanny."

"Are you, indeed?" he said, the words more like a soft aside.

As he came to the bottom step, the rest of him fell under the scattered light of the entrance. He was a large man, she noted instantly. Tall and solidly built, even under the elegant lines of his white shirt and gray slacks. But it wasn't so much the man's size, that made her want to lean back, as the man himself.

He stood with a kind of complete self-possession very few men could master. His bearing was rigidly straight, giving the appearance of being coldly withdrawn, from the stiffness of his spine to the intense scrutiny of his eyes. Right at the moment, those pale blue eyes were raking her up and down with an indifference that made her shiver. People said that her brother Cagney could stare down the devil himself, but those people had clearly never met this man.

"You're too young," he said flatly.

For a full minute, she couldn't find her voice. She could only hear the litany of the little voice inside her head. *You're not ready for this, Liz. You're too small-town for this, Liz. This isn't what you'd been expecting.*

No, she'd been expecting someone a bit more...fatherly, she supposed. Not this harsh man with his lean face and powerful build. Taking a deep breath, she forced herself to speak.

"I know that, sir," she found herself saying in a slightly tremulous voice, her Southern accent growing thicker with her nervousness. "But, given the experiences of the last three nannies, the agency thought perhaps youth would be a better approach."

He didn't say anything, his eyes once more raking her with clinical scrutiny. It wasn't just that she looked young, he forced himself to acknowledge. It was the fact that she was so damn beautiful. Her eyes looked almost black in the dim light, deep midnight pools of uncertainty and doubt. Combined with the pale hue of her skin and the luxurious fall of her mahogany hair, it was enough to bring any red-blooded man to his knees.

But he wasn't a red-blooded man, he reminded himself unemotionally. He was a brilliant scientist, a workaholic inventor, a man who had already learned his lessons from a woman far more beautiful than innocent Miss Guiness.

Still, her beauty annoyed him. So did the traces of fear in her eyes.

"How old are you?" he asked, keeping his voice distant.

"Twenty-five," she answered.

"And you think," he asked crisply, "that you can control a six-year-old boy who has already gone through three nannies in three months?"

She nodded.

He turned away without further comment. "You may stay the night," he said over his shoulder. "In the morning, I will call the Bradford Agency and tell them to send over a more mature alternative. Miss Pram will show you to your room."

Already his broad form was disappearing down the dark hallway, his shoulders vanishing from sight. Without giving it another thought, she went after him, leaving her bag abandoned in the foyer.

"Wait," she called out desperately. The word seemed to echo down the hallway, but no reply came. Uncertain, but not willing to give up so quickly, she continued to follow. Her boots rang out on the wooden floor, and even through her overcoat she could feel a draft.

The darkness was so complete, wrapping around her, caressing her cheek...how could one hallway be so long? she thought dimly. And how could it be so cold?

Then, abruptly, a light glowed ahead on her left. Her steps quickened as she hastened toward it. There she found another room, a small den. In the center stood a large cherry desk and behind the desk sat the imposing Mr. Keaton, his back to her as his fingers danced over the keyboard of a sophisticated-looking computer.

She went straight to the desk, clearing her throat. He swung around, his eyes telling her he'd known she was there all along.

"Is there a problem?" he asked curtly.

"Yes, sir," she managed to get out before the words could die completely in her throat. He raised one eyebrow expectantly. She tried to continue, but it had been such a long day and the effects of being, for the first time, so far away from home suddenly hit her. She'd had such great hopes that this would be her calling, her answer to finding a new life after all those horrible months, when her old life had ended with a senseless shoot-out in front of the local movie theater. But now she was here and the house was so big and dark and her employer was so cold and dark, and...

She realized in that moment that she was probably going to cry.

Sitting behind his desk, Richard watched it all play out across her face. She really did seem to be a guileless creature, young and fresh and open. In time, she would learn the armor necessary to get through life, but now her face was an open book. And the pain he saw there tore at him.

Fiercely, he looked away, trying to focus his concentration on some abstract theorem until she got a grip on herself. Chaos theory, Richard. Cite examples of chaos theory.

It didn't work. He could still see her midnight eyes filled with pain, and he hated himself for his weakness.

He found himself motioning her to a chair. "Why don't you have a seat?" he said quietly, relieved that his voice was still dispassionate.

She nodded silently, not trusting herself to speak.

He gave her another minute to compose herself, then probed, "What is it you would like to say, Miss Guiness? And for God's sake, stop calling me sir."

The sting of tears was beginning to fade, and after another long moment, she had control again. She tilted her chin, willing herself to talk to this intimidating man. This was her new life. She had worked hard for this, prayed for this. Besides, she didn't know what else to do if it didn't work out.

"I realize that I'm young and all," she began, her words slow and not as firm as she would have liked, "but I've been thoroughly trained by the agency, and they have the utmost confidence in me, Mr. Keaton. You can be sure they wouldn't have sent me all the way here if they didn't think I was up to the challenge. The truth is, Mr. Keaton, your son is, well, precocious, for his age, sir. He's already caused the resignation of three wonderful and highly qualified nannies. As you can well imagine, nothing like that's ever happened before—"

"Miss Guiness," Richard interrupted. "I believe Andrew is well beyond precocious."

She nodded. Yes, in fact it would seem that Andrew was closer to unbridled genius. The boy had taken it upon himself to read all sorts of bizarre statistics, which he recited to anyone who would listen. As she recalled from the file, Andrew Philip Michael Keaton had asked the first nanny, Ms. Gregory, if she'd known that each day one hundred seventy-eight babies were conceived by artificial insemination. Ninety-six with donations from people they knew, and forty from anonymous sources. Andrew had then gone on to suggest that artificial insemination might be a suitable option for her. When Ms. Gregory had attempted to reprimand him, he had written a formal statement in his defense claiming first amendment rights, not to mention that punishing an individual for issuing true and factual information was unjust censorship. All this from a six-year-old child. Further incidents had followed until

Ms. Gregory, an older, very conservative woman, had resigned.

After that, it would appear that Andrew had become even
more literal. During Ms. Haverford's term, he'd refused to
bathe for five weeks on the grounds that, on average, one
American drowned in the bathtub a day. Then for three days he
had refused to eat because he'd read that ten people choked to
death a day in the United States alone. When the little monster
finally did start eating again, all he'd wanted was Coca-Cola
because nine hundred and fifty thousand Americans drank
Coke for breakfast, therefore he should, too. Shortly there-
after, Ms. Haverford had ruled him completely uncontrollable
and had resigned her position.

Then had come the interesting case of Mrs. Louis. A mid-
dle-aged wonder, Mrs. Louis was rumored to have an angel's
touch with children. Calling her in had been the agency's
equivalent of marshaling the cavalry. There was no child Mrs.
Louis couldn't tame. And, indeed, for the first few weeks, Mrs.
Louis had seemed to be doing well with Andrew. Then there'd
been a series of tense dark nights. Andrew kept having nightmares, and before long, Mrs. Louis was claiming nightmares,
too. One night, she'd simply run screaming out of the house,
wearing nothing but her long flannel nightgown. She had refused to go back in the Keaton household, even to retrieve her
clothes. When the agency had drilled her on her improper behavior, she had firmly stated there was nothing in the world that
would make her return to that house and that was all there was
to it. Finally, they had decided that Andrew had set something
up to terrify the woman. So they had given her a leave of absence and looked around for a new approach to the "Andrew
Dilemma." They'd decided upon Liz. She was young, fresh and
energetic. Perhaps she would have the imagination and cre-
ativity necessary to deal with such a difficult charge. Now, if
only she could convince the father of that.

"Mr. Keaton," she tried again, clearing her throat. "Andrew definitely is beyond precocious. That's precisely why I was
sent. I grew up with four older brothers and I've always been
around lots of children. I truly do love them, and maybe, just
maybe, I can think of a new approach for the little gu—for your

son, sir. And honestly," she rushed out suddenly with a fresh burst, "I really think I can do it. I am young, but I have lots of energy. I even have a degree in English, so perhaps I can keep up with Andrew's reading. Please, at least give me the chance."

Her eyes were so earnest in the shadows of the den. They were beguiling, drawing him in when he already knew better than to be such a fool. Still, it was hard to remember the lessons learned from Alycia, looking at such dark blue eyes and such an open face. Alycia's beauty had always possessed a fixed, almost porcelain nature—the type of beauty meant for show, not touch. This girl before him, however, exuded a natural freshness, a wholesomeness he hadn't seen in far too long. Her eyes seemed to care....

He frowned once again, steepling his hands beneath his chin as he contemplated this newest turn of events. He should just send her back. This arrangement would never work. So Andrew had already gone through three nannies in three months. Surely the agency could still do better than some mere girl. He didn't want someone this inexperienced. He didn't want someone this... beautiful, this feminine. No, the older, Mrs. Pram, variety was much better. Beauty, after all, had a way of blinding a man, confusing his senses. He wasn't interested in such distractions, and he'd already learned his lesson well enough by now. No, he liked his solitary life. He liked his work. He liked the emptiness that surrounded him.

She really did have such a fresh, earnest face. And those dark blue eyes. A man could dream of such eyes forever.

Perhaps he should at least give her a chance. Perhaps she really could tame the brilliant monster mascarading as his son. Perhaps...

He kept his voice neutral, unsteepling his hands from under his chin.

"All right," he said firmly, trying not to notice the brilliant light of relief that flashed in her eyes. For one instant, her face broke into such a wide smile that he couldn't remember his next sentence. Then abruptly she was leaning forward, doing her best to look calm and professional. It was disconcerting. "Let's just go over a few details," he said curtly, trying very hard to keep his stern composure. "As I'm sure you know from the agency, the position is full-time, with every other weekend off. You will be staying in the room adjoining Andrew's, and you will be expected to be available whenever he needs you. While it may seem very demanding, Andrew generally likes to keep to himself so it shouldn't be as difficult as it may sound. Do you understand?'' he said stiffly.

She nodded, her eyes still burning with a mixture of relief and earnest determination. He'd never had such a hard time keeping his concentration.

"Traditionally," he continued quietly, "Andrew likes to eat breakfast at seven, lunch at noon, and following the custom of his grandparents, tea at four. Dinner is served at eight. Currently, he has no tutor or formal schooling arrangements, although he has been studying on his own. I expect you'll find him filling most hours by reading. I will leave it to your own judgment as to how to manage his time. If there is ever an emergency, you can find me in the left-hand tower." His face grew very serious and grim. "That is where I work," he warned darkly. "And I am a very busy man. I do not want to be disturbed. Any unnecessary interruptions, Miss Guiness, and your stay with us will be a short one. Is that clear?''

His voice was so ominous, all she could do was nod with large round eyes. At least he was letting her stay, she consoled herself. But even then, she could feel a slight uneasiness in her stomach. This was her new life now, but it certainly wasn't going the way she'd imagined.

"Good," Richard was saying curtly. He turned away to buzz a small intercom on the corner of his desk. "Mrs. Pram will be here shortly to take you to your room and to introduce you to Andrew. Any last questions?''

She shook her head. She'd never met a man quite so efficient, quite so completely impersonal. No, this definitely wasn't how she'd pictured things. How could one man seem so distant? And what really went on behind those shuttered blue eyes of his?

For a moment, she was almost tempted to pry. For a moment, she wanted to stand up and touch his arm, just to see what he would do. She was accustomed to warm, caring people. She was accustomed to the easy laughter and casual interaction of her large family, the indulgence of her solid, teasing brothers. She didn't know how to handle a man so completely remote.

Did he ever laugh? Did he ever, even for a minute, let go of his stern composure? She found herself guessing no, but didn't think she had the courage to ask.

"Good," he was saying briskly from behind the desk. "Then that will be all."

With that, he turned away completely, his attention returning to the computer in front of him. Feeling rather awkward, she rose from the chair. She wrung her hands in front of her nervously. Should she just walk away? What?

Abruptly, one last question came to her. The dossier the agency had shown her contained a full bio on Mr. Keaton. But Mrs. Keaton was a blank, leaving Liz to believe they must have divorced, with Andrew obviously living with his wealthy father. But she had to know about visitation rights. Should she be prepared to turn over Andrew to Mrs. Keaton whenever the boy's mother came?

"Excuse me," Liz ventured. "I have just one last question."

Richard turned enough to pin her with one sharply raised eyebrow.

"When does Andrew's mother visit? Is it on the weekends when I'll be gone, or does she ever come during the week, or..."

She let the rest of her sentence trail off, waiting for an answer.

She never expected how dark and cold his face became.

"Alycia Keaton is dead," he told her flatly. "Do not speak of her again."

"Oh," she said, that one statement taking her completely off guard. Abruptly, she felt its impact in her gut. Her eyes began to swim, a dozen pictures suddenly flooding her mind. Nick, picking her up in his shiny black Mustang. Nick, standing beside her at the altar, his young face so serious and strong as he looked into her eyes. Nick, jumping in front of her at the first sound of the gunfire. Nick, down on the sidewalk, his blood on her hands as she tried so hard to make it stop. Nick, handsome, strong Nick dying in front of a stupid, small-town movie theater. Nick. Even here, she could still see his face. Why couldn't it have been her, instead?

The thought was so strong, it almost overwhelmed her. With sudden effort, she dragged it in. It had been a year now—she was supposed to be getting better. She was supposed to be moving on with her life.

Swallowing resolutely, she turned and headed for the door.

Behind her, Richard Keaton watched her with intense concentration. He'd looked up just in time to see that look in her eyes, that look of absolute pain, of agonizing emptiness. He knew the expression well, for so many times he had seen it in his own. But he'd never thought to see it in a girl so young.

Just for a moment, he wanted to call her back. Just for a moment, he wanted her to turn around so he could see her eyes, and see if what he'd seen had really been there at all.

But after all these years of the emptiness, he found he didn't know the words anymore. And so he watched her disappear into the long, dark hallway instead, listening to the echoing of her boots on the hardwood floor as she walked away.

He turned back to the computer screen. She was just the nanny, he reminded himself firmly. And he was a man who knew better.

Mrs. Pram led Liz through the dimly lit halls in silence. Every now and then, if Liz asked a direct question, she would receive a curt one- or two-word answer. In such a strained manner she managed to learn a little about the immense house where she would now live.

The main structure of the house had been built shortly after the Civil War, when the first Keaton made his fortune in steel factories. With all the additions made by future generations, the house now consisted of forty-five rooms, which divided into two wings to form a V-shaped structure. The west wing contained the rooms for the family, while the upper east wing had been designated for servants. The main structure of the house contained the formal rooms, including the entranceway, the kitchen and dining room, a study, two ballrooms and a grand library. Since the current Mr. Keaton wasn't given to entertaining, most of the main structure was closed up. The right-hand tower was also closed, though Mr. Keaton used the left one for his work. From what she'd seen so far, most of the house hadn't been redecorated since its inception.

Dark portrait oil paintings of kings and queens hung next to dim gas lamps in the hall. The doors all appeared to be made of thick, heavy wood, and the crimson Oriental runner down the center of the hall was becoming threadbare in the middle, its gold and black scrolls already faded from time and traffic.

All in all, it was a far cry from the cozy white ranch house where Liz and her brothers had grown up. But then, wasn't that what she'd been looking for? a voice in the back of her mind whispered. She had wanted to get away....

"Your quarters," Mrs. Pram was saying. The door was open, so Liz went ahead and walked in. It was a nice room, its new furniture and bright decor a startling contrast to the rest of the house. The hardwood floor was covered with a thick blue rug and the furniture was made of white-painted pine. A four-poster bed sat against the far wall with a blue and rose comforter, while a rose chaise rested not far from it. There was an armoire for her dresses, as well as a dresser against one wall and a chest of drawers at the end of the bed. It was a very nice room, looking as if it had come straight out of a magazine, she thought with surprise. And it was obvious that it had been redone very recently. Why? Surely no one had gone to all that trouble just for a nanny.

But she had no time to pursue the matter because to her right a door swung open abruptly and she found herself face-to-face with someone who could only be Andrew Philip Michael Keaton. He looked like an angel was her first thought. His hair glowed a flaxen blond under the lights and his skin maintained a pale translucence against the darkness of his navy blue suit. He must take after his mother, she thought, because except for his stiff bearing, he certainly didn't look like Mr. Keaton.

"You are the new nanny," the boy said, and even though it was impossible to clearly see his eyes behind his rather thick glasses, Liz could hear the accusation in his voice.

She took a deep breath and called all her training to mind. Everyone had always said she had a way with children. That was one of the reasons she'd decided to become a nanny when it had become clear to her she needed to get away if she ever wanted to get on with her life. Now, of course, was the moment of truth.

Kneeling so she would be on eye level with him, she extended an easy hand and a friendly smile. "Yes, I am," she said slowly, her drawl evident. "I'm Elizabeth, but you can call me Liz. And you must be Andrew."

"Andrew Philip Michael Keaton, the first," the boy informed her haughtily. Then he threw in for good measure "You dress like a peasant."

On that note, Mrs. Pram crossed to the armoire and opened it to reveal a row of neat gray suits.

"Miss Guiness has not had time to put on her uniform yet, Master Andrew," the head housekeeper said primly. "You will have to excuse her."

From across the room, Liz eyed the rows of starched pressed suits with dismay. She was supposed to keep up with a six-year-old boy wearing those? Then again, given his choice of attire . . .

Still, she just couldn't picture herself in such constricting clothes. Surely the uniform didn't matter *that* much. Maybe she could take up the matter a little later with Mr. Keaton. For now, she would just have to stall.

She tried to change the topic instead. "Why, thank you for showing me the uniforms," she said brightly. "Now, then, I believe Andy and I would like to get better acquainted, wouldn't we, Andy?"

"I most certainly would not."

Liz managed to maintain her smile even then, though it was starting to strain the muscles around her mouth. Where was the insecure little boy just waiting to be loved? Not even Mary Poppins had had to put up with this. Well, all she could do was forge blindly ahead.

"Tough," she informed him, trying valiantly to maintain her smile. "Mrs. Pram," she said casually, "I think you may continue with your other duties now. I can take care of things here."

"Mrs. Pram, I order you not to leave," Andrew immediately countered with his clipped young voice. "Don't leave me alone with her," he ordered. "Forty-nine Americans are murdered a day, and many of those by people they *know*."

Despite herself, Liz couldn't quite keep the shock off her face. So he really was a walking stats book. And not very pleasant stats, at that. What was she supposed to do about this?

"Nonsense," she told him firmly, adopting her mother's best no-nonsense tone. "I'm here to take care of you, not harm you." But he was still glaring at her with such a distrustful mean expression she couldn't quite stop the next words from rushing out. "Besides," she found herself saying, "I'll only kill you if you drive me to it."

"Did you hear that," Andrew said immediately to Mrs. Pram, who was watching the interaction with avid interest. "She *threatened* me." Then he abruptly whipped out a small spiral notebook from his inside breast pocket and promptly began scribbling something down.

This time she didn't try reason. If this little interaction was anything to go by, the child clearly needed solid, consistent discipline. Or four older brothers who didn't take any guff. Without asking, she simply swiped the notebook from his hands. Then, turning to Mrs. Pram, she said in her most practiced, authoritative voice, "Please excuse Andrew and me." The woman still didn't move, so Liz took a deep breath to say it one more time. But perhaps her determination showed now, for the older woman turned and without so much as a backward glance, marched out of the room.

That small victory achieved, Liz glanced down at the small notebook. "Infractions Committed by Nanny Number Four," she read out loud. "I guess that must mean me."

Andrew gave a small dignified little sniff before trying to grab the notebook back. Having grown up with lightning-quick Garret, however, she was quicker. "Infraction number one—threatened being of Andrew Philip Michael Keaton, the first, with death," she read out loud. Looking up at the angry little boy, she said, "Well, Andy, that's a very serious charge."

Andrew nodded his head furiously, grabbing the notebook from her hands and scribbling yet another notation. "Infraction number two—refusal to call Andrew Philip Michael Keaton, the first, by proper name," he stiffly read to her when he was done writing. "You may call me Master Andrew if you desire, but 'Andy' is out of the question."

"I see. How about simply Andrew?"

"*Master* Andrew."

"You may call me Liz," she attempted cheerily.

"You're a nanny, your title is irrelevant," he informed her. "I can call you whatever I choose."

She gave this last comment a little more thought. If the boy truly was insecure, he seemed determined to hide it behind an armor of snobbery and disdain. While the Bradford Agency had gone into great depth about such things as proper nutrition, exercise and education for a healthy, happy charge, there were no clear guidelines as to dealing with a brat. You simply had to use your best judgment. From what she'd seen, she was convinced a little bit of small-town upbringing would do this child a world of good.

Her mind made up, she looked at him with warm, dark blue eyes.

"I'm going to call you Andy," she informed him with a firm but easy smile. "Andrew is a name of respect, and if you want to have respect, you must show respect. When you can do that, then I will call you Andrew."

He glared at her a minute, but she refused to back down. It was a small battle of wills, but she'd grown up surrounded by strong-willed people so she figured she ought to have the advantage. But just as she was beginning to congratulate herself on her handling of the situation, he once again began scribbling furiously in the notebook.

"Infraction number three," he told her. "Refusal to wear proper attire."

She could only agree with this one. She really didn't want to wear those starched gray things, and after a moment's consideration she decided it would be better if she didn't. The agency had assigned her to the Keatons because traditional approaches weren't working with the child, so it was felt that creative handling might do better. And that was exactly what she intended to do—which meant no uniforms. "I think these clothes will just have to do," she told him, indicating what she was currently wearing.

This time instead of the usual glare, she received a slightly more puzzled look.

"You're a nanny," he told her again as if this ought to have some special meaning for her. "You *have* to wear a uniform."

She shook her head. "As a nanny, I'm supposed to help you grow and learn. And I certainly can't do that in a uniform. Besides, you definitely can't ride a horse in suits like that, or play catch, or go to a park, or fly a kite, for that matter."

His confusion cleared immediately.

"I don't do any of those things," he informed her promptly.

"You're only six," Liz reasoned with him. "You're still allowed to try new things. I believe that option is open until you're at least ten or so."

He frowned. "You're making fun of me," he accused.

She tried to shake her head no, but it didn't do any good.

"I don't like you," Andrew said, and his lower lip began to jut out suspiciously. It was the first sign of normality Liz had seen, though, and she was actually relieved by this newest display. However, she truly didn't want to upset him, so she decided to change the topic once more.

"What do you like doing?" she asked as a means of declaring a truce.

"I read," he told her. "I have been reading since I was three. My father taught himself how to read when he was two. How old were you?"

"Probably at least six or so," Liz admitted, and was given a disdainful glance for her obvious inferiority. She chose to ignore it. "What kinds of things do you like to read, other than statistics on how many people are murdered a day, that is?"

"That is an important statistic," Andrew informed her. "You have to be careful, you know. There are lots of bad things out there." He seemed to eye her for a minute, then, with a speculative gleam in his eye, he dropped his bombshell. "My mother was murdered."

In spite of herself, Liz could not quite keep the shock from her face. Mr. Keaton had said his wife was dead, an event that must have been traumatic enough for a young boy. But he'd never hinted at murder, and that seemed such a strong charge. Then again, she thought with a small internal grimace, after exactly one hour in this dark house, what did she know? She was definitely going to have to speak with Mr. Keaton in the morning. Now, why didn't that settle her nerves at all?

Andrew was still looking at her, his bright blue eyes still speculative. Not knowing the truth, she decided the safest course was to change the topic yet again.

She stood, stretching out her cramped knees. "I'm hungry," she declared. "It's too late for dinner, so how about a late-night snack?"

"Dodd does not allow snacks."

"Dodd?"

"The cook," Andrew said impatiently, his voice clearly implying that he was speaking to an idiot.

"Well, *I* would like a snack, so we'll just have to think of something," Liz told him, and without a backward glance, she headed for the door.

"Snacks are bad for you," Andrew said, but she noticed that he followed her.

She shrugged her shoulders. "Then we'll just have to live dangerously."

There was silence for a bit, only the sound of their shoes striking the wood floor as they journeyed down the long hallway.

"What are you going to eat?" Andrew asked after a while.

"Hmm. Preferably something with chocolate."

"Two million, one hundred and sixty thousand Hershey's Kisses are produced a day," he volunteered.

"Really?" she asked, truly impressed this time. "Well then, we'll just have to eat some of them."

She wasn't sure if he was convinced, but he continued to follow her into the foyer, where she turned around in circles, realizing she had no idea where the kitchen was. Finally, giving her another condescending glance for her efforts, Andrew showed her the way to the kitchen.

The mysterious cook was nowhere to be seen, so Liz seized the opportunity to raid the pantry. There was no chocolate to be found, but eventually she did stumble upon some strawberry ice cream in the freezer. It would do the trick, she decided.

She carried it and two bowls she'd found over to the small wooden table.

"Only servants sit there," Andrew informed her.

As long as her day had been, she was almost afraid to ask. "And where do you sit?"

He led her into an adjoining dining room. There rested a formal dining table of rich mahogany wood, set up to serve sixteen. Overhead was another dimly lit chandelier. She took the ice cream back to the wooden table.

"Sit," she informed him curtly. Not waiting for him to obey, she began scooping ice cream into the bowls.

"Two hundred and twenty-five Americans receive nose jobs a day," Andrew said behind her.

She handed him a bowl with two small scoops of ice cream. "Eat."

He seemed to debate this for a minute, but when it became clear she wasn't going to wait for him to decide one way or the other, he went ahead and sat on the other side of the table.

For the next ten minutes she was at least blessed with silence. Spooning in the ice cream bite after mechanical bite, Andrew seemed content to simply stare at her. For her part, she did her best to concentrate on the smooth, creamy texture of the sweet dessert sliding down her throat.

The house was very different. The owner much too distant, the child much too somber. But the ice cream at least, the ice cream tasted like home.

And sitting there, finally at the point she'd been dreaming of reaching for six long months now, she wondered once again if she'd done the right thing. That was the problem with small towns, she knew. They became your life, your identity. And maybe it wasn't too bad. Until that identity became too much to handle. Until the memories were too much to bear and you knew you would never be able to progress unless you simply left. Maybe in this cold house she would forget Nick. Maybe surrounded by the mysterious Mr. Keaton and his insecure son, she could finally put the past behind her.

But then again, looking at the intense little boy sitting across from her, she wasn't so sure anymore. He was watching her with unblinking eyes, eyes that brought back the unbidden image of Richard Keaton, standing in the foyer. Such a dark and powerful man. What went on behind those eyes? What did those eyes see, and what did those eyes feel?

She'd talked to the man for nearly an hour, and she had no idea at all.

And Alycia Keaton? Andrew said that his mother had been murdered. Surely such a thing could not be true.

Under the dim light of the kitchen, she found herself shivering.

She'd run from one dark tragedy. But where she'd arrived, she wasn't so sure of at all.

Chapter 2

After an exhausted night's sleep, Liz awoke to an abrupt piece of news. Richard Keaton had left.

Late in the night, he'd been called away to some sort of scientists' convention in Geneva. According to Mrs. Pram, this kind of impromptu travel was not unusual. It seemed that Mr. Keaton maintained a fairly unstructured and highly irregular schedule. At any rate, he would be gone anywhere from five days to two weeks. And that was that.

The announcement certainly caught Liz off guard. She didn't know whether to feel relieved, for surely Mr. Keaton must have some sort of confidence in her to leave her alone so soon with his child, or to feel absolutely panicked, because indeed she was alone with a rather devious child. And then, of course, there was the fact that she got the fun job of telling little Andrew his father was gone.

Andrew didn't say anything when she broke the news. But his bearing became even stiffer, his shoulders more rigid. She could see his need for toughness with such clarity, it hurt. When Richard came back, she vowed, she would have a serious discussion with him on his life-style.

Andrew was extremely difficult that day, rattling off his morbid statistics right and left. How many people died of cancer a day. How many people choked to death a day. It truly was overwhelming, and it was all Liz could do to keep her composure amid such morbidity. The child needed to get out, she decided firmly. He needed sunshine and activity and normality. Anything but all those darn statistics.

He also needed a firm hand.

That set the tone for the next twelve days. Andrew tested, she resisted. Andrew wore his stiff blue suits, she wore her flowing cotton skirts. She took him out to the pool, and when he refused to swim, she swam, anyway, leaving him to watch from the sidelines. Sooner or later, she was convinced, he would join her. But he seemed to be even more stubborn than she. She took him out to the stables, and when he refused to mount the horse, she rode it around the arena alone. Andrew didn't go on picnics, she took him, anyway. It was a battle of two wills, and at the end of the twelfth day, when she finally tucked him into bed, the winner was still far from certain.

One thing was for sure: she was certainly earning her keep.

It was now after nine o'clock, and her time was officially her own. The first few nights, she'd spent learning the house. But with all its sprawling hallways, that was easier attempted than done. On the third night, she'd discovered the library in the west wing, and every night since, she'd gone there. It was a beautiful room, large and lined with row after row of leatherbound books and intricate wooden paneling. A thick crimson and gold Oriental rug padded the hardwood floor, while delicate Tiffany lamps accentuated carefully arranged reading spots. With a roaring fire in the stone fireplace, it was the only room in the mansion that felt at all comfortable.

Now she settled down on the overstuffed leather sofa to enjoy one of the many classics that lined the walls. She was almost completely engrossed in *Wuthering Heights,* her imagination lost in the haunting intensity of the Yorkshire moors, when the hair on the back of her neck prickled and she looked up.

He was there.

"Hello," she said softly and the word seemed to reverberate through the arched ceiling of the room. He looked tired, she noticed immediately, no longer standing quite so tall and dignified as he had that first day in the foyer. The gray hair at his temples glowed under the faint light of the hall, making him look, all at once, more stately and more exhausted than ever.

"I see you found the library," he said at last and the words were completely devoid of emotion. He had been on a plane for the last fourteen hours, and of the past twelve days, he'd only slept about twenty hours. He was exhausted and all he really wanted to do was collapse. But there were phone calls to make and meetings to confirm and diagrams to check and equations to compute, and . . .

And there was this woman, with her long brown hair falling down the back of the chocolate-colored couch, the strands gleaming a burnished copper by the firelight. This woman in her deep purple skirt and brilliant pink blouse. This woman with her silver bangles on her arms and her dangling earrings tangling in her hair. This woman with the most beautiful midnight blue eyes he had ever seen. Once more her smile was open, once more the look on her face was genuine and warm.

How many times in the past twelve days had he seen her in his mind's eye? How many times, after endless hours of computations and arguments, had he returned to his hotel room only to be haunted by images of her?

He'd only seen her for one day, damn it. And she was his son's nanny, he shouldn't even remember what she looked like. But he did. His damned scientist's mind had remembered every little detail, from the way her hair curled down around her face, to the delicate arch of her cheekbones, to the haunting intensity of her eyes. Mostly, he remembered the way her face had lit up when she'd smiled at him that once, as if every bit of her had felt that smile.

"I like your collection of books," Liz managed to say as she swallowed under the intensity of his gaze. It seemed an eternity had already passed since he'd walked into the room, and she'd spent it all pinned under the scouring examination of his eyes. But nothing showed on his face. He'd stared at her for several long moments, and she still had no idea at all what he was thinking. It seemed that even tired, Richard Keaton remained as elusive as ever.

"I didn't select them," Richard said abruptly, indicating the books as he pushed himself away from the doorframe. His lips thinned into a grim line and he crossed the room to the small bar. There was a decanter of brandy out and he poured himself a stiff glass.

"Would you like something to drink?" he asked curtly.

"I'm fine," she replied softly. What went on in that mind of his that he always looked so controlled and grim?

She found that she really wanted to know. This was her new life now, and in a way, this was her new home. Certainly it would be easier if she could at least carry on a simple conversation with this man.

"How are things coming?" Richard asked abruptly, surprising them both with the sound of his voice. "I see that you are still here."

"Well enough," Liz said, hope flaring at the possibility of conversation. "Andrew's trying, but he hasn't driven me to murder yet."

"Is he eating?"

"Yes."

"Sleeping?"

"I'm actually not so sure about that," she said honestly. "I think he may be reading on the sly, after lights-out, but I have yet to catch him in the act."

Richard merely nodded.

"How was Geneva?" Liz asked after a bit, setting the book aside once and for all as she took in the man in front of her.

"Busy."

"Did the conference go well?"

"Well enough."

"You look tired," she said softly.

"I am."

"You're not much for conversation, are you?"

"So I've been told."

She smiled at that, not noticing the way his hand suddenly trembled at its impact. He was still as reclusive and reserved as she remembered. But she could try, couldn't she? After all, Mrs. Pram wasn't much for friendly overtures, and as much as

Liz honestly liked Andrew, it would be nice to have some adult conversation from time to time.

The thought of Andrew, however, brought her to a more sobering point.

"I imagine," she began slowly, "that you would probably like to spend some time with your son now that you're back." Not waiting for his reply, she rushed on. "I had planned to take Andrew fishing, but I could cancel that if you'd like."

"Fishing?"

Liz smiled wanly. "It's part of my campaign to get him out of the house more. I have to tell you, he's a rather morbid child."

"Is it working?"

"Not yet," she admitted. "Now he brings his books with him and reads while I do whatever."

Richard nodded, but remained silent, his eyes focused on the fire while he slowly turned the glass in his hand.

"So would you like me to cancel my plans? Perhaps he would enjoy it more if you took him fishing," Liz pressed. Andrew needed his father; it didn't take a rocket scientist to see that.

"I don't fish," Richard said, and whether he'd intended it or not, in that instant he sounded exactly like his son.

"Then do whatever," Liz prompted. Why was he so cold to the idea? Andrew was his son, for goodness sake. His only child. Somehow, she would have thought that with the mother's passing away, the father and son would be even closer. Yet . . .

"That won't be necessary," Richard said abruptly. "Continue as scheduled, Miss Guiness."

She paused now, getting the distinct idea that Mr. Keaton was indeed determined to avoid his son. On the other hand, she was just as determined that the two do something together, if only for the sake of her six-year-old charge.

"What about joining us for lunch?" she suggested levelly.

"I have an appointment."

"Tea? Dinner? A midnight snack? I'm sure it hardly matters to Andrew, as long as he gets to see you."

"I don't know if that will be possible just yet." Once again, the words were emotionless.

They began to anger her. How could he ignore his own child? Couldn't he see how insecure Andrew was? Couldn't he see how much his own son missed him? Maybe that was the problem. Maybe with all his science and experiments, he didn't understand how children worked. She selected a new tack.

"He talks about you a lot," she said softly. "He has really missed you."

But whatever response she was hoping for, it wasn't what she got. Once again, the words were clipped and cold.

"Miss Guiness, Andrew has not seen me in five years. He doesn't even know me."

"But I think he'd like to," she countered immediately, not willing to give up.

The words were coaxing, tugging at him, but he fought them off with another sip of the brandy. Yet, deep inside, he felt the depths of his turmoil swirl again. The guilt, the uncertainty, and perhaps most of all, the vulnerability. He had cared once for Alycia and Andrew. Sometimes, late and tired as he was now, he could almost remember other nights, when he'd looked down at the sleeping baby, and had felt his heart constrict in his chest. But Alycia had destroyed that, as she'd destroyed everything that had ever meant anything to him.

He couldn't look at the boy without seeing her. And he couldn't look at the child without wondering... Alycia's death had been her final victory, leaving him alone with all his doubts. Andrew was the symbol of that triumph, the small blond reminder of Richard's vulnerability, and all the things the tenth smartest mind in the nation would never know.

"I am a busy man," he finally said. "You and Andrew will just have to accept that."

She looked at him a long time from across the room on the couch. His coldness intimidated her, but she drew up her spine against it. She'd never been a timid person, she reminded herself. She'd led a sheltered life, but it wasn't as if she'd been hiding from the world. There simply had never been the need to explore it until now. But here she was, and darn it, this man was being stubborn. She would not let him scare her into silence with his scowling face and cold eyes.

"I can't," she said suddenly out loud, her chin coming up as she openly challenged him. "Andrew is your son, and he needs you. You are his father, and you need him."

His lips turned wryly, but he hid it by downing the last sip of brandy. Putting down the glass, he turned to face her with dispassionate ice-blue eyes.

"If you cannot accept my terms," he said curtly, "you are free to leave."

The finality, the coldness of the statement, shocked her. For a moment, she felt a rush of panic. She'd blown it. She'd pushed her employer too far, and now she would be sent home. But after the panic, came the anger. How could he be so distant toward his own child? How could he possibly be so cold?

She couldn't understand it. All her life she had been surrounded by the easy laughter of a large family. She was accustomed to sharing, touching, reaching out. She'd already called home twice in the twelve days she'd been here to tell everyone she was all right and get her mother's advice on handling her young charge. That was the way the Guiness household worked. Everyone was there for everyone.

She didn't understand the Keaton kind of remoteness at all. And she could not accept it.

"Look," she said at last, sitting up straighter. "I know I'm overstepping my bounds here, but I really feel you should reconsider spending more time with Andrew. He's in a new environment now, in a large and lonely house. He's insecure." Her voice grew more earnest. "He's scared. And his own thoughts offer no comfort. He thinks his mother was murdered."

The last words were spoken softly, but she could see the impact even across the room. The man froze completely, his face turning to utter granite.

"He knows?" Richard questioned harshly.

She could only nod.

He laughed, a mirthless sound in the firelight. "Of course, the Wynstons told him. That would be something they would do. Take the child and turn him against me completely. Anything to advance their petty war. I should have known."

"The Wynstons?" she questioned quietly, feeling confused. *He knows?* Not, what a foolish thought, but *He knows?* Good God, was it true?

"Alycia's parents, of course." And then, because he was tired, he found himself saying, "Andrew is right, after all. Alycia was murdered."

He could see her eyes go wide with the impact of the confirmation, and it prodded him on.

"Everyone thinks I did it."

If he'd been trying to shock her, Liz thought vaguely, well, then, it had worked. She was shocked. She was sitting on a leather sofa with so many thoughts running through her mind, she didn't know where to begin to sort them out.

Could he really have murdered his wife? And if so, why hadn't the agency warned her about this? Surely they wouldn't send her to a house where the father was a suspected murderer. But then, if no charges had ever been filed, it would be just like the prim and proper Bradford Agency not to mention something as undignified as rumors in the file. She supposed there might be legal implications, as well, such as slander, but still . . .

Could this man be capable of murder?

Looking over at him, she couldn't be sure. His face looked so harsh in the shadows, his eyes so cold. He had an aura of power around him, an aura of total control. And his features gave away nothing—no hint of softness, no hint of anything at all.

She shivered slightly on the sofa, and immediately his sharp eyes caught it.

"So, my dear Miss Guiness," he drawled from across the room, "do you think I did it? Do you think I killed my wife?"

He shouldn't be prodding. A part of him knew that. But he was tired and the brandy was rolling through his veins even as the bitterness gnawed at his gut. He wanted to know. He wanted to know what this beautiful, fresh creature thought of him. He wanted to see the disgust and horror in her eyes now, so he could replay it in his mind night after night after night. So he could block her out of his mind completely.

"I ... don't know," Liz said at last, the words halting. She grappled for a complete thought. "I don't know any of the details, so I guess I can't come to any conclusions at all. I mean, *did* you kill your wife?"

It seemed like a rather inane question. Would a true killer actually answer yes? But she was still feeling frazzled and rather out of her league. It was the best she could do.

He smiled his mirthless smile once more.

"Would you believe me if I answered that?" he asked roughly.

"I don't know," she found herself uttering yet again. "I don't really know you yet."

She was trying to be honest, trying to recapture her hold on the situation. Perhaps he would at least give her credit for her honesty.

But he didn't.

Instead, his face grew darker, and for a fraction of an instant, his grip on the brandy glass tightened until his knuckles grew white. Then abruptly, he set the glass down, his face returning to its traditional, dispassionate state.

"It doesn't matter," he said curtly. "It doesn't matter at all. Now if you will excuse me, Miss Guiness. I believe I have some work to do."

Then, just as abruptly, he turned and walked out of the library. She could do nothing but watch him leave, the doubt and uncertainty sharp and cold in her mind. For a minute, she wanted to call him back. She wanted to search his face for any kind of emotion at all, anything she could latch on to. Anything she could believe in.

Because she was far from home, in a dark house with echoing halls and moaning drafts. In a dark house with a child who rattled off death statistics, and a man who might be a murderer.

What had she done?

In a moment of crashing despair, she wished desperately that she could turn back the clock. It would be one year earlier, and she would be home in bed, curled in the warm embrace of her husband. She would stretch out and roll over, safe in the arms of the man she had loved to one extent or another, for all her life. And he would wake up, and brush her cheek and look at her with his warm hazel eyes. And . . .

And there was no going back. Nick was gone. It had taken her months to come to terms with that grim fact. At first, right after the murder, she hadn't been able to eat, she hadn't been able to sleep. Her oldest brother, Mitch, had flown in from his FBI job in D.C. to be with her. When he'd had to return, Cagney had taken a short leave of absence from the D.C. police to hold her hand. Even Garret, who served as Navy SEAL for classified missions that even Mitch couldn't access information on, had come. He'd materialized one night in her bedroom, and talked her to sleep. When she'd awakened the next morning, he'd been gone. Finally, Jake, the Harvard man and middle brother, had called from Singapore or wherever he was making his latest fortune. He'd started a scholarship in Nick's name and had told her jokes until she'd laughed through her tears.

Everyone had been there for her, but mostly, she'd had to acknowledge that her past was over. Nick was dead, and she was still alive.

She'd known then that she had to do something with that, had to build some sort of a new life. The girl from North Carolina wasn't so fragile, she'd survived the worst so far. She would survive this, too.

She would do some checking on Mr. Keaton, she decided. Find out what kind of man he really was, and what indeed had happened to his wife.

Perhaps she would even find a clue as to what went on in those remote pale blue eyes of his in the dark hours of the night.

Whatever small progress Liz had made with Andrew quickly deteriorated with his father's sudden appearance and then equally sudden disappearance. Liz tried to inquire as to the whereabouts of Mr. Keaton several times, only to be informed by Mrs. Pram that he was working and could not be disturbed. Which left her alone with a six-year-old prodigy who was deeply intent on ruining her sanity.

"Five thousand nine hundred and thirty-seven Americans die a day," Andrew announced over breakfast the next morning.

"I see," Liz replied patiently. She launched into her new tactic, formulated late the night before when it was two in the morning and she still couldn't sleep. "And how many Americans are born?"

"That's over two hundred people dead every hour!" Andrew continued intensely.

"Yes, but how many people are born?"

"That's four people every minute! That...that means by the time you finish eating your eggs, forty people will have *died*." His eyes were growing rounder in his agitation, and Liz was fast beginning to lose her appetite.

"That may be," she said as calmly as she could while she set down her fork. "But I believe over *fifty* new babies will have been born in the United States alone in just the time it takes me to eat my toast."

Andrew processed this information, his eyes blinking rapidly behind his glasses. "How many minutes does it take to eat your toast?" he demanded to know.

"Let's say ten minutes, for simplicity's sake." Liz was beginning to get accustomed to Andrew's ways by now, and sure enough, thirty seconds later he was spitting out the answer to his mental computations.

"You're wrong!" he informed her haughtily. "With ten thousand, five hundred and one Americans born each day, that would be an average of roughly seven a minute. Thus, seventy, not fifty, Americans are born by the time you finish your toast."

"Either way," Liz observed, "more Americans are born than die. Perhaps you should spend more time dwelling on *that* statistic instead."

He scowled, stubbornly pushing away his plate and folding his arms in a typical sulk.

"Come on," Liz said resolutely, pushing back her own plate. "The weather is beautiful. Let's go do something outside."

"I don't want to."

"You haven't even heard your options yet."

"I don't want to."

"You don't want to do anything at all?"

Andrew shook his head vigorously.

"How about climbing a tree? Wait, wait, let me guess. You don't climb trees."

Andrew nodded his head.

"Well, then, maybe we could just go outside and sit on the grass. I could read you a story, or better yet, you could read *me* a story."

"I don't read stories."

"Well you must be reading something because there's a suspicious glow under your door at night."

"I turn out the light," Andrew declared defensively. "The rule is lights out, and the light is out."

"Ah, but lights out includes all lights. Even flashlights."

His eyes flickered suspiciously, but he didn't say anything.

"Well, you must be doing something with all those books you carry around with you. What was it you had yesterday?"

"The 1995 Universal Almanac."

"You were reading the *Almanac?*"

"My father read the phone book when he was three," Andrew told her proudly.

"I see," Liz said, and nodded gravely. "So did you read the phone book, too, or did you decide to start with something that had a little more meat?"

Andrew looked a little less certain now, but after a bit, he nodded.

"Well, then," Liz said abruptly, and stood up, "why don't we go outside now, and you can tell me about what you read yesterday."

"The grass is wet," Andrew said immediately. "It will stain my suit!"

"Then wear jeans."

"I don't—"

"I know, I know, Andy. *You don't wear jeans.* Well, I tell you what. Just for today, if you wear your jeans, I will wear my uniform."

Obviously, the exchange had potential, for Andrew was now eyeing her crimson and jade skirt with a speculative eye.

"The whole uniform?" he questioned. "Even the tie?"

Liz sighed, and wondered how soon she was going to regret this. Still, she really wanted to get the child outside more—for both their sakes. "Even the tie," she agreed.

"All right," Andrew said at last with a decisive nod. "Deal."

That was how Richard found them an hour later, both sitting on a blanket in the yard. He took in Andrew with an appraising eye, noting the jeans that looked brand-new and the sweater that was still creased from being folded in a box. His sharp blue eyes found Liz sitting straight and formal, with her legs curled primly to one side. Liz, who looked stiff and uncomfortable in her straight gray skirt, short gray jacket, starched white blouse and stranglingly serious black tie. Looking at her in this new restrictive attire, Richard frowned. And unconsciously, as a person might search for signs of familiarity in someone he knows but does not immediately recognize, his eyes scanned up and down her figure. It wasn't until he noticed the large silver hoops in her ears that his forehead cleared.

"Hello," he managed to say, and cleared his throat. They both looked up simultaneously, and it was hard to tell who was the more startled. Andrew's eyes blinked several times in rapid succession, and Liz's face registered shock. She, however, was the first to recover, reaching out her hand in welcome.

She'd told him to spend more time with his son, and now here he was. Even if she did have her doubts about him, even if he did sometimes scare her, she had to at least appreciate that. Besides, Andrew was watching.

"Welcome," she said as casually as she could. "Andrew was just telling me about absolute zero on the Kelvin scale. Would you like to join us?"

Richard nodded, looking somewhat uncomfortable. He had recognized them from a distance, in fact it was Andrew's hair that had given them away. In the bright burning light of morning, the boy's fair locks had glowed like an angel's halo—that is, if there were any such thing as angels or halos. And from a distance, as Richard had walked toward them, the child had looked so much like his mother, it had made his breath catch in his throat. Even now, up close, the blond, blond hair, the blue, blue eyes—it was Alycia all over again. Grimly he faced yet again the fact that he could spend all day looking for something of himself in the boy, and never find one trace. Not one.

Already regretting approaching them, Richard moved to the empty place on the blanket and sat down carefully in his brown slacks and long-sleeved oxford shirt. His eyes squinted uncomfortably against the brightness of the sun. It had been a long time since he had been outside on a day like this, something that did not go unnoticed by Liz.

"Andrew," she prompted. "Go ahead and continue."

The child blinked his eyes several times again, looking first at the rare presence of his father, and then back at Liz. He looked very nervous, Liz thought. Nervous, and not at all the haughty young man he pretended to be.

"Andrew," she said again. "It's okay."

"Zero degrees Kelvin," he said quickly, his round eyes still glued on his father. "That's . . . minus 273.15 degrees Celsius, or minus 459.7 degrees Fahrenheit."

Richard nodded. "Very good," he told Andrew, and the boy sat back with a quick, almost shy nod of acknowledgment. "And where did you learn this?"

But Andrew just sat there, staring with uncertain eyes at the man before him.

"He read it in the *Almanac*," Liz supplied after a bit. "It's his newest choice in reading material. According to local legend, you, yourself, read the phone book at age three, something Andrew has taken very seriously."

Once again Richard nodded his head. "So I did," he said softly. "So I did."

The lapse in conversation became awkward, and Liz searched to fill the void. "Andrew," she said, "why don't you ask your father about Geneva."

But Andrew merely turned expectant eyes onto Richard, his mouth still tightly shut.

"I attended a conference of world scientists," Richard said shortly. "We compared notes on some things, exchanged information on others. Really, it wasn't anything exciting."

Another lapse. Social graces obviously didn't run in the family, Liz decided.

"And what project are you working on?" she asked presently.

"Capacitors."

"Oh." It appeared he wasn't going to explain, so finally she gave up and asked, "What exactly is a capacitor?"

"Capacitors store energy in the form of an electric charge," Andrew said suddenly. Both Richard and Liz looked at him in surprise.

"That's right," Richard said. "Capacitors store energy. For example, things like rechargeable shavers and batteries have them."

Now both Richard and Andrew were staring at her with their blinking eyes. Miniatures, Liz thought abruptly. They looked like perfect opposites in their coloring and features, but in actual mannerisms, Andrew was a perfect miniature of his father, right down to the rapidly blinking eyes. Lord help her, she thought. She was having enough problems surviving one Keaton, let alone two.

"Perhaps Andy could visit you at your lab," she suggested into the silence. Andrew immediately turned to Richard expectantly, and in that instant Liz feared she had made a grave mistake in even mentioning the idea. But then, after a long moment, Richard nodded slowly, and both she and Andrew breathed easier.

"That could be arranged," Richard said quietly, and then, as if that was as much as he could take for one afternoon, he stood up quickly and dusted off his pants. "I have to go back to work," he said curtly. "I will see you both later."

"Perhaps for dinner," Liz said.

"Perhaps."

She nodded, watching him turn and walk away with speculative eyes. He moved gracefully, yet economically for such a large man. And his tailored slacks and shirt revealed a lean, powerful build. Come to think of it, she'd seen calluses on his hands—so how exactly did a man who supposedly locked himself in a lab all day come by such muscular tone and definition?

And what had brought the man who, just yesterday, had said he wanted nothing to do with his son, out here to join them on the blanket? She frowned, her eyes narrowing in thought. She had four brothers, she thought she knew a thing or two about the male species. And right now, she was sure there was more to Richard Keaton than met the eye. A lot more.

She would get to know him better, she thought determinedly, her head nodding unconsciously. Not for her sake, she told herself. But for Andrew's.

Chapter 3

The opportunity came as the clock struck midnight and she was curled in her favorite chair in the library. As the cavernous room had a habit of growing chilly at night, she had lit a small fire in the fireplace and pulled the chair closer to the welcoming warmth of the flames. Once more she was lost in the burning love of the Yorkshire moors, and once more she knew instantly the moment that he entered the room.

Neither acknowledged the other right away. She remained with her head in the book, even though she was no longer following the words. And he remained in the doorway, watching the way the firelight reflected off the long gleaming strands of her hair and accentuated the delicate planes of her face. She was wearing another flowing skirt, this one covered with fall leaves. Over it, she sported a long, cream-colored knit sweater. This outfit suited her better, he thought. For some reason, he hadn't liked her in the uniform. She looked more comfortable now— comfortable, natural, fresh. And lovely, oh, so lovely.

He frowned to himself and entered the room.

"Would you like a drink?" he asked her as he crossed the room to the brandy decanter for his habitual fare. She still hadn't looked up from the book, but he could feel her awareness even across the distance that separated them. It filled him with a primitive satisfaction.

"All right," she agreed, surprising them both.

"Brandy?"

"That would be fine."

He poured the two snifters, feeling the unwanted tension build in his stomach. He'd come down from his tower tonight knowing she would be here. He'd come down sooner than he should have, and much faster than his normal steady steps took him. Because he wanted to see her. He wanted to watch her hair glow by the firelight, he wanted to feel the probing of her midnight eyes on him. He wanted . . .

His face grew dark, and his eyes grew cold as he pushed the thoughts away. She was his son's nanny, he told himself—nothing more. But he still wasn't quite thinking in those terms when he took the glass over to her. And he certainly wasn't thinking of her as a nanny when her hand brushed against his to take the glass. Instead, the muscles of his stomach tightened reflexively as a bolt of pure desire rocked through him.

He willed the response away with unrelenting determination, retreating to the opposite chair.

Liz didn't say anything, hiding her own thoughts by taking a sip of the brandy and letting it blaze a fiery trail down her throat. She'd only had brandy once before, and the strength of it startled her. She could already feel it, a low, curling burn deep in her stomach. But it didn't seem to quite calm her nerves.

The atmosphere of the room had changed radically upon Richard's entering, she realized with a start. Suddenly the quiet coziness of the room seemed to spark, smoldering now with an unrelenting awareness. All at once she felt self conscious, wondering if her hair was too unruly, the sweater too bulky. When she lifted the glass for a second sip, her hands were trembling slightly.

She shook her head against the sensations. It was just nerves, the usual awkwardness of being around an unfamiliar person, she told herself. After all, though she had lived in this house for nearly two weeks now, she'd hardly exchanged half a dozen words with the man across from her.

It looked as if he'd had a rough day, too. His hair lay dark and tousled across his forehead, and his usual pristine dress shirt had the top two buttons undone. She found her gaze resting on the tantalizing glimpse of black, curly chest hair, strong and virile against the white of his shirt. When she realized she was staring, a low blush infused her cheeks as she glanced sharply away. What in the world was the matter with her?

The silence was becoming unbearable.

"So how was your day?" she asked finally, the question sounding unbelievably inane to her. He looked almost tired, but the grim set of his features made it impossible to believe he possessed such a human weakness.

He didn't answer, his eyes seemingly intent on the dancing flames. He shrugged, maintaining his remote composure.

"Are you making much progress?" she tried again. Her cheeks still felt flushed. She should probably slow down on the brandy; the room was really becoming warm and her hands were shaking.

"A little," Richard said shortly, taking another sip from his snifter.

"Enough to start getting more sleep soon?"

"I don't sleep much," he said simply. No, he didn't like to sleep. He didn't like to close his eyes, and see all the pictures that came to his mind—like *her* blond hair, and brittle blue eyes. Like her scorning laughter, her porcelain face twisted in petty rage.

A muscle in his jaw clenched, but then he forced himself to relax. It was all over. The wicked witch was dead.

He almost smiled at the dark humor, but his lips no longer remembered the motion.

"Are these capacitor things really so important?" Liz asked. Up this close, she could see the clean line of his jaw, the way it clenched and unclenched as he unconsciously rolled the brandy glass between his hands. He had a strong face, highlighted by sharp, penetrating eyes. There was nothing awkward about his features, nor anything soft. He certainly didn't look like any scientist she'd ever known. In fact, he didn't look like *any* man she had ever known, not even tall, dark and handsome Garret, who made all the girls swoon. Richard was too removed, too distant, too controlled. He looked like a man carved from granite, but for some unfathomable reason, she wanted to lean closer to him.

Her hands trembled even more as she glanced down at the amber drink gently swooshing in the confines of the heavy crystal glass.

Had he really killed *his wife?* whispered her inner voice. *Was he really that cold?*

She had no answer but the shiver that crept along her spine.

As she watched, Richard gave a dismissing shrug in response to her question and took another sip from his glass.

The silence reverberated through the room, straining her nerves. She found herself watching his hands, the way they rotated the glass around and around and around. He had long, lean fingers and wide palms. His hands could probably hold a basketball quite easily. They were strong, too, she would bet. Capable hands that could manipulate delicate wires as easily as they could crush a tin can—

What about someone's neck? that tiny voice piped in again insistently. *What if they had curled around the delicate curve of a woman's neck, and—*

She cut off the thought with a horrified mental shake. She had no business thinking such things. She hardly knew the man at all, let alone what had happened to his late wife. Surely Liz knew better than to base judgments on mere gossip.

She dredged up a neutral topic. It seemed far better to keep talking.

"It was nice of you to stop by this afternoon," she said after a moment. "Andy has done nothing but talk about you since then." She stopped, but he didn't say anything, so after a while, she continued, determined to develop a conversation. "What made you stop by? After our conversation last night, I didn't expect to see you."

He had no answer, watching the firelight. He had never intended to visit them. He had only done so because he had come downstairs and Mrs. Pram had informed him in her highest and mightiest voice that "that woman" had "Master Andrew" wearing "*jeans.*" That in itself hadn't concerned him, but it had tempted him into glancing outside as he was about to climb the stairs to his tower. And then . . . How did a logical man like himself rationalize the rest? They had simply looked so...so... *right* out there. The bright blue of the blanket against the lush green of the yard, the glowing blond of Andrew's hair shimmering against the deep darkness of her own as she had leaned over to hear him better. He had looked outside, and his feet had done the rest.

Like now. Just like now. He shouldn't even be in here, he thought abruptly. What was he doing, sipping brandy with this woman, sitting in front of a fire with her? As if the cozy, domestic scene were natural. How long had it been since he had sat in this library with another person? How long since he had tried to carry on a casual conversation?

Who was he trying to kid?

The silence had dragged on so long, Liz had given up hope for an answer.

"Will you really arrange for Andy to come to your lab?" she prodded. "It would mean the world to him."

Richard nodded. "I told him I would," he said tautly, keeping his eyes on the flames, his hands once more absently twirling the glass in his hand. The child had seemed so eager. It would have been unnecessarily cruel, even for him, to have told Andrew no.

"Do you work by yourself?" Liz asked presently. The effort at conversation was beginning to be almost too much, but she was yet determined to make it work. Anything was better than just sitting, watching the lean fingers of his hands twirl the glass.

He nodded again, his wintry blue eyes finally glancing up to meet her own. "Yes. Most of my tests are run on computer, so I don't really need any assistance."

"It must get lonely at times," Liz ventured gently.

"Mostly it's just frustrating."

"What is your goal right now? What are you working on?"

"Finding an ideal dielectric to enhance the capacitance of a supercapacitor."

"Oh. Well, that explains everything."

For a moment, he paused at her humor, as if it had some-how startled him. But he quickly recovered his indifference, mustering his control.

"It's not that technical," he told her brusquely. "Basically, a capacitor consists of two small sheets of, say, metal, with a substance—a dielectric—between them. There are several tra-ditional minerals that are used as capacitors—aluminum ox-ide, tantalum and the like. But to build a supercapacitor with the storage ability that I'm aiming for, those substances would take up too much room, making the capacitor huge. And I don't want that."

"I see," Liz said. "So you want to build something like a battery?"

Across from her, Richard nodded and took another sip of his brandy. Unbidden, other images rose in his mind of other con-versations. Yes, the person across from him should have blond hair, almost white. And she should be wearing something filmy and pink and looking at him with huge, china blue eyes as he babbled on and on about his work and his lab until he realized that she understood none of it. And really didn't care to, ei-ther.

"Something like that," he said with a shrug, letting the sub-ject trail off.

Across from him, however, Liz's mind was racing on its own.

"What does a capacitor look like?" she asked. "Surely it isn't exactly like a battery, or you would simply use that."

He turned his brandy glass in his hand once more, then took another sip.

"Don't worry about it," he said abruptly. "It's not that in-teresting."

Across from him, she frowned. He was definitely shutting her out, and for whatever reason, it made her angry. She was tired of all this mystery, and darn it, she was curious now. She'd never known anyone who had made a capacitor before.

"But I want to know," she responded stubbornly, her fore-head crinkling into a small frown. "I really do."

The words pulled at him, threatening his control. He didn't want to talk about his work. He didn't want, for one minute, to wonder if she truly *was* interested. Because he'd been down this road before, damn it. And he wasn't so big a fool as to make the same mistakes twice. He was different, he'd learned that long ago. His mind worked faster, too fast, his inventions were important to him, too important. Other people, they just didn't understand these things. And he didn't want to try, he didn't even want to start, to make the effort only to look over and find her yawning, as he had found Alycia doing time and again throughout their marriage. "Well, really, dear, it's not as if it's anything interesting."

"Forget it," he said out loud, his features grim. "Perhaps when you bring Andrew to the lab, you can see them for yourself."

It was, however, too late. Liz was easily as stubborn as he was, and she really did want to know.

"How big is a normal capacitor?" she quizzed. She glanced around suddenly, then picked up her discarded book. "Is it bigger or smaller than a book?"

He turned then, and that was his undoing. She was looking at him with those big clear eyes so unlike any eyes he'd ever seen. The dark blue color should have made them mysterious, should have made them unreadable. But instead, her eyes possessed an open unrelenting determination that drew him in, tempting him with their apparent sincerity.

"It's smaller than a book," he said tersely, staring into her eyes even as he told himself to shut up. "In fact, a normal capacitor would be the size of—" he looked around for an immediate reference point, and his eyes landed upon a simple silver ring she wore on her right hand "—like this," he said, and without thinking about it, he moved over to the couch and picked up her hand. "This small stone here, the sapphire, is about the right size. And traditionally, a capacitor of this size can store ten to the—" he looked up suddenly to find her face just inches away as she leaned closer to see "—ten to the negative six farads," he finished softly.

"That's not much energy?" she asked, glancing from the ring to find him right in front of her. His eyes are intense, she thought hazily. Beautiful pale blue eyes. Lost in his much larger grip, her hand began to tremble once more.

"No," he was saying. "A charge like that would be used up instantaneously." His hand was still holding hers, but neither moved. Neither *wanted* to move.

It was a stunning contrast, Richard noted absently, his mind taking in the scene with almost clinical detachment. The pale beauty of her small, soft hand lying in the encompassing strength of his own large palm. Her fingers looked fragile and delicate, but he could imagine them having a strong, earnest grip to go with the rest of her. Hadn't she talked of fishing, and horseback riding? He could see these hands on the reins, controlling the stubbornest of horses with the lightest of touches.

And he wondered . . .

He looked up to find her eyes watching his with a kind of dazed breathlessness. Then his eyes wandered down a little farther to the red flush of her cheeks and the parted moistness of her lips. If he leaned forward, just a couple of inches . . .

She licked her lips, and the man of pure logic lost his rationality. He leaned over abruptly, and claimed her lips with his own.

She went rigid with the shock, her lips suddenly stiff under his as her eyes opened wide. But his lips were warm and moist against her own, his tongue darting out to trace delicately around her lips and an electric thrill shot through her. Suddenly, she found herself moaning in his arms. Her lips opened, her eyes closed, and she welcomed him in.

His blood raced at her submission. He moved forward, pressing her against the couch as his tongue plunged into the heated recesses of her mouth. She tasted fresh and sweet, her arms wrapping around his neck with a pure passion that filled him with raw satisfaction. There was nothing coy or artificial here. She welcomed him with honest desire, and he took her with primal need.

He explored her mouth, wrapping his tongue around her own and feeling her move against him in response. His hands dived into her hair, tilting back her head to plunge deeper. He heard her moan, he heard her sigh and he thought if his body got much harder he would be crippled for life.

He forgot about the library, his lab, the dielectric that eluded all his efforts. He thought of only the taste of her lips, the smell of her skin, the sound of her small sighs of satisfaction.

His lips moved to her ear, and delicately, deliciously, he nipped at her earlobe. She sat up with a small gasp of surprise, the electric jolt of desire catching her completely off guard. Her skin felt hyperaware, every nerve ending attuned to his touch. She wanted to taste his skin, she thought suddenly. She wanted to run her hands through his hair, flatten her palms on the warm flesh of his chest.

She wanted. Oh, God, she wanted . . .

Nick had never touched her like this.

The thought penetrated out of the blue, and all at once, her eyes flew open.

"Oh, God," she whispered, and the next thing he knew she was pushing him away with desperate hands. She didn't even stay on the couch, the shocked energy propelling her off the sofa until she was standing before the fireplace, wrapping her arms around herself tightly. In her face he could see a kind of dazed horror, the kind one might experience after awakening from a nightmare.

And then it hit him. Of course. She was horrified that she was attracted to him, horrified that he, a man thought to have murdered his wife, would dare to kiss her.

Why shouldn't she be horrified? he thought harshly. He was a man who'd lost all hope of redemption long ago.

His eyes became the cold blue slate developed from years of practice, his bearing suddenly stiff and straight. He drew back into himself completely, and in a matter of mere seconds, was once again Richard Campbell Louis Keaton, III. Distant. Proud. Cold.

Liz still hadn't said anything. She could only stare at him, this dark man before her. And then she found herself looking at his lips, the shocked attraction fizzling through her once again. Angrily she told herself to stop it. She wasn't supposed to be feeling these things. She didn't *want* to feel these things.

All her life her emotions had belonged to one man. From those first awkward moments of adolescence to those that had marked the pure joy of maturation, all her attention had been for Nick. Yet here she was, just one year later, riveted by a stranger and the way he'd touched her. She found herself shivering, and wrapped her arms tighter around herself. What was wrong with her? She and Nick had been so in love, and certainly, she had enjoyed his touch a great deal. They'd shared sweetness and passion, the gentleness of two young people falling in love. Yet compared to what this man had just done to her senses, what they'd shared might as well have been from a Disney movie.

Richard Keaton was not a boy. No, he had kissed her like a man.

She couldn't take it. The guilt and doubt and confusion swirled inside her like a suffocating mist. She needed to leave the room.

She didn't want to go yet.

What was she doing? What in the world was she doing?

She turned away completely, approaching the fire as if its heat might afford her some kind of protection against the tension that was slowly strangling the room.

"I should be going now," Richard said curtly behind her, his face still ominous. But he didn't move.

She nodded, her eyes stricken as she took in the golden flames. "Yes. It's getting late." She didn't step away.

She needed something to hang on to, she realized. Some small, simple conversation to restore her view of the world. Then she could pretend this entire evening had been filled with nothing but casual conversation, getting to know her charge's father. The rest, well, she could write it off as a flukish event brought on by an overly tense atmosphere. Perhaps *Wuthering Heights* wasn't the best reading material for her....

But she needed to say something, anything, to get the evening back on track. Normalcy. She needed normalcy. When nothing better came to mind, she latched on to the question of his work.

"So," she began, the word slightly shaky while her back remained to him. "When, when you find this...dielectric thing, what will you do?"

Richard didn't answer right away, he was still watching her, still feeling the raw anger and tight passion in his gut. But then he let it go. What did it matter, what she thought of him? It wasn't as if the entire town hadn't already tried him and found him guilty. He'd spent the past five years listening to all the whispers behind his back when he went out, feeling all the curious stares. It wasn't important.

So after a moment he went along with her little game. It wasn't as if he cared, he told himself. It wasn't as if he cared at all.

"The biggest breakthrough would be for solar cars," he said finally, his voice distant and professional. "As the sun is only available for half a day, the major challenge is in trying to store the energy acquired during those hours for use after the sun goes down. Currently, such storage capacity requires the use of almost six hundred pounds of batteries. The weight alone is prohibitive. With the proper dielectric, however, it should be possible to build a supercapacitor that could store the necessary energy while weighing, say, fifty pounds. That, at least, is the theory."

She nodded, seizing the words. "But finding the right dielectric is hardly easy."

"No, it isn't easy at all. But sooner or later, I will do it." He said the words with such quiet conviction they were easy to believe. And she did believe him. If his dossier, and for that matter, his son, was anything to go by, the man was a virtual genius. She imagined he could do pretty much anything.

Like kiss.

She clamped down on the thought with a horrified gasp, once more rubbing her arms in unconscious agitation.

"Are things improving with Andrew?" Richard's voice cut in, his penetrating eyes still detailing her every action. She seemed upset, and for the first time, he wondered if it might have to do with more than him. He knew nothing about her at all, maybe there was something else— But then he dismissed the thought with a mental shrug. What did it matter? She wouldn't be around much longer, anyway.

"A little," Liz said after a moment, trying to focus on the change in topic. "I'd still like to get him out more. He's too hung up on all those books and depressing statistics. It's not natural for a boy his age."

"I was like that when I was his age," Richard observed quietly. Let her understand now, he thought. Let her understand just how different he was, before she started getting any ideas, any expectations otherwise.

"What? You spent breakfast quoting how many people die every minute, as well?"

"No. But I did, after all, read the phone book, not the *Almanac*."

"Doesn't it bother you?" she asked abruptly, whirling from the fire to face him for the first time. "He's your son, for God's sake. Aren't you concerned?"

"That's what I hired you for, Miss Guiness," he said slowly, and already she could see him tensing, the cold formality dropping like a shield between them. Yes, she thought it was something to be concerned about. Something *abnormal*, wasn't that the word they all liked so well?

"It's not that simple," she began, but he cut her off easily.

"I believe we've already covered this matter, Miss Guiness. As I told you before, your job is to take care of Andrew, not analyze my relationship with him. Besides," he said tightly, "I don't think even that will be your concern for very much longer."

She eyed him warily, her focus now completely on the conversation at hand. "What do you mean?"

The solution had occurred to him while he was in Geneva, and after some thought, he had decided it was a good one. It solved the problem of taking care of the child, and at the same time removed the child from Richard's immediate concern. It was a perfect solution, benefiting Andrew and himself. He didn't know why he hadn't thought of it sooner.

"Andrew is six years old now," he began slowly, "and as you know, a very precocious child. I've been exploring educational options for him, and at his age, I feel he is more than capable of entering private education. There are a few excellent schools in Germany—"

"Boarding schools, you mean!"

"Yes. They are boarding schools, but their curricula will give him incredible opportunities."

"What?" she cried, her voice genuinely outraged. Her temper flared, seizing all her previous guilt and confusion and converting it straight to anger. She couldn't believe what she was hearing. It was bad enough he fairly ignored his son, but to get the child back after five years only to ship him away again . . . ! Not if she could help it. "Intelligence and opportunity are the least of Andrew's concerns," she informed him vehemently. "What he needs is a stable, secure, loving environment to help teach him a little about the other side of life, such as living!"

She crossed toward him, and this close, he could see her blue eyes flashing midnight fire. He smiled at her coolly, even as desire once again knotted his stomach.

"I believe, Miss Guiness, that you are a bit of a romantic."

"Now what is *that* supposed to mean?" she demanded hotly, her gaze narrowing dangerously.

"You seem to think," Richard said dispassionately, "that the important things in life involve experiencing things like emotions and sentiments and playing. I disagree."

The ridiculousness of the statement was enough to stall her temper. "What do you mean you disagree? What do you think life is?"

"I think it is reasoning, I think it is logic. I think it's man's search for progress, man's mastering of the resources left to him. In short, it is something precise, something definable and something reasonable."

"You can't be serious."

"But I am," he said grimly, the intensity of his features almost enough to make her believe him.

"Well, I don't agree," Liz declared firmly, her own face intent. "And I don't think you should send Andrew to a boarding school. For goodness' sake, that child is giving himself enough of a textbook education, as it is. He doesn't need more lessons. He needs a father!"

"It is not your concern," Richard repeated coldly.

"Oh, yes it is," Liz told him, her jaw tightening stubbornly. "It is *very much* my concern. My job is to look after him. And do you know what I see? I see a scared little boy who idolizes his father. And I see a father who, for whatever reason, is perfectly intent on ignoring his own son. And I think that's a great tragedy."

Richard's lips thinned dangerously at her description. "Don't meddle in things you know nothing about," he warned.

"Well, how can I know anything," she retorted, "when you tell me nothing."

"It is not your place—"

"Oh, spare me," Liz cut in, her fragile emotions roaring out of control once and for all. "You cannot draw invisible boundary lines and hope to chain me in with them. I already know you don't have the highest opinion of me, Mr. Keaton, but when I took this job, I took it with the intention of doing my best. And if I have to tear down every last particle of your self-control, if I have to pry through your deepest darkest concerns to learn why you avoid your son, I will do it. If you don't like it, fire me."

She let the remark hang in the air, filling the vaulted ceiling with a tight, heated tension. Her cheeks were flushed, her chest heaving. Abruptly, their gazes locked, and the air between them heated another hundred degrees.

Damn it, she wanted to kiss him. She wanted to grab his head and savage his lips with all the rage and frustration boiling in her veins. And one look at his darkening eyes told her that he would give as good as he got.

"If you want to run," he spoke suddenly, his voice low and curt, "you'd better go now. Or I won't be held responsible for the consequences."

With a small cry of distress, she whirled and fled from the fired atmosphere of the room. Because she just wasn't ready for the consequences yet.

He watched her go, saying nothing, doing nothing. And he sat there in silence for a long while after, listening to the echoing remains of her anger in the vaulted ceilings of the library, watching the flames of the fire burn down, sipping his brandy.

His deepest darkest concerns?

No, he told himself. The words had only been said in anger. She wasn't serious about them, and even if she was, what could she find out after all these years?

Still, he had to admire her conviction. And in all honesty, he was impressed by how she'd handled the boy thus far. If only she knew . . . But she didn't know, and he would never tell. Alycia's death had sealed so many secrets, there was no use in disturbing them now.

Finally, he rose, his eyes unreadable as he picked up the book she'd been reading, to put it away. *Wuthering Heights,* he read to himself as he crossed the room to the empty slot on the shelf. He had read it himself a good thirty years ago. The eternal love of Catherine and Heathcliff, storming through the Yorkshire moors. He hefted the book into place, his fingers resting for a moment on the fine leather cover.

Maybe he had even believed in such things as eternal love back then, so many years past. It had been a long time ago, a very long time ago.

But you could never go back.

Liz thought about it all night, turning the evening's events over and over in her head as she lay in bed and stared at the ceiling above her. He'd kissed her. She'd let him. She'd wanted to kiss him again.

She rolled over in the bed, and stared at the far wall with dismal eyes. When she had determined, back in Maddensfield, that she needed to start her life over again, she hadn't meant to change *everything.* She hadn't come looking for this. Especially with a man who looked like some dangerous arch- angel most of the time.

The guilt churned her stomach once more, and her midnight eyes grew bleak. Nick was dead. He'd died in her arms on a sunny afternoon, and he'd taken with him all the dreams she'd ever had about her life. She'd loved him. God, how she'd loved him. A part of her still hurt, and even after twelve months, a part of her felt empty.

But he would never lie beside her again. He would never grin down at her, and squeeze her hand with impulsive emotion. She would never again wrap her arms around his strong shoulders, and bury her face against his neck. What they'd shared was gone, all lost to a senseless tragedy.

Now there was just her, and she had an obligation to live.

She rolled over to the other side, now staring at the door and still not finding answers. She'd liked Richard's kiss. She hadn't expected that. Half the time, she didn't think he even liked her. Half the time, she couldn't tell what was going on in his mind at all. But when he'd kissed her . . . Once more, she found herself shivering.

She tried lying on her back, and gazing at the ceiling instead, but it didn't make the truth any easier to face. She was attracted to another man. She'd *kissed* another man.

She squeezed her eyes shut, but the knowledge remained. Richard wasn't anything like Nick. He didn't look like Nick, he didn't act like Nick and he certainly didn't kiss like Nick. But he was Richard, and she'd liked being in his arms.

For a moment, she was tempted to call her mother. Her mother would know what to say. But then she sighed deep in the bed. No, she wasn't a child anymore. She was a woman and she could deal with this. Her life was changing, and she would figure out how to handle Richard Keaton, one way or another.

Abruptly, she frowned in the darkness and her thoughts became determined.

For whatever reason, the infamous Mr. Keaton seemed intent on keeping his distance from his own son. He had said he was no good for the child. Perhaps he was afraid, perhaps he didn't know how to get along with children.

Therefore, it would simply have to be her duty to prove to him otherwise. Mr. Keaton wanted to keep distant. Mr. Keaton wanted to keep his logical, cold little world intact. Mr. Keaton was about to be in for a surprise.

Because Liz had no intention of leaving Mr. Keaton alone. In the time she'd been here, she'd already grown fond of little Master Andrew, and he needed his father—and whether he admitted it or not, Mr. Keaton needed his son. No, she had no intention of letting Mr. Keaton avoid his own child. She would be charming, she would pretend she had given up on trying to bring them together. Then she would be free to "accidentally" force son and father together as much as possible. She would let Mr. Keaton see just how nice it would be to have Andrew in his life. And then . . .

And then they would see who was talking about boarding schools.

Yes, she thought as she finally drifted off to sleep, she would charm Mr. Keaton and help him learn about his son. For Andrew's sake. But a little voice inside her whispered, *Not only for Andrew's sake.* She steadfastly ignored it.

Chapter 4

"Flour."

"Flour."

"Salt."

"Salt?"

"Yes, salt."

Andrew passed her the salt. "Is that all?"

"Mmm ... baking powder. The stuff in the red can."

"Is that everything?"

She looked at the recipe once more. "Sure looks like it. Now stir."

She handed Andrew the bowl of soon-to-be brownie batter and he looked at it questioningly. Perched on top of a counter, he was still in his suit, but she had managed to get him to take off his jacket for the occasion. Liz herself was wearing a fiery fall skirt with a deep crimson sweater that was currently covered by a long white apron. The apron was, in turn, covered with large splotches of butter, sugar, vanilla, and now flour, as well. She had even managed to get some of the flour in her hair, despite her attempts at making sure the long strands were pulled back with a loosely tied ribbon.

But Liz wasn't about to worry about her hair now. She had gone to bed last night feeling angry and woken up ravenous. Her nerves felt on edge, and every time she contemplated facing Richard, a slow flush covered her cheeks. Maybe he would take her up on her rash words and fire her. Maybe he would kiss her again. At this point, she wasn't sure which worried her more. But as the morning had progressed without any sign of his granite countenance, she had finally relaxed enough to turn her attention to her stomach. Face it, she told herself, this nanny business was simply going to require large doses of chocolate if she was to survive. And the kitchen, for all its size and substance, didn't carry much in the way of chocolate, so she'd decided that they would just have to make their own.

It had taken her the better half of the morning and threats of a mental breakdown to squeeze the kitchen from the head chef, Dodd, but at last she had worn him down. So now, at precisely one o'clock, she and Andrew began the Great Brownie Experiment.

Through a small trick of cruel fortune, Andrew had managed to make it an entire six years without ever making brownies, a situation she was trying to rectify, though it had brought them a few problems. For starters, he had "cracked" the egg by pretty much flattening it against the outside of the bowl. But with a little coaching, he was moving right along and she was sure she could turn him into a brownie connoisseur in no time at all.

"How do you know when it's all mixed?" he asked. He had been stirring the batter with great concentration for the past few minutes, and was currently eyeing the brown goo with a mixture of suspicion and distrust.

"Taste it," she informed him as she greased the square pan.

"I need a bowl and a spoon, then," Andrew said.

"What for? You're holding a bowl and spoon now."

"Not this bowl and spoon," he explained patiently. "A bowl and spoon suitable for tasting."

She merely waved a flour-enriched hand at him. "You can't use a spoon to taste brownie batter. It dilutes the flavor. I'm sorry, but a straight finger is the only way."

"But that is unsanitary!"

"Well, I promise not to tell."

He looked at her with open doubt for a minute longer, but when it became apparent that she was truly serious about the matter, he gave the batter another suspicious glance and touched it with a tentative finger. When it didn't bite back, he proceeded to poke it a little more, and then with one last uncertain glance, he bravely stuck his finger in his mouth.

His eyes widened in speculation, his head tilting to the side for just one moment, eyes blinking rapidly with the verdict.

"Well, is it good?" came a distinctly male voice from the doorway.

Both Liz and Andrew turned abruptly, Andrew almost falling off his perch on the counter. There, standing in the doorway, was a nicely dressed but definitely unfamiliar man.

"Who are you?" Liz asked blankly.

"Blaine," Andrew answered for the stranger. "Uncle Blaine."

"Right you are, kiddo. Hey, nice tie." The man smiled the wide beaming smile of a born playboy. He dressed the part, too, Liz thought. Complete with a polo shirt and leather shoes. And considering that it was early October, his suntan had most definitely not come from these parts. He certainly didn't look like Richard, so perhaps the man was Alycia's brother. Given the blond looks and open manner, she figured that was a safe bet.

"Nice to meet you, Blaine," she said politely, reaching out her hand only to realize that it was covered with grease and flour from the pan. With a small laugh, she let her hand drop back to her side.

"And what brings you here?" Blaine asked, his eyes busily skimming her graceful figure as he leaned against the doorframe in a nonchalant pose. "Richard's tastes must be improving."

"She's my nanny," Andrew said suddenly, and the possessiveness in his voice was so intense it caused Liz to look at him sharply. The bowl of brownie batter lay forgotten in his hands, and his features had almost completely frozen over. For whatever reason, it seemed that Andrew did not like his Uncle Blaine.

"A nanny," Blaine repeated, and his voice revealed his shock. "My, my, nannies have changed since my day. I must say, the improvement is almost enough to make me wish I was six again."

The flattery was so blatant, Liz's eyebrows shot up in surprise. No, he certainly wasn't anything like Richard.

"Seriously," he told her, "I don't mean to harass you. I'm just a little surprised. It's been a long time since I've stopped by this place to find a beautiful woman cooking in the kitchen. Richard must be getting out more than anyone has realized."

"I wouldn't say that," she assured him. "As I said, I am just a nanny."

Blaine nodded, but the look in his eyes was speculative. "So what are you two cooking?" he asked suddenly. "Should my friends and I be staying for dinner?"

"No," Andrew said flatly, earning another sharp look from Liz. But Blaine just shrugged it off.

"Still sore about the ghost incident, huh, kiddo?"

"The ghost incident?" Liz questioned.

Andrew glared, Blaine laughed. "Yeah," Blaine answered. "I visited the Wynstons last year around Halloween and dressed up as a ghost Halloween night. I thought I'd let the kid experience a little of the Halloween spirit, you know, and knocked on his door. Hey, how was I to know you were so afraid of ghosts?"

"I'm not afraid of ghosts," Andrew said sharply, and behind the thick guard of his glasses, Liz could see the growing signs of his agitation. "One thousand, six hundred and eighteen Americans undergo plastic surgery a day for purely aesthetic reasons," he said loudly, his voice accusatory.

Blaine raised his eyebrow, but had the good sense not to respond.

"It's time to put the brownies in the oven," Liz interrupted tactfully. "How about you do the honors, Andy?"

"I don't want to," he said stubbornly. "Eight hundred and eighty-six people are cremated a day."

"Andy, all you have to do is pour the batter into the pan."

"Each day four thousand, nine hundred and twenty-eight are buried."

"Andy—"

"I bet some of them are still alive!"

"You're right, Andy, I'll take care of the brownies." The child was growing agitated very quickly, and Liz took the bowl from him carefully. "Andrew," she said calmly, "the brownies are supposed to cook for half an hour. How many seconds is that?"

"Every day, fourteen children die in the United States alone."

"Andrew. Tell me how many seconds." But his eyes had gone wild, dashing from Blaine to her to Blaine with blooming anger, and most disturbing of all, fear. "Eighty-one Americans kill themselves a day."

She had no choice. She grabbed his shoulders and shook him hard. "Calm down, Andrew," she said sharply. *"Now."*

"Easy little man," said Blaine from behind her. "Easy, Andy."

"Don't call me Andy!" Andrew shouted suddenly. "Only Liz can call me Andy. Only Liz, only Liz, ONLY LIZ!"

"Andrew!" she said again, starting to feel desperate. "Andrew, calm down. What's the square root of 6,561?"

He looked at her with glazed eyes and she shook him once more. "The square root of 6,561?" The numbers at last seemed to penetrate, his eyes slowly coming back into focus.

"Eighty-one," he said haltingly.

"Good, Andrew. Very good. Are you okay now?" She kept her voice level and looked at him closely. Never had she seen him become this upset this fast, and frankly, it had scared her. She was tempted to hold him close, but he was generally so reserved that she was afraid it might set him off again.

"Yes. May I go to my room now?" he asked. "I forgot to bring down my book."

She hesitated a moment, but then, with a final look at his somber eyes, she nodded her head. "The brownies will be done shortly," she told him. "And remember, they're best fresh."

He nodded, grabbing his jacket and awkwardly hopping down from the counter as quickly as he could. In a matter of minutes, he was fleeing from the kitchen.

"Sorry," Blaine said as soon as the boy had left the room. "I didn't mean to upset him like that."

She looked at him sharply. Andrew's reaction had scared her, and looking at this man's unrepentant face didn't help. "Andrew's a very sensitive child," she said curtly. "You ought to be more careful around him. The ghost incident should have been a hint about that."

The cool, midnight look of her blue eyes would have done her brothers proud. Blaine found himself uncharacteristically flushing in embarrassment.

"All right, all right," he said, throwing up his hands in mock surrender. "I honestly didn't mean to upset Andrew. Kids just aren't my strong suit. But I swear, I will be gentler in future."

She nodded, then sighed, the worried look never leaving her eyes.

"It couldn't have been just you," she said pensively as she poured the batter into the pan and slid it into the oven. "So he doesn't like you." She shrugged as she straightened. "Half the time I'm not sure he likes me and I've still never seen him like that."

"Well, living with those grandparents, who can blame him?"

She looked at him intensely for a moment. "You mean, your parents?"

Blaine looked momentarily confused, then gave a small laugh as his face cleared. "No, no. The Wynstons. Richard's and my parents died when we were in our teens."

Liz could only nod, trying to digest this new information all at once. Apparently, this golden playboy was Richard's brother, not Alycia's. And their parents were dead.

"I imagined you never met the dearly departed Wynstons?" Blaine stated.

Liz shook her head. "No, I didn't."

"Well, they were nice enough people, but quite frankly, they never recovered from Alycia's death."

"Richard's first wife."

"Uh-huh. And let me tell you, their house was practically a shrine to their daughter." Blaine pushed himself away from the doorframe and wandered over to the refrigerator. He continued to talk as he opened the door and examined the contents. "Every room, every hallway, every nook and cranny of that house had at least one picture of her, or a riding trophy, a favorite doll, a burning candle. Frankly, I'm thirty years old and the place even give me the creeps after a while."

"And Andrew was there for five years?" Liz asked, trying to keep her voice casual as she absorbed this unexpected fountain of information.

"Well," said Blaine as he took out a plate of cold cuts and imported cheese, "if the Wynstons' original plan had worked out, Andrew never would have come back. As far as they were concerned, they'd already lost their only child to Richard, and they certainly had no intention of losing their only grandchild, as well. But then nature had its own plan, it seems. Want some cheese?"

"What do you mean they lost their only child to Richard?" Her forehead furrowed in consternation.

"Come on," said Blaine. "You know what I mean. Or if you don't, then you're the only person in the state of Connecticut that hasn't heard the rumor."

"Oh," she said shortly and busied herself with wiping the counter. "You mean that Alycia was murdered?" She held her breath, trying to appear nonchalant as every nerve ending tensed for his reply. There were so many things she didn't know about Richard, and so many things she wasn't sure she had the courage to ask. Blaine, on the other hand, seemed bent on doling out information as casually as candy. "What exactly happened?"

Blaine looked at her queerly for a minute, his attention temporarily diverted from the food. "She was pushed from the right-hand tower," he said quietly, "five years ago."

Liz froze, the image in her mind of a woman plunging to her death just too strong. It had happened here, in this house. In spite of herself, she shivered.

"How do you know," she asked in a strained voice, "that she was pushed?"

Blaine shrugged, returning his attention to the cold cuts. "There were signs of struggle in the tower, plus the way she fell. The police had some trajectory type thing worked out for that. Richard could probably explain it better. Finally, there was just knowledge of Alycia herself. She wasn't exactly the suicidal type. You could say she believed in living life to the fullest."

"Oh." And all of a sudden, Liz didn't know what else to say. Somehow, she hadn't really wanted to believe any of it. Somehow, she had wanted to believe that Richard had told her his wife was murdered just to scare and intimidate her. But now it appeared it was definitely true. Alycia had been pushed from the right-hand tower, and everyone believed Richard had done it. She couldn't hold back another shiver.

"Didn't the police investigate? Surely they've found the killer by now," she said casually.

"It's been five years and they still haven't found anything conclusive," Blaine said, shrugging and rolling a slice of roast beef together with one of Swiss cheese. "They drilled Richard enough, that's for sure. I mean, everyone knew how much he and Alycia fought. Hell, sometimes I thought you could hear their screaming matches down in Haiti. Then, of course, there was the matter of his not having an alibi. He said he was working in his lab." Blaine shrugged. "He's always in that lab, but no one's ever there with him to confirm it. I don't know. In the end, the police only had circumstantial evidence, so they gave up. I doubt we'll ever know who did it now. Unless, of course, the diary's found."

Liz rubbed her arms. This whole conversation was making her nervous. When she'd told Richard last night that she was going to find out his deepest darkest concerns, this certainly hadn't been what she'd meant. Good God, and the man lived with this every day—knowing someone had killed his wife, knowing the killer was still out there.... And knowing that society had already found him guilty of the crime. No wonder he was so withdrawn.

"The diary?" She latched on to this with hope. "What do you mean by that?"

"Oh, Alycia always kept a daily diary. She liked to let everyone know about it, used to say half of Connecticut's wealthy had their secrets recorded in those pages. That's hard to believe, though. No one with half a brain would tell their secrets to Alycia." Blaine shuddered overdramatically. "That would be a bit like feeding a tiny piece of raw steak to a Doberman and thinking that would satisfy it. Still, there are probably some interesting things in that book. Maybe some of them would tell us who killed her.''

Liz frowned. "Surely it can't still be lost after five years?"

Blaine just shrugged. "Alycia was a very clever woman and she liked to keep her secrets. God knows where she put the damn thing."

Liz found herself filled with unease. The more she learned of Richard and his ex-wife, the more uncomfortable she became. Alycia didn't sound like a very nice woman, though Liz hated to think ill of someone she'd never met, especially someone who had died so tragically. This whole family was nothing like her own, that was for sure. Her brothers would certainly never stand in the kitchen and practically accuse one another of murder. Not even hot-tempered Garret and cool-eyed Cagney, who had enough differences between them to keep mealtimes interesting.

She didn't like this environment at all, and she was beginning to understand why Andrew maintained such a morbid streak.

"Andy's not that bad of a kid," she said out loud, more to herself than to Blaine. "He just needs a little attention, that's all. Not to mention some sunshine."

Blaine gave her a sideways glance. "Well, you two seem to have hit it off, all right. *Andy?* How did you ever convince him to let you call him that?"

"Last I knew," she confessed, "I still wasn't allowed to."

"Oh, well." Blaine shrugged. "Don't suppose you know if my brother's around?"

She shook her head and smiled ruefully. "Frankly, he doesn't tell me anything about his schedule. He seems to be slightly addicted to his work."

"Slightly?" Blaine responded wryly. "Just slightly?"

"Has he always been like that?" Liz asked hesitantly.

"Always," Blaine confirmed. "I think my first memory of Richard is of him taking his play mobile apart. He probably would have gotten it back together again, too, except that I swallowed one of the pieces. Tough break."

"Was your father like that, too?" she pressed, ignoring the bit about the piece he'd swallowed. She wanted to learn as much as she could about the cold, dark man for whom she was now working.

"My father? No, not that I remember. We don't really know why Richard is Richard. There's a sneaking suspicion, of course, that maybe they swapped babies at the hospital. You never know."

"Well, it seems to have paid off for him," Liz said in his defense. And all of a sudden she felt angry toward the blond playboy in the kitchen. Richard was his brother, after all, yet Blaine seemed perfectly insensitive toward the man. It bothered her. Maybe because she wasn't ready to dismiss Richard as an oddity quite yet. She'd seen his eyes, and heard the sharp bleakness of his voice.

She'd felt the raw hunger of his kiss.

She forced the thought away, not wanting to remember that moment. She was just feeling compassionate, she told herself. Because she did know how abnormally smart the man was—just as Andrew was exceedingly brilliant. And over the course of the past eleven days, she was beginning to see just what that meant for a child Andrew's age. His intelligence set him apart, alienating him from both children and adults until he belonged nowhere, with no one. She wondered if it really got any easier in adulthood.

But Blaine was shrugging again, a gesture she was definitely beginning to associate with him. "Yeah. Richard's the successful one. Me, I'm more dedicated to enjoying life. I figure, there are people out there that do nothing but work. So someone should at least do nothing but play. What do you say, nanny? Wanna play with me?"

The buzzer for the brownies went off, saving her from answering. A minute later she was pulling a small pan of rich brownies out of the oven. The wonderful scent of warm chocolate wafted through the air and she inhaled deeply, not bothering to stop the sigh that escaped her. Warm chocolate. It soothed her immediately. Chocolate was definitely the key to solving life's problems. She inhaled deeply once more.

"Mmm. It has been much, *much* too long."

Blaine was watching her, thinking the same thing himself, but not exactly in the same context. "Are you going to share?" he asked when he finally trusted himself to speak.

"I don't know," Liz said. Her eyes had cleared now, the sadness of the earlier conversation melting away under the on-slaught of rich, warm chocolate. "Brownies are pretty special. Besides, Andrew helped make them, so you'll have to ask him. Perhaps you could convince him to declare a truce."

Blaine gave her a doubtful look. "I told you, children were never my strong suit."

"Oh, I believe you, but I'm not letting you off the hook, either. Remember, be gentle."

"All right, all right. I'll go up to his room and see if he'll at least come back down."

"Better yet," Liz said after a minute, "why don't you take him up a small plate of brownies and a glass of milk. Knowing him, you'll probably have to take a knife and a fork, as well, but who knows, maybe chocolate will soften him up."

"And if he starts getting upset again?"

"Just call for me. I'll be right here holding down the fort. Remember, don't take any of the statistics personally. I think they're just his means of defense."

"Then I'd hate to see what his offense is like."

She smiled at that. "Somehow, I think we'll both wind up finding out eventually. Now, on to your mission. Stand sharp, and remember, never let him smell fear."

"Great, now I really feel confident."

"You're a grown man, you can handle it."

He managed to stall a few minutes longer, but when it became apparent that Liz was serious, and furthermore, that she was more than capable of evading his advances, he gave in gracefully and headed up the stairs. Then he went and found his friends.

It was the start of a long afternoon for all of them.

The evening, however, was hardly any better. Blaine had somehow managed to reach his brother, and using whatever sort of leverage brothers use, managed to drag Richard downstairs for dinner. When Liz first walked into the room, leading a sullen Andy behind her, she practically stopped in her tracks at the sight of Richard sitting at the table. It wasn't only the fact that he'd never joined them for dinner during her entire stay thus far, it was how he looked at the table. The imposing room with its formal table and towering chandelier seemed to shrink with his mere presence. Sitting stiff and tall at the head seat, he looked exactly like who he was—the master of the house.

It made her feel strange, a part of her wanting to reach out and touch him, if only to verify that he was flesh and blood. She wanted to feel the warmth of his skin, the roughness of his callused palms. She wanted to know the man, not the cold master with such rigid bearing that faced her on this night.

But instead, she simply seated Andy and then herself. The table practically drowned in the ensuing silence. Blaine appeared fifteen minutes later with three friends in tow, interrupting their soup course and hardly taking notice. He had barely sat down, when he began to more than make up for Richard's lack of conversation.

"Liz," he said, by way of introduction, "This is the gang. Jillian." A tall, elegant blonde nodded coolly. "Parris." He appeared to be a dark-haired version of Blaine, and grinned flirtatiously at her. "And finally, Greg." Greg was tall and thin, nodding toward her gallantly as his dark eyes glinted with quiet humor. Liz found herself smiling at all three, while Richard looked on darkly from the head of the table.

"And how long will the Gang of F—" he tripped over the word for a moment, then forced it out. "The Gang of Four be staying this time?" It had once been the Gang of Five, when Alycia had been alive.

Blaine merely looked at his brother in blatant unconcern, then turned his attention to Liz. "We all met at Princeton," he explained, and Parris and Greg confirmed this with a nod while Jillian merely watched in reserved silence. "Generally, we like to pop in four or five times a year, just to see how my dear brother is doing, of course."

Richard didn't say anything, but his jaw tightened at the thinly veiled sarcasm. The tension of the room was nearly thick enough to cut with a knife.

"I understand you're the nanny," Parris cut in effectively. "If we promise to be good boys, will you play with us, too? Jillian just isn't fun anymore."

Jillian raised her eyebrows at this, but the beginnings of a smile tickled at her cool lips. Liz found herself staring. Were they all this outrageous?

"Ignore Parris," Greg supplied easily, as if he'd read her thoughts. "After spending ten years running around with Blaine, he's become somewhat of a handful. I don't think they're a good influence on each other."

"And just who would be a good influence on them?" Jillian quizzed dryly.

"Satan," Andrew suddenly quipped, looking at them all darkly. The conversation came to an abrupt halt.

"Andrew," Richard began quietly, his face impassive as he cut his steak, "you don't insult guests, no matter what you might think."

Andrew's eyes shot up at this unexpected reprimand, but it seemed to be highly effective. Rather than pouting, as Andrew usually did when Liz uttered such things, Andrew suddenly sat straighter and peered out at Blaine's group with the most benign expression Liz had ever seen. She was going to have to remember this trick.

"In answer to your earlier question, brother dear," Blaine said smoothly, "we're not really sure how long. Jillian had a hankering to ride the horses, and you know we can't deny her anything. Besides, there's just not much going on this time of year. As usual, we'll be taking care of ourselves. I'm sure it's not a problem."

Richard just nodded, knowing it wouldn't have mattered even if it was a problem. Though Richard managed the estate, the house legally belonged to both him and Blaine. Blaine, with his jet-setting ways, wasn't around much. But when he did decide to pop in, it was generally unannounced, and he and his gang always left just as abruptly. There were times that Richard thought they did it just to annoy him. They'd all been close to Alycia. While they might sit at his table, eat his food and smile, he had no doubt what really went on in their minds, particularly in Parris's. Alycia had told Richard she'd had an affair with the man. Of course, that hadn't been her first fling and it hadn't been the one that had truly hurt.

His fingers tightened on his knife, but then he forced his grip to relax. He chewed mechanically, and let his mind wander to his dielectric. It was either that, or watch Liz sitting so calmly beside Andrew and remember how her lips had tasted under his own. And realize how Blaine, Parris and Greg were looking at her, as if they, too, wanted to take her lips—

He pushed his food away. He wasn't hungry anymore. He wanted to go back to his tower, and curl his hands around his weight set instead. He suddenly had a lot of tension to burn.

Trying to ease the unsettling atmosphere, Liz spoke up, asking Richard if she and Andrew might visit his lab in the afternoon. Richard nodded curtly. Andy piped up and asked him if he liked brownies. Richard nodded again. Undaunted, Andy promised to make his father brownies. Richard nodded yet again.

Liz was almost grateful by the time the dinner ended. Blaine and his friends took off for a roaring night on the town, and though they told her she was more than welcome to join them, she waved them off on their own. They were a little beyond her small-town speed. Besides, she wanted to get her hands on Richard, if only to rebuke him for his unenthusiastic response to Andrew's brownie offer.

Whatever was plaguing Richard, however, was enough to keep him in his lab for the rest of the night. Liz retreated to the library for her customary night reading. But this time she stayed long past midnight, waiting for the sound of footsteps. Waiting...

But he never came. She tried telling herself it was irrelevant that she had come to the library merely to read and relax after her rather intense day. But that didn't explain why the pages she'd been reading blurred suspiciously after the midnight hour came and went. That didn't explain why at each small creak and groan of the house, her pulse jumped, her senses focused intensely on the sound. But only silence filled the house, and save for her own solitary presence, emptiness filled the library. At one, she finally gave up her vigil, and returning the book, damped the fire and retired.

Even then, sleep was a long time coming.

"Liz. Liz, wake *up*."

"Hmm?" She made a noble effort to bat the hand away, but it managed to persist.

"Liz. Liz, you have to get up *now*," the young voice insisted.

With a small sigh, she peeled open an eye. The room was pitch-black, but just faintly she could make out the form of one Andrew Keaton, complete with round glasses and a bathrobe.

"What time is it?" She yawned, her eyes still trying to penetrate the darkness.

"Four twenty-two."

"In the morning?"

He nodded.

She sat up sharply. "Is everything all right?" she asked quickly.

Once more he nodded, causing her to sink back with a relieved but tired groan.

"Go away, Andy," she told him and snuggled back down in her bed. "I don't work before at least seven."

"But Liz, we have to make the brownies for today."

She sighed, collecting her tired wits. "Andy," she managed to say levelly enough, "you and I both know how much I love chocolate, but not even I make brownies at four in the morning."

Andrew's lip jutted out suspiciously. "You said you would help me," he said with a small quiver in his voice.

"And I will, Andy. Around ten or so."

"The brownies won't be done in time!"

"Andrew," she said, starting to lose whatever meager patience she possessed at four in the morning, "it only takes about an hour to make brownies. And we are not meeting your father until one. There is plenty of time, even if we start at ten. Now, *go to bed*."

But he still wasn't moving, and after one long, droopy-eyed moment, she realized he wasn't going to. Good God, four-thirty in the morning and she had to deal with this? What in the world had possessed her to take this crazy job!

"Andy," she started out firmly, mustering her small supply of energy. "Go to bed. Now!"

Once again, he simply stared at her. "I can't," he said after a minute, and this time the quiver in his voice was more noticeable. She looked at him carefully, by now fully awake in spite of herself.

"Is something wrong?" she asked him once more.

He shook his head, but his lower lip was still trembling.

"Andrew, if there is nothing wrong, why won't you go back to bed?"

"There's a ghost in my room," he whispered softly.

She sighed. A ghost in his room. She should have known. Probably just the aftereffects of the memories Blaine had invoked. Well, at least this was more standard ground when dealing with six-year-olds. When she was his age, she had had her fair share of run-ins with a bogeyman or two.

"I'll tell you what," she whispered back. "Why don't we go back into your room together, and turn on the lights, and look in the closet and under the bed. I'm sure that will scare the ghost away for good."

"But she'll come back."

"She?"

He looked at her stubbornly, his face pale.

"She will."

"How about we leave on one light?" Liz said slowly. In spite of her best intentions, she was beginning to feel a little bit nervous herself. *She?* Why had he called the ghost a she? She shook her head firmly to clear the thought. Andrew was a spooked child, they would turn on some lights, that would be the end of it. "What do you say, Andrew?" she tried again, keeping her voice confident and light. "Will that help?" He still looked less than certain, but finally he gave in with a small nod.

Throwing back the covers, she took his hand and led him to the door separating their rooms. She had to feel her way carefully in the dark, going around her bed, and then over to the wall. Suddenly, looking around, she began to understand just how scary the rooms might seem to a six-year-old boy. In the blackness, the ornate carvings of the armoire began to take on the twisted bearings of gargoyles and the floor of the old house squeaked beneath her feet, echoing through the empty old house.

Andy tightened his grip on her hand, and she squeezed his as much to comfort him as herself. Slowly, she pulled open the door.

Andrew's room was even darker than her own, the curtains pulled tight across the window until only a sliver of light crept through. The dark closet seemed like some hideous, gaping mouth, and the table and chairs blended together into a hairy gothic beast. Suddenly, she wasn't feeling so confident anymore and phrases she'd heard all too recently began to sound off in her head.

"Alycia was murdered."

"I doubt we'll ever know who did it."

She swallowed heavily. It was just the house, she tried to rationalize. It was an old house, and with its creaky boards, vaulted ceilings and ornately carved trim, well . . . it fed the imagination.

But then something moved suddenly on the left, and she jumped, causing Andrew to yelp.

Their reflections. It was just their reflections in the mirror. Her nerves couldn't take any more; she looked desperately for the light switch. Her hand found it and gratefully flipped it— nothing.

No light. Nothing. Oh, boy.

"What was that?" whispered Andrew shrilly. "What was that sound?"

"I don't hear anything," Liz whispered back, but in that instant, she did.

Something was scratching at the window. Or someone.

"Alycia was murdered."

"I doubt we'll ever know who did it."

Oh, this was not a good time. Desperately, she flipped the switch again and again. And still the darkness reigned, still the scratching sounds whispered across the room.

Andrew whimpered slightly at her side, his grip on her hand now cutting off any hope of blood supply. Grimly, Liz swallowed and squared her shoulders. She did not believe in ghosts, and she was not going to let a creaky old house with faulty electricity get to her. Besides, Andrew needed her. That simple realization lent her strength.

"Stay here," she said to him now. "I'm going to open the curtains."

But Andrew shook his head frantically in the darkness, his grip on her hand tightening even more. "Don't go," he whispered desperately. "The ghost will get you. She will, she will, she will."

"Andrew," Liz managed to say calmly enough given the fact she was standing in a pitch-black room where the lights wouldn't work and strange noises were coming from the window. "You read all the science books. You know ghosts don't exist."

"But they do," he said softly. "*She* does."

In spite of herself, she shivered in the darkness. She? Must he continue to call his fictional ghost a she?

"I'm going over there, Andy," she said at last. "Now, you can either come with me, or stay here."

There wasn't much hesitation; he went with her. Together, hand gripped tightly in hand, they crept their way along the wall, Liz using her other hand to guide them.

The scratching grew louder.

"I want my dad," Andrew whimpered, and quite honestly Liz agreed with him wholeheartedly.

"It'll be okay," she tried to reassure him, but was reaching the point where she could barely reassure herself.

"Alycia was murdered."

"I doubt we'll ever know who did it."

She was beginning to hate her own imagination. Ghosts do not exist, she tried repeating to herself over and over again. Not even in spooky old houses. But then the scratching grated across the window again, and her heart stopped beating in her chest.

They were a few feet from the dark hanging curtains and there was only one way to do it. Liz drew a deep breath, closed her eyes and yanked the curtain back.

Andrew screamed, she jumped, and came face-to-face with several long, ugly tree branches.

"Geez Louise," she breathed, her heart coming back to rest in her chest, where it thumped madly. "It's only a tree, Andrew. Only a tree."

By the silver moonlight that was streaming in, she could see his face. It was chalk pale, his eyes the size of saucers. She shook him gently, and he immediately buried himself in her arms.

"It's okay, sweetheart," she told him in a soft Carolina voice meant to soothe his nerves. "Honestly, Andrew. Everything is all right. Now take a deep breath. Relax."

But just as she said the words, the door banged open with a crash and both she and Andrew jumped once more in fright.

"What's wrong?" demanded the unmistakable voice of Richard. Liz sagged against the wall in relief, Andrew still wrapped tightly around her.

"Good God," she breathed. "Don't ever do that again. You just gave me a heart attack!"

The candle he was holding flickered until it caught both her and Andrew in its wavering light. "I thought I heard someone scream," Richard said tersely, his winter-blue eyes slicing through the darkness. "Is everything okay?"

Liz nodded, even though Andrew was still shaking against her. "A tree outside Andrew's window just gave him a fright. But it's all right now, isn't it, Andy?"

The boy's pale face turned to peer out from the comfort of her stomach. "I w-w-want the lights on," he said tremulously.

Richard set the candle on the dresser, taking in the boy's ashen features. The child was honestly terrified and it occurred to him all at once that this was the first time he'd seen Andy act as a child. The sudden urge to reach out, to stroke his hair in parental comfort was almost overwhelming. He fought it grimly, willing himself to keep his hand at his side. The boy didn't need him. Richard could see just how tightly Andrew clung to Liz. The child trusted her, trusted her as absolutely as Richard had seen him trust anyone. And he also noted the way Liz reacted to him, one arm curved around his shoulders, offering him the comfort and security he needed in the jumping shadows.

He couldn't quite take his eyes from the picture, even as he willed himself not to be affected by it.

"The electricity is out," he said. "Will a few candles do?"

But the candlelight merely flickered across the room, casting light and shadows at random. It added to the spell more than it helped. Andy pressed closer to Liz. Her hand stroked the top of his head to soothe him.

Richard watched the motion, feeling raw emotion surge through him. Why did she look so right with the child? Why did she look as if she cared? Didn't she know she was just a nanny? Didn't she know she wasn't supposed to belong?

He'd been avoiding her all day, trying to forget last night and the way she'd felt in his arms, the way she'd looked at him in horror immediately afterward. He wanted her out of his dreams, out of his mind. He'd even avoided the library, determined to prove to himself that it didn't matter. But he'd thought of her just the same. Hunched over his damn equations, it was her picture that burned into his mind.

And now she was here, standing just seven feet away with a terrified child wrapped around her leg and nothing but a thin T-shirt for cover.

His grip on the candle holder tightened.

"Are any of the lights working?" Liz asked.

Her hair was tumbling down, framing her face in sleepy disarray. He turned his face away. "I haven't checked the whole house," he said shortly. "But I assume the problem is with the power lines, and therefore, yes, the whole house is without electricity."

"What if we go back to the library?" Liz suggested. "We could light another fire in the fireplace and sit down together there." She looked at Andrew's drawn face. "Would that make you feel better, Andrew? Maybe we could even roast some marshmallows."

He looked uncertain, but after a moment, he nodded. "All right," he said quietly.

She looked at Richard. "How does that sound?"

It sounded like a cozy domestic scene. It sounded like three souls huddling up together against the cold, dreary darkness.

It sounded like something he definitely shouldn't do.

But he found himself nodding, anyway.

There was a small shift then, Andrew releasing his death grip on Liz at last. The boy walked forward tentatively, attempting to be brave. But with the shift, Liz became fully exposed to Richard's gaze for the first time. Like a drowning man, he took in the sight, the short jersey T-shirt just skimming the top of her thighs, her legs, long and slender stretching out before him. He'd seen women in silk and he'd seen women in lace. But he'd never seen a woman as sexy as this.

He thought his knuckles might break with the effort at control.

"Couldn't you at least put on a robe?" he managed to ask tightly.

Liz glanced down at her old football T-shirt, apparently just realizing how little she was wearing. "Sorry," she muttered, heading for the door that connected her room to Andrew's.

"In future," Richard cut in, "perhaps you should consider more appropriate sleepwear when on duty."

"You're right," Liz told him dryly. "From now on, I'll sleep in all those lovely uniforms you purchased."

She vanished into her room before he could reply, which was probably just as well. His nerves were wound impossibly tight, too tight, to deal with such things as Liz in only that T-shirt.

"Let's go downstairs," he said abruptly. Andrew nodded, but it seemed to Richard that the child's eyes looked slightly accusatory, and he felt even worse. Then suddenly the little boy glanced at the jumping shadows, and stuck his hand tightly in Richard's grip.

Richard nearly jumped himself at the unexpected gesture. Andrew had not touched him since his arrival. Richard had thought that it was best. But now, the little hand tucked so securely in his own massive grip, Richard felt something strange and tight grip his chest. It felt almost like pain.

His face grim in the darkness, Richard led Andrew downstairs in complete silence. With studied detachment he noted that the scared little boy disappeared with each step, until soon it was the somber child-genius that walked by Richard's side.

It's better this way, Richard reminded himself. Yet in his mind's eye he could see the scared Andrew, clutching at Liz.

Liz, in her simple T-shirt, holding the child, giving him the comfort he needed.

She was the first touch of warmth this old house had ever seen. But she was six years too late.

Chapter 5

Sometime shortly after six, the lights came on with a small flicker. Liz's eyes had already drifted shut and Andrew was curled next to her on the leather sofa. Only Richard was still awake, sitting in the chair by the fire.

As her vision cleared, Liz had the impression of a lone man, his gaze dark and intent on the dancing flames. Even now, in the dawning hours of the morning, nothing gave him away. His features were as impenetrable as before, his hand tapping lightly on the arm of the chair to the silent rhythm of his own private thoughts. He glanced up only when she finally raised her head.

"The lights," she said softly, her voice husky with sleep.

He nodded, his eyes skimming briefly over her bathrobed figure before returning once more to the flames.

"It's morning now," he said, his own voice quiet in the vaulted room. She and Andrew had been asleep for the past hour, curled together so softly and snugly it had almost hurt to look at them. How was it that one woman could integrate herself into things so quickly? Even looking at her now, her hair mussed, her eyes soft with sleep, he could feel his stomach tighten, his pulse leap.

He'd looked at her a hundred times in the past hour. And each and every time he'd thought of how her lips had tasted beneath his own. Sweet, lush and willing. His body hurt with the relentless ache, and there was nothing he could do about it. Not after the way she'd looked at him after that kiss, her eyes filled with such horror. He wouldn't go through that again, he simply wouldn't. Besides, now golden boy Blaine was back, and he'd seen how Blaine looked at her....

It would only be a matter of time. Not that he cared. The tenth sharpest mind in the country was much too smart for such emotional drivel as that.

"You should go back to bed and get some rest," he found himself saying, his voice expressionless and curt.

She nodded, glancing over at Andrew.

"He almost looks like a six-year-old when he sleeps," she whispered.

Richard could only nod his head in agreement. Lost in slumber, Andrew's defensive posture was gone. Now he was simply a little golden-haired boy, worn out by the day's activities. He was curled into a little ball, his glasses lying beside him. He looked...vulnerable. Once more, Richard felt his chest tighten. Once more, he steeled himself against the intensity of the emotion.

"Do you think you can carry him back to his room?" Liz asked, keeping her voice low. "It seems a shame to disturb him."

He should have said no, but instead, he found himself nodding. He got up, and picked up the weight of the child easily. The boy barely stirred, his head falling soft and comfortable on the solid expanse of his father's shoulder. Richard followed Liz out of the library, and willed himself to be strong.

Carrying the child, however, he felt himself assaulted by a thousand and one sensations. Years ago he had carried this same child, but then the small one-year-old frame had been a whisper against his chest, a tiny, fragile burden. Now the very same child was a solid weight against him, firm and warm with five years of growth. The smell of baby powder was gone, but the simple burden of a child's trust remained.

They came to the bedroom. Liz smoothed back the rumpled covers of the twin bed, silently gesturing for Richard to lay Andrew down. As gently as possible, he complied, setting the boy down.

Abruptly he felt the loss, the warmth of his small charge replaced immediately by a rush of cold air. He'd come in as a father, but stood now as a lone man; he hated himself for noting the difference.

Andrew stirred, muttering in his sleep. But then, with a sigh, he rolled over and Liz pulled the covers snugly over him. Wanting to keep him warm, she tucked the edges of the blankets securely around his neck.

She glanced up in time to catch Richard staring at the child with the most intense look on his face. And for a moment, there was a flash of rippling emotion in his pale blue eyes that could only have been yearning.

Then suddenly it was gone, and once again his face was the smooth dispassionate slate of before. She still couldn't stop herself from reaching out her hand and laying it on his arm.

"Thank you," she whispered.

His eyes fell to her hand, small and feminine on his arm. Emotion ripped through him once more and the temptation to take her into his arms, to hold her if only for a fragile moment, was almost too strong to resist. He steeled himself against desire willing the weakness away. He was a solitary man; it was the way it was meant to be.

Looking up, he met her expectant gaze with his own dispassionate stare. "For what?" he asked tonelessly.

"For coming to Andy's room when you heard the commotion. For taking him down to the library for comfort. For carrying him back up to bed still asleep. He needs those things, you know."

Her voice was beguiling, the soft, velvety drawl trying to penetrate his control to find the emotion she'd witnessed so briefly. But his control was too strong, and once more he was the cold, intimidating man she'd known before. He simply shrugged, looking at her with his wintry blue eyes. "You should get some sleep, too," he said simply. "It's been a long night."

She nodded, letting her hand fall away. Whatever he had been thinking was lost. He'd already told her that his relationship with his son was not her concern, and he seemed intent on keeping it that way. Still, she'd seen the look in his eyes. The man obviously cared for his son more than he was willing to admit. She just needed to show him the way, and he would come around. She was convinced of it. This night made it clearer to her more than ever just how much Andrew needed his father. And how much Richard needed his son.

"You should get some rest, as well," she whispered, leading the way out of the room. "You work too hard, as it is, and tomorrow—well, today—is going to be a big day."

"What time are you coming to the lab?" he asked.

"Let's say two or so. And we'll bring the promised brownies."

She saw his face twitch into what might have been a wry smile. It made the remembered words of beratement for his earlier cold treatment of the brownies die on her lips.

"Yes, the brownies," he repeated dryly. "See you then."

She nodded, the words suddenly making her nerves tingle. *See you then.* They sounded so full of promise. His pale gaze was on her, and abruptly she became aware of the limited clothing beneath her robe. Unconsciously, her hand clutched the top of the terry cloth together, and his eyes looked at her with a knowing glint. She blushed, thinking she ought to disappear into her room now, but standing in the hall like an idiot instead. Then, without any direction from her, her own eyes settled upon his lips.

The air sparked, and a stomach-tightening burn of awareness filled the dimly lit hall. And just when she should have stepped back through her doorway, she found herself taking a small step forward.

An experiment, the voice at the back of her mind whispered. *Just to see if two nights ago in the library had really happened.* Then his lips came down abruptly and she wasn't thinking anymore.

His lips were as hard as she remembered, hungry and demanding. They slanted over hers harshly, demanding her participation even as they dared her to step back. His tongue plunged into the warm recesses of her mouth, caressing her deeply as she sagged against him. Her arms wrapped around his strong shoulders for support, her fingers finding the silky spikes of his midnight hair. He tasted like brandy, fiery and beguiling. She pressed closer, wanting to feel more, to taste more.

Dimly, she became aware of his hands on her bathrobe, pushing the terry cloth aside until his hands could plunder inside. They curled around the small of her waist, then caressed up her back to press her closer. She was still gasping from the impact, when his palm stole forward to cup her breast.

She gasped, her eyes turning black with desire as they fluttered open to meet his gaze. His eyes were no longer cold, she thought hazily, but seemed to burn with a fierce need that sent more tingles down her spine.

And she desired him with an intensity that suddenly scared her. She wasn't ready for this, wasn't ready to feel anything quite this powerful. But even as she began to draw away, he pulled her closer.

His lips claimed hers once more, but this time they were no longer demanding. Instead, his tongue delicately outlined the lush fullness of her lips as if it had all the time in the world. He tasted one corner of her mouth, and even as her lips parted with breathless anticipation, he ignored the offering with keen discipline. He dipped his tongue into the other corner of her mouth, hearing her light moan. She was sweet and exquisite, at once bold and bashful. Slowly, he penetrated her mouth with his tongue, tracing the line of her teeth, then finding her tongue to tangle with his own.

Her knees gave out under the slow onslaught, her senses overwhelmed by the sheer sensuality of his kiss. But he held her up easily, his fingers strong and warm on her waist. She had never felt so tiny and feminine. . . .

His tongue probed deeper, and her arms tight around his neck, her breasts aching and heavy against his chest. He licked the inside of her mouth languorously, delving slow and sure, seeming to relish each voluptuous movement.

She moaned again and he felt it in every burning cell of his blood. Slowly, relentlessly, he pulled away.

It took her a good sixty seconds to realize he wasn't coming back. She had to bite her lips to keep herself from moaning in loss. Her eyes fluttered open, the lids heavy with the desire. At once, she became aware of his gaze hard upon her face. His eyes no longer looked at her with raw passion. Instead, they glittered with a dark combination of rage and reluctant hunger.

"Do you want me to stop?" he growled softly.

The words doused her passion as quickly as a cold shower. She became aware of her compromising position, of how long they'd been kissing. A dull flush crept up her cheeks, and her hands scrambled to pull her robe back together. Richard watched her movements with cynical eyes.

"You're too old to play the virgin," he said mockingly.

She stiffened, and for one moment, she was tempted to hit the man. But then she tightened her robe with the rigid control and pride she'd learned from growing up with four mercilessly older brothers. She looked him straight in the eye, her midnight gaze not giving an inch.

"My apologies," she said curtly. "I didn't mean for this to happen. I can assure you, it won't happen again."

This time Richard stiffened, his pale eyes growing even colder as they homed in on her. Slowly, he reached out and touched her cheek, no expression crossing his face as she flinched.

"Only fools make promises," he said softly. He knew why she was turning away, he remembered that look of horror in her eyes after their last kiss. She didn't trust him, she was afraid of him. Fine then, he sentenced himself savagely. Perhaps it was better this way. God knows he would have done better with Alycia if she'd ever had the slightest bit of fear.

He let his eyes fall to her lips one last time, taking in the full, bruised softness of their form. Then his gaze swept up, full of mocking intensity.

She swallowed heavily under that stare, her mind filling with too many sensations—the feel of Richard's kiss, the intensity of his gaze. Then she remembered Nick. Sweet Nick, down on the ground with so much blood—

Her control wavered, her shoulders folding forward as the first sliver of pain washed through her. For one instant, she swayed on her feet, the exhaustion and mental strain almost too much.

Richard saw her waver, and his eyes narrowed with new and sudden puzzlement. He'd seen the pain in her eyes, her face was so damn open. It was the same sharp sliver of emotion he'd seen that first day when she'd sat in his office. He didn't understand it, and he didn't like things he didn't understand.

But that didn't stop him from suddenly reaching out a hand to steady her elbow. Her midnight blue eyes swept up, and he saw gratitude. It made him feel like an absolute lout.

"You should get some rest," he said forcefully, hating the way she tied his insides into knots when he knew better than to be manipulated by a woman. For all he knew, this was some grand charade on her part to keep him off balance. God knows, Alycia had performed similar tricks in her lifetime. Though, over time, he'd come to realize her China blue eyes never completely lost their hard, metallic glint.

Liz simply nodded, steadying herself. The worst of the anguish passed, as it usually did. Now she was just left with the feeling of emptiness and vulnerability. Sometimes, she hated that more, especially when looking at this dark, unreadable man before her.

"Thank you," she whispered simply, and before her control completely gave out, she pulled away and disappeared inside her room.

Richard let her go, swearing one soft, succinct word under his breath. But it was aimed as much at himself as at the situation. He didn't understand her. And he didn't understand himself when he was around her.

He scowled as he stormed to his own room, and even in the light hours of the morning, sleep was a long time coming.

Liz rose at nine to the sound of movement from Andrew's room. Rousing herself completely, she set about getting ready for what indeed would be a busy day. She didn't allow herself to think about last night, or the kiss, or Richard's reaction. She was attracted to the man, she would allow herself that much— even if it did fill her with a twinge of guilt. Sooner or later, this situation, her being attracted to someone, was bound to occur.

All she needed was more time. And someone less formidable than Richard Keaton.

Well, she'd meant what she'd said last night. She had no business cultivating his kisses, not when she barely knew the man, and not when she still felt unsure about him. From now on, except where Andrew was concerned, she was going to stay clear of him.

She had no sooner stepped out of her room than she walked straight into Blaine, who was standing in the middle of the hall, still dressed in his clothes from the night before. He gave her a startled look.

"What were you doing in there?" he asked her sharply.

She looked at him blankly. "That's my room."

He appeared genuinely shocked. "So that's the way it is. I guess I should have known. One doesn't exactly hire a nanny of your years for her 'experience.'"

Liz looked at him with wide eyes, outrage immediately bristling at the blatant insinuation. "And just what do you mean by that?" she demanded.

"Oh, come on," Blaine said with a careless gesture of his hand. "You can't tell me you're staying in the room adjoining Richard's and you're not involved with him. But honestly, you could have just admitted it straight out. I wouldn't have thought any less of you."

"I have no idea what you are talking about," Liz told him firmly. "My room doesn't adjoin Richard's, it adjoins Andrew's. And speaking of Andrew, I have an appointment with him to make brownies. So if you will excuse me—"

"Wait a minute," Blaine said sharply, grabbing her arm as she tried to push past him. "Let me get this straight. Are you telling me that Andrew has the room adjoining this one?"

"Of course," she informed him, her voice prim.

"Well, I'll be damned," Blaine breathed to himself, relinquishing his grip on her arm. "Richard actually went ahead and did it. He talked of it for the longest time, but I hadn't realized he'd actually done it."

"Done what?"

"Changed the rooms," Blaine explained slowly. "You, my dear—and Andrew—are now living in what used to be the master suite. Split rooms, of course. You have to remember just how old this house is. After the accident, Richard talked of moving out of the suite. For a while, he even muttered about boarding the whole thing up. But I guess he went with a little redecorating instead. I wonder where the old boy is holed up now."

"Wait a minute," Liz echoed this time, a frown furrowing her forehead. "You're telling me that I'm in Alycia's half, and Andrew is in Richard's half?"

"Yes. That's it."

She couldn't help herself; she shivered. She had a six-year-old waking her up in the middle of the night because a "she" ghost was in his room, and now she learned that she was occupying the rooms of a woman who had been murdered.

Oh, she was definitely a long way from Maddensfield now.

"What was she like?" Liz found herself asking suddenly. "Richard's wife, I mean."

"Alycia?"

"Yes."

"What? You've never asked him about her?"

She gave Blaine a narrow look. "It's hardly a simple thing to bring up. Besides, I'm just the nanny, and it's really none of my business. I'm only curious, that's all."

"She was beautiful," Blaine said abruptly, and his eyes were no longer looking at Liz, but peering back into the past. "She was the most beautiful woman you'd ever seen."

"How so?" Liz prodded.

"Her hair was exactly like Andrew's," Blaine said. "Her eyes, too, that delicate China blue color. She had perfect, refined features, with just a hint of vulnerability. Men are real suckers for that kind of thing."

His lips curled a little with the last words, and Liz couldn't miss the undertone of self-loathing. She looked at him intently, trying to picture this woman. "So all men really liked her?" she said slowly.

"Oh, yeah. When she debuted, every man went after her."

"But Richard won?"

Blaine only nodded.

"She must have really been something," Liz said after a bit, "to pull Richard away from his work." And on the heels of that thought came a thin streak of what seemed suspiciously close to jealously. She pushed the emotion away.

"She did in the beginning," Blaine was saying. "Hell, you wouldn't have recognized Richard back then. He actually cut back to forty-hour work weeks. He had a single yellow rose sent to her each and every day. He recited poetry, he danced, he romanced. It was truly amazing. I'd never seen him like that. Never have since, for that matter."

Liz just nodded, feeling the prickles run uncontrollably through her. Danced? Romanced? She couldn't even get the man to carry on a conversation.

"He must still miss her," Liz said shortly. "What a shame."

Blaine looked at her sharply then. He laughed, but it wasn't a pleasant sound. "Miss her? I honestly doubt that. Richard might have picked out the most beautiful woman for himself, Liz, but he also chose the most ill-suited. Alycia was an outgoing sort of girl. She liked attention, she liked the social scene. She liked to see and be seen. And, well, Alycia liked men. All kinds." Once more, bitterness laced his words, and the smile that twisted his face looked out of place after seeing his earlier, flirtatious ones. "Richard never was a good judge of women," he said flatly.

"And you are?" Liz quizzed with an arched eyebrow.

"Hey, I wasn't the one holed up in a book for all of childhood," Blaine told her. "One of us had to have a life."

"If you're so experienced, why didn't you marry Alycia?"

But Blaine backed off the suggestion with a wave of his hands. "Marriage? Me? I don't think so."

Yet there was something in the way he said those words that made her look at him again. So he wasn't the marrying type, she could buy that. But let the challenge of the most sought-after woman slip by? She definitely couldn't see *that*. And all at once she wondered just how deep the sibling rivalry between Blaine and Richard ran. One brother was bookish and hard-working. The other was a playboy and fun-loving. But the bookish one had gotten the girl, at least, temporarily. Somehow, she just couldn't see that sitting well with Blaine. God knows, if last night's dinner had been anything to go by, there was tension between the two.

"I really need to get downstairs," she said finally. "But thanks for the conversation."

Blaine nodded, his eyes moving past hers to stare at the door she'd closed behind her. He frowned. "Fine, fine," he said almost absently, then he looked down at his clothes. "I ought to be getting to bed myself."

Liz's eyes widened at the apparent indication he'd just returned from last night's revelries. He and his gang were definitely a fast crowd. Shaking her head, she brushed past him and continued down the hall. When he called out behind her, she turned. "Liz, since your room does adjoin only Andrew's, I take this to mean that you and Richard aren't involved, correct?"

She managed a small smile. Involved? No. They were only two strangers who were drawn to the library by firelight, two strangers who had shared a kiss or two that had made matters worse.

Richard had once danced, and romanced a woman. The words came to her unbidden, taunting her. Underneath that steely reserved man lay the heart of a romantic. She wanted to know that man, she thought suddenly, her forehead furrowing once more. She wanted to know what made his features so grim at night. She wanted to know what kept him awake in the early-morning hours.

And she wanted to know what thoughts crept into his mind when he looked at his sleeping child with such heartrending yearning.

She wanted to know the real Richard Keaton.

Blaine was still looking at her with expectant eyes.

"No," she said slowly. "We aren't involved."

She continued her way downstairs.

Promptly at two, Liz led Andy to the left-wing tower with the promised plate of brownies in hand. For all of Andy's previous enthusiasm to see his father's lab, now that the moment had finally arrived, his face was tight with tension. He'd been silent all morning, dark circles rimming his eyes from the long night before. Liz had actually begun to wish he would rattle off his incessant statistics, anything other than this strained silence.

"Are you excited?" she asked him now.

He nodded, but the look on his face negated the gesture.

"Come on, Andy," she tried. "We're visiting your father in his lab. You can see what he does, where he works. It'll be great."

In point of fact, she wasn't so sure. Given the family's conversational abilities, she had already figured out that it would be a long afternoon for her. But she was determined to get the two to interact. There was still Richard's threat of sending Andy to a boarding school, something that she believed more than ever would be disastrous for the child. The father and son needed to become better acquainted. From what she'd seen, both were brilliant. They ought to fit together perfectly.

They were nearing the top of the three stories of long winding stairs. Chilly drafts swept by them every now and then, but for the most part, the old tower was better lit and heated than the rest of the house. The carved stone steps were worn in places, an indication, Liz figured, of how much time Richard spent going to and from his lab.

At the top of the stairs was a solid wooden door. Giving Andy one last reassuring look, Liz raised her hand and knocked. Abruptly, the door opened.

Richard stood there, dressed in dark blue slacks and a blue and white pin-striped shirt. His face, while as controlled as ever, seemed extra tense. Liz had the sneaking suspicion he was probably just as nervous as his son.

She smiled a friendly, easy smile, and thought her face might split from the effort.

"Good afternoon. Here we are. Oh, and, of course, the brownies." She handed him the plate with hands that were only trembling mildly. He looked at it dully, as if he wasn't quite sure what to do with it. Then, seeming to collect himself, he stepped back, motioning them to enter while he set down the plate on a nearby table. Taking a deep breath, Liz led Andy into the room.

It certainly wasn't what she'd expected. Somehow, in her mind, she had pictured something scattered and random like a mad scientist's lab filled with bubbling test tubes and Bunsen burners. Instead, laid out before her was a very efficient, well-organized work area. The circular expanse of the room had been broken into three main areas. On the right was a large desk on top of which sat a sizable and modern-looking computer, as well as a phone and a fax machine. Straight ahead was a long white table covered by large equipment that sported a multitude of dials and long dangling attachments. To the left of it sat a huge wooden table that was covered with reams of paper. Along the wall a curved shelf system held jars filled with various materials and oils, while what looked to be rocks were scattered throughout the room.

The biggest surprise, however, was the full nautilus system and the StairMaster directly next to the door. Liz found herself sneaking a look at Richard's well-toned physique with new insight. Unbidden, her eyes drifted down to his hands, all sorts of thoughts—thoughts she'd sworn not to have after last night—flitted through her head. She cast them off viciously. When had she become such a fool?

She looked over to see Andy taking in the lab with huge eyes.

Turning to Richard, she forced her shoulders to relax and the smile to reappear on her face. Another minute longer, and they would be able to slice up the tension in the room and serve it with side orders of stark nervousness.

"It's very impressive," she told him, keeping her voice easy as she motioned to the room. "Could you give us a small tour?"

Richard nodded, looking from her determined face to Andrew's intense eyes. He could feel a small tremor again, the distinctly unfamiliar feeling of nervousness. Damn it, whatever had possessed him to agree to this? He didn't have time for these types of things. And he didn't like standing here with this woman in his lab. It was too intrusive, he thought sharply. He wanted some area untouched by her damn smile. One place where he could be and not remember her lips beneath his own, or that look of anguish cutting through her eyes.... His jaw tightened, and he forced his attention back to Andrew instead.

The child was looking at him with that intense look that tore at him. Even he could tell the child wanted to adore him. He didn't want that, but he seemed powerless to stop it. Damn. What had he gotten himself into?

But both remained looking at him. There was no backing out now. Keeping his face expressionless, he motioned to the desk.

"This is where I work," he began tonelessly. "As I've mentioned before, I'm trying to find a new dielectric for a supercapacitor. Originally, I began by manipulating some of the more common substances used as dielectrics—"

"Mica, aluminum oxide and tantalum," Andy rattled off, interrupting him.

Liz could only stare at the child, while Richard nodded his head approvingly. He looked at the boy with surprise. "Very good. Those are some of the more prominent examples."

Andy ducked his head in a sudden rush of shyness, and in spite of himself, Richard almost smiled at the boy. Once, he'd probably looked just like that, he realized. Once, he'd wanted so badly to learn, while being embarrassed by how much he already knew. He was tempted to lay a hand on Andrew's shoulder, and only held back at the last minute. Distance, Richard. Distance.

"As I was saying," Richard began again, trying to recapture his toneless voice. "I began by examining the mica, aluminum oxide and tantalum that Andrew just mentioned. But after some brief experimentation, I realized the only way I would ever get the storage capacity I needed was to find a new substance altogether. With the computer here, I'm trying to model some different possibilities. I still have a ways to go, I'm afraid."

Andy nodded, his serious eyes blinking rapidly behind his glasses as he followed his father around the room. Liz watched the child, keeping slightly behind. It was obvious to her that he was enthralled by the lab and the work Richard was describing. Even she found herself intrigued. She'd never known anyone who was looking for an entirely different substance to serve as a battery. What if he succeeded? What would it be like to drive around in a solar car?

"What does the equipment over there do?" she asked, wanting to keep the conversation moving.

Richard nodded, his eyes still not quite able to meet her own. He concentrated on Andrew instead and the boy's quick blinking blue eyes. He really did look so much like Alycia. And yet, when he blinked like that . . . Richard had to shake the notion away. It was pointless to look for himself in the boy. He knew better.

He led them over to the second workstation he had set up. "This is where I test the substances," he explained, pointing to a small black box with several knobs and a small, lined display screen. "This first, smaller box is an LCR meter."

"It measures inductance, capacitance and resistance," Andy supplied.

"Is this what you've been reading late at night?" Liz asked. "You know, after bedtime, when you bring the flashlight out?"

Andy remained mutely silent. Liz couldn't help herself. She smiled down at his rebellious face, and then, giving in to the impulse, she ruffled his hair affectionately.

"You're a wild kid, you know that?" she teased.

Andy seemed unsure how to react to this teasing.

"It's very interesting," he defended himself sullenly.

"I'm sure it is, Andy," she said, not wanting to make him feel self-conscious. "And you've obviously learned it very well. Hasn't he, Richard?"

Richard nodded, having watched the interplay with silence. Once again he found himself amazed by how naturally she interacted with the boy. She seemed to know how to tease him, yet also when to take him seriously. And that motion, that roughing of the hair. It was done so easily, and bespoke so much affection.

He couldn't stop the thought from appearing. He'd never seen Alycia do that with the child. After those first few months, he couldn't recall her paying much attention to Andrew at all.

He shook the thought from his head. A nanny was supposed to take care of a child. Liz was doing her job, that was all. He should be grateful she'd been able to keep Andrew under control so far. It allowed him to concentrate more on his work.

He returned his attention to the matters at hand. "The LCR meter is good," he explained to Andrew and Liz, "but I needed something that could measure capacitance to a finer degree. So, last year I added the impedance analyzer you see here. While the LCR measures out to four digits, the impedance analyzer measures to eight digits. It's more accurate, but the machine is also a great deal more sensitive and requires careful calibration."

Andrew nodded, still looking serious. Liz, however, was feeling rather lost.

"What exactly do these machines do?" she asked, trying to put all the pieces together in her mind.

"Basically, they allow me to test different substances for their various properties of inductance, capacitance and resistance," he answered. She still looked lost, so he forced himself to backtrack. It had been a long time since he'd talked about his work to anyone other than scientists. He told himself he preferred it that way, but suddenly, he wanted her to understand. More important, he wanted to be capable of making her understand. If only because she was trying to and no one else ever had.

"You see," he said, and for the first time some of the dispassion went out of his voice and was replaced by excitement instead. "I need something that can store a great deal of energy, so, I need something with high capacitance, and yet it has to have low resistance—to easily take the electric charge. This substance has to be small and light. A supercapacitor."

"Have you found the right dielectric?" Andy asked, his voice hushed as he looked at his father with expectant eyes. The atmosphere of the room had changed until it seemed sparked by something new and exciting. It was like standing at the edge of the world, seeing a whole new terrain opening up ahead.

Slowly, Richard shook his head, but his eyes remained determined. "Not yet," he told Andrew. Then, unexpectedly, he smiled at the boy, "but I'm close."

Andrew flushed with the warmth of that smile, and all of a sudden, his blue eyes were sparkling with uncontrollable enthusiasm behind his glasses.

"It's so exciting!" Andrew breathed with joy. He looked at Richard with shining eyes that seemed to slam right into his gut.

He was supposed to be unfeeling, Richard thought faintly. He was supposed to remain distant. But how could anyone remain unaffected by such a wonder-filled, awestruck gaze? And to make matters worse, Liz was standing there, too, looking at him with her warm, open eyes that said so clearly how happy she was with the way things were going. How happy she was with him.

Suddenly, after all these years, he was a scientist with an audience. He found himself unsure of what to do. He led them over to the next workstation in a small daze.

"Here's where I take notes on the results and work out some of the calculations," he said quietly. "The computer can do it, but a lot of the time when I'm hot on an idea, I prefer to scribble it out on paper." He shrugged. "I think better seeing all the scratchings."

Andy nodded, and Liz smiled at him once more. "I'm glad I'm not the only one that still likes to do things by hand," she told him.

He nodded, turning away quickly so he wouldn't have to see that smile. He felt like a drowning man, he thought grimly, assaulted on all sides by things he didn't want to see. He moved over to the shelves.

"Here," he said, picking up what looked to be a lump of coal. "This is mica. It was used primarily in the thirties, forties and fifties as a capacitor. Feel it."

He handed it to Andy, glad to have their attention focused on something else for a change. Andy took the rock into his serious little hands, turning it around and around as he looked at it with intent eyes.

"It's a mineral," he offered shortly. Then, apparently having had his fill of it, he handed it to Liz.

Liz looked at it with equal fascination. As an English major, she'd taken few science classes and definitely didn't consider it her strong suit. Still, this search for a substance that could hold huge quantities of energy fascinated her. And she was especially captivated by the way the mica felt in her hands. It looked like coal, but had a strange texture. Experimentally, she rubbed it lightly with her finger. A paper thin section flaked off into her hand. Intrigued, she rubbed again and was rewarded by another incredibly thin layer peeling off at her touch.

"I've never seen anything like it," she remarked, looking at Andy and Richard. "It looks so solid, but it's really all these incredibly thin layers."

Andy's forehead crinkled, he was clearly annoyed he hadn't made this discovery on his own. Looking sullen, he took the mica back from her. Liz let him have it, unconcerned.

"Is that what you're working with?" she asked Richard, her eyes excited.

"Actually, I'm working with versions of it," he said, having a hard time taking his eyes from her. "I've been coupling it with other minerals, manipulating some of its molecules to come up with a whole new substance."

She held out the bits that had rubbed off the stone. "Look at how thin those layers are. It's amazing."

He, himself, had been playing around with the mineral for so long that he no longer noticed such things. But now he found himself deeply engrossed by the fragile-thin layers lying so carefully in her hands. He took her hand in his own, studying the slices intently.

Instead, however, he found himself noticing all the fine details of her hand. The delicate lines that streaked across her palm, the rounded curve of her thumb, the elegant lines of her fingers. She had small hands, matching the rest of her graceful build, but they were capable hands, he was sure. He could imagine them smoothing a child's hair, bandaging a small scrape, and yes, even making brownies.

He bet they would feel soft against a man's cheek, and for a minute, he almost tested out his theory. But then he looked up from his scrutiny, preparing to pull himself away. And found himself captivated by her eyes. The easy warm glow was gone. Now, her midnight eyes had darkened to almost black, and they were watching his with a mixture of rapt fascination and slow yearning. He watched her gaze shift, felt the heat of her eyes upon his lips. He watched her stiffen and felt his jaw tighten as he followed her thoughts. She was remembering last night, the way he'd treated her. The way she'd reacted. She'd promised not to let such things happen again. He could suddenly kick himself for having allowed her to swear such a thing.

The rest of his body, already hard from her mere look, agreed with his statement. This was ridiculous, he thought suddenly. They were attracted to each other and they were both adults. They should just be open about it, get the lust out of the way. Then, he was sure, they could go back to an easy working relationship. He was sure of that.

His eyes settled on Andrew's blond head as the boy examined the other minerals on the shelf. Now was not the time. But maybe later, tonight. When she came to the library...

He let her hand go, and whether he knew it or not, his eyes were filled with enough promise to bring a fiery heat to her cheeks.

"Is..." The word had come out so faint, she tried again. "Is there anything else you'd like to show us? We'd hate to keep you from your work too long."

He shook his head, but his gaze had fallen to her lips once more.

"Then thank you for letting us come," she managed to tell him politely, feeling her hands tremble as she turned her eyes to Andrew. She held out her hand for the boy and he walked back from the shelves to her. Richard saw the interchange, and again marveled at the easy way she had with the boy. In the months Andrew had been in the house, Richard had never seen the child as relaxed and well-behaved as he was now.

"Will you be joining us for dinner?" Liz asked carefully.

"I have too much work to do," Richard answered automatically, then found himself frowning over the foreign disappointment that stabbed his chest. He pushed the sensation away. He was a scientist, a workaholic. Besides, he'd promised to keep distance between himself and the boy, and if the past twenty-four hours were anything to go by, he wasn't doing a very good job of it.

Liz nodded, feeling her own mixture of relief and disappointment that she decided she would rather not question. "Well, good luck, then, and hopefully Andy and I will be seeing you later. What do you say, Andy?"

"Thank you," the child intoned, his eyes looking around the lab one last time. They swooped up to meet his father's eyes. "If you find the right dielectric, will you tell me?" Andy asked breathlessly. "Can I come see you test it?"

There was a tense moment of silence and while no expression ever crossed Richard's face, Liz could see the indecision warring in his mind. Unconsciously, she held her own breath, willing him to say yes. For Andrew. Please, do this for Andrew.

Abruptly, Richard moved his head in a small nod.

It seemed to him Andy's face lit up before his very eyes.

"I can hardly wait," the child said breathlessly, and the worship returned to his gaze.

Richard simply nodded again, recognizing that even as he shouldn't be encouraging the boy, he still couldn't quite seem to stop. He would check into those boarding schools, he thought curtly. The sooner he sent the child away, the better it would be for them all.

With a parting nod, Liz led Andy back down the stairs, the solid wooden door closing firmly behind them.

Alone at last in his lab, Richard went back to the computer to work. But it seemed to him, suddenly, that the lab was very big and very empty.

And everywhere he looked, he could see the expectant eyes of Andrew.

And the midnight blue eyes of Liz.

He sat down at the computer, and drawing upon all his self-control, so hard-earned in the past six years, he willed himself to work.

Chapter 6

He managed to work for several hours, but it was more like shuffling than true work. He calibrated the impedance analyzer, he manipulated the results of the tests. But it seemed no matter what he did, he could feel the restlessness gnawing away at his gut.

From the tower window, he watched the daylight fade outside, saw the night roll in. Another fall storm was brewing, he could hear it in the low howl of the wind as it swept outside the tower. It sounded like an animal to him, raging with a mournful howl. It tugged at his concentration even more, calling to him.

The sun fell completely, until the only light in the lab came from his two desk lamps and the bluish glow of his computer screen. He should flip on the bright overhead light, he thought, but standing at the second workstation, he still didn't move. Absently, his hands moved over the multitude of dials of the LCR meter. He adjusted, calibrated, fine-tuned. But he never actually hooked up anything to the waiting probes for measurement. Instead, he stood, listening to the wind howl and feeling the countdown in his stomach.

Deep and far off, he heard the boom of the grandfather clock as it counted out the late hour.

Unbidden, her image rose in his mind. He saw her midnight blue eyes, gazing at him with a soft smile, locking on his lips with heat. And he pictured the way Liz gazed down at Andrew's golden head, how she held the child's hand, how she soothed the child's worries. What was she doing now? Probably tucking Andrew into bed. Did she read the child a story? It sounded like something she would do. She would read him something wholesome and good, like *Winnie the Pooh,* maybe, her soft Carolina voice weaving a beguiling tale. Richard's imagination couldn't fill in those blanks; fables and fairy tales had never been a part of his own childhood regimen.

And after she'd tucked Andrew in? Blaine would find her, if Richard knew Blaine at all. It had been bluntly obvious at last night's dinner what Blaine thought of Liz; the man's eyes had been all over her. And there had been all those subtle little comments that really weren't subtle at all....

Blaine would probably find her. Good, old brother Blaine.

The thought filled him with anger, and Richard looked down to find himself clenching the worktable with whitened knuckles. He forced his hands to relax. It wasn't his concern, remember? He felt an attraction, but that was only natural for a man who'd been holed up in a tower for five years. Sooner or later, he would have her, and that would be the end of it. They would fall back into their routines, and even that wouldn't be for too long.

After all, Andy would be going to boarding school soon. It was for the best, he reminded himself. He saw how the child had looked at him this afternoon, with too much adoration, too much awe. He never should have allowed Andy to get that close; he'd sworn not to let it happen. But last night, when Andrew had slipped his hand into his own, he had felt a tightness in his chest he hadn't been able to control.

He wouldn't care, he thought firmly. He'd been down that path and he wouldn't travel it again. Especially when he knew the truth about Alycia and her son.

Andrew would go to boarding school, Liz would move on to a new assignment, and he would continue with his work. Neat, simple, logical.

He moved determinedly over to the far wall and snapped on the overhead lights. Suddenly the dim shadows were gone, banished by three hundred and fifty watts of electric light. It seemed even the wind dimmed its mournful cry, silenced by the penetrating white glare. Richard crossed over to the table, picking up some mica on the way. It was time he got serious. He was a scientist. His work was his life. It never betrayed him. It got him through everything.

But the restlessness gnawed at him even as he put the probes in place. The emptiness hammered in his stomach even as he adjusted the last dial, flipping the switches on. Abruptly the graphs appeared on the LRC meter, readings registering as he selected the appropriate settings. But there was no satisfaction in looking at these numbers, he realized suddenly. No sense of urgency, no glow of intrigue.

There was nothing but the restlessness, the emptiness and the lonely cry of the raging wind.

The numbers were just numbers. They didn't smile or laugh or tease.

And they didn't look at him with midnight blue eyes.

The thought came from nowhere, and he quashed it instantly. He would not think like that, he wouldn't. He had a life here, damn it. He'd been to hell and back and it was this one room, this lab, that had kept him sane. The lab was his sanctuary, the one place where his brain did not make him a freak, but a master.

Even as he thought this, however, the grandfather clock in the foyer struck midnight. He could feel the chimes reverberating up the spiral stairs until they rang deep and true through his tower, drowning out even the wind.

And with every reverberating bong, his restlessness grew.

His feet moved before he had given them a conscious command to do so. They simply started walking, and before he knew it, he was rounding the long spiral stairs. He never actually formulated a destination in his mind; that would have been too much like granting conscious permission. He just let the restlessness move him forward.

He came to the library as the last chime of the old clock faded into the distance. Already he could see the golden glow of the fire. And there on the couch pulled closest to the flames was Liz.

He went in.

Her head came up as he entered, her long mahogany hair falling away from her face. Myriad emotions flickered across her face to vanish before he could capture even one of them. Still, he could see the quick rise and fall of her chest as her breath quickened.

She was wearing a terry-cloth robe this time, the navy blue color accentuating the deep mysteriousness of her eyes. The robe belted at her waist, pooling around her tightly curled legs. Even from this distance he could catch a glimpse of a gently curved calf.

The muscles in his stomach tightened once more, and this time it was *his* breathing that accelerated.

God, she was beautiful by firelight. Open and honest and with a glance that caressed a man like warm velvet.

He crossed over to the safety of the bar, moving away from the heat of the flames.

"Brandy?" he asked at last, refusing to look at her.

"No, thank you."

Perhaps she remembered what had happened the last time she'd accepted. He sure as hell did.

Taking a steadying sip of brandy, he walked to the fireplace. Maybe the heat from without would cancel the heat from within.

Liz watched him approach, her eyes drawn to the breadth of his shoulders, the trimness of his figure. She shouldn't be noting such things, she thought in a distant corner of her mind, but she couldn't quite keep her eyes away, either. Once more it struck her how he moved, with such firmly restrained power, with such complete and utter control. He sat down now, just ten feet away in the supple leather of the deep chair. Looking down at her lap, she could see her hands tremble. The whole atmosphere of the library had become charged with his presence, she realized suddenly, as if before it had been merely waiting, and now, it was alive.

Remember last night. She forced the thought through her mind. *Remember how he mocked you and how you swore to keep your distance.* She had no reason to get involved with this man. She was here for Andrew, nothing more.

But her hands still trembled on her lap, and she couldn't stop herself from recalling the feel of his lips upon her own.

"How . . . how did this evening go?" Liz asked shortly, her drawl more pronounced with her nervousness.

"The same," Richard answered tautly, keeping his eyes on his glass.

"Did you make any progress?"

"No."

The conversation stalled, and in the silence, she could feel the tension tightening her stomach. A log popped in the fireplace, and she jumped nervously. With a self-conscious smile, she curled her legs inward even more, adjusting her robe around her.

From the chair, Richard stole a short glance. The flickering flames cast her face in shadows, darkening her eyes, and her hair looked on fire as it tumbled down her back. He could follow its line all the way to the graceful curve of her waist.

He wanted to follow his gaze with his touch.

He took another deep swallow of the brandy, willing it to burn the thought away.

It didn't help.

"Andrew was very excited about your lab," Liz said at last. "He did nothing but talk about it during dinner."

Richard's face froze for an instant, and she could practically feel him come alert.

"How was dinner?" he asked slowly.

Liz shrugged. "The same, I suppose. Dodd prepared poached salmon, it was excellent."

"And Blaine? Did he like the salmon, too?"

"He ate it," Liz supplied, puzzled by the question. "I don't recall his commenting on it one way or the other. Though Jillian claimed she'd had better in Seattle, and Parris told her she wouldn't know good salmon if it swam onto her lap. Or something like that."

"I see. And after dinner, what did you do?"

Liz frowned slightly at the curtness of his questions, but gave in with a small shrug. Perhaps he was finally becoming interested in the household, she couldn't complain about that. "I convinced Andy to play dominoes with me," she said. "He complained that it was all a matter of luck, but I think that's because I beat him two out of three times. He did very well, though, for his first time."

"Did Blaine play?"

This time she could hear the cold suspicion in his voice. Obviously the rift between him and Blaine was larger than she suspected. She tried to keep her voice light.

"Actually, Andy and I were too boring for the Gang of Four. They decided to make a field trip into Manhattan. I imagine they'll be out all night again."

Richard nodded, sinking back slightly against the chair. So Blaine had gone out for the evening. The thought made him much happier than it should.

"What else did you and Andrew do today?" Richard asked shortly. He could feel her gaze upon him, and it filled him with a mixture of anticipation, desire and denial. He'd thought earlier that if he could simply take her, that would ease his relentless hunger. Now he sat immobile, half-afraid to even touch her. What if he did possess her and that didn't ease the ache at all? He hated the doubt, he hated the confusion.

And he wanted to reach over and grab her for another burning kiss.

He took a deep swallow of the brandy.

"—visiting your lab, I took Andy outside for a bit," Liz was saying, startling him back to attention. "It really was a beautiful day out, though it was chilly. We walked around, looking at all sorts of things."

"A walk?" The disbelief was obvious in his tone as his hands began their familiar rotation of his brandy glass.

Liz followed the motion with her eyes, feeling the nervous restlessness again. He had such strong hands. She could still feel those fingers tangling in her hair, arching her head back to deepen the kiss. She could still feel how that palm had felt, cupping the weight of her breast. What would it feel like to have those fingers warm upon her breasts, rolling her nipples with his strong, callused fingertips?

She licked her lips and had to take a deep breath to regain her scattered thoughts. "Yes, a walk," she answered faintly. She swallowed, and tried again, with her voice louder this time. She still couldn't match the curt coolness of his own, however. "I told you I wanted to get Andrew out more. We went around the grounds, mostly, visited the stables."

He digested the news in silence. Stables? He hadn't been out to the stables for over a year. In the beginning, he'd ridden with Alycia. But then she'd taken to riding on her own, or with Blaine. After a while, he'd stopped asking, and he'd stayed clear of the stables altogether. Some habits died hard. But, of course, the stables were still there. Blaine and his friends still used them, so the bill was paid accordingly.

"What did you think?" he asked after a bit.

"You have some beautiful thoroughbreds," Liz told him honestly. "Whoever selects your stock has done an outstanding job."

"Do you ride?"

"I used to. It's been awhile, though. My parents sold their own horses a few years ago. The upkeep was too much for them."

"You can ride the horses whenever you like," Richard offered.

She looked at him speculatively. "What about you? Do you ride?"

"I don't have the time," he began, but she dismissed what she knew was an excuse with a wave of her hand.

"What's the point of maintaining such fine stables if you don't take the time to enjoy them?"

"I'm not that good with horses," he told her.

She leaned forward, intense now. "You can learn, though. I can show you, if you don't mind. In fact, why don't you come out some day with Andrew, and all three of us can go riding together? We'll just walk around some of the hills, take it nice and easy."

The enthusiasm was welling up in her voice, the freshness returning to her eyes. He wondered dimly if she was even aware of the transformation. When he'd first entered the library, her uncertainty had made her mysterious and beguiling. Now, her energy made her fresh and invigorating.

He wasn't sure which woman was more dangerous to him—the vulnerable one, or the enthusiastic, energetic one. Once more, he wanted to kiss her relentlessly. He wanted to hear her moan against his lips, he wanted her arms curled around his neck. He wanted to know that she wanted him as much as he wanted her.

He stood abruptly, and walked over to the far corner of the fireplace, as if that would put enough distance between them.

"Does Andrew ride?" he asked tightly, trying to keep his mind off her body and on the conversation.

She tilted her head at his question, hit once more by his apparent lack of knowledge about his own son. But then she shrugged, her eyes lingering on his tall frame instead. "No," she replied. "Andy gave me some song and dance about all the people that were killed in horseback-riding accidents."

"And yet you plan on taking him riding, anyway?"

"I think it would be good for him," she said honestly, wondering why he insisted on keeping his back to her. "I assure you, I'll take all the necessary precautions such as insisting that he wear a riding helmet and the proper gear, but sooner or later Andy needs to learn that statistics aren't real life, and that enjoyment is as much a deciding factor as anything."

"Enjoyment, Liz?" He turned, and the dark glow she saw in his wintry eyes made her catch her breath. All of a sudden, he didn't look cold at all. Instead, as his heated gaze swept over her curled form, she felt all the breath leave her body. "Do you know what I would enjoy right now, Liz?" he asked intensely.

She shook her head, her eyes never leaving his face as her mouth went dry.

"I would enjoy kissing you, Liz. I would enjoy tasting your lips once more. I would enjoy hearing you whisper my name while your arms wrapped around my neck." He took five steps toward her, until he could peer down at her with glittering eyes. "Would you enjoy that, too, Liz?"

She shivered, feeling her throat work even as she fought the answer. She'd promised herself she would keep her distance after last night. He was too dangerous, this man leaning over her like a predator sighting its prey. And he knew more about kissing than any man had a right to know. She shivered again, and closed her eyes.

"What do you want?" she managed to say.

He leaned even closer, until she could feel the whisper of his breath against her lips. One inch more, and the rough burn of his whiskers could caress her soft cheek. She had to clench her fists to keep from closing that inch.

"Why do you close your eyes, Liz?" he quizzed softly. "Why do you turn away when we both know what's going on here? Are you afraid of me?"

Barely, just barely, she shook her head.

"Do you find me cold?"

Once more, that near-imperceptible motion.

"Is it Blaine?"

Her eyes flew open with shock, then jolted as she became fully aware of just how close he stood. "No," she whispered firmly. "This has nothing to do with Blaine."

"Then what, sweet Liz. What?"

She floundered, not knowing what to say when he remained so close she could smell the scent of fresh soap and spicy aftershave on his cheeks. She wanted to feel that five o'clock shadow, rediscover the soft fullness of his knowing lips. She wanted her arms around his shoulders, her breasts flat against his chest.

"I don't think," she said, then licked her lips nervously, feeling the heat of his gaze following the motion. She took another breath and tried again. "I don't think you really know me at all."

"What does that have to do with anything?" he asked levelly.

She flinched at the words, looking down at her hands on her lap. She felt the sting of tears against her eyelids. She should have seen that coming. There were times when she liked to think there was someone real beneath his granite exterior, someone who *had* danced and romanced and delivered a single yellow rose every day. But that person seemed to be gone, and the Richard she knew was a dangerously attractive man who seemed just as hard on the inside as he appeared on the outside.

She was out of her league. And even knowing that, she still wanted to kiss him.

She drew herself up. "I don't think this is such a good idea," she said softly, forcing her midnight eyes to meet his own glittering gaze. He frowned at her words, and she could see the first glimmer of frustration in his eyes. Once more, he dropped his gaze to her lips, and once more, she felt herself hold her breath in anticipation.

"I take it back, then," he said, low and sure as his gaze swept across her face. "If it makes such a difference, I do know you, even better than you think. I bet you believe in happily-ever-afters. I bet you believe in knights on white horses, and endless love like in *Wuthering Heights*. I bet you drink fresh-squeezed lemonade in the summer, and daydream in clover fields of discovering true love. You find the silver lining in every cloud, searching out more and more adventures because you honestly believe they will all end well. Am I right, Liz? Tell me that I don't know you."

His eyes burned into hers, daring her to deny his description. But if he thought she would surrender, or even be outraged, he was wrong. Instead, he found a deeply troubled face looking back at him, emotions flickering across her eyes faster than even the fire's shadows.

"No," she whispered. "No, you don't know me at all."

Her hands revealed her agitation, twisting the robe's belt over and over again. He watched the motion, then glanced back up, trying to find her eyes.

She turned away sharply, but not before he had seen. The impact of the sight floored him, and he felt a sudden coldness in his chest. Twice before he'd seen that look, that sliver of deep pain and raw anguish.

"Did you love him that much?" he found himself asking, the words harsher than he'd intended. It had to be a man. Only something as cruel as love could strike someone that deep.

She looked at him slowly, nodding her head. He could tell she was trying to remain calm, but she certainly hadn't had the practice he'd had. Her face was too young to hide its mysteries. Instead, the pain flickered through in open revelation.

He found, this time, he was the one that had to look away. He straightened, giving them both the distance they suddenly needed.

"He was my husband," Liz volunteered finally. She took a deep breath, willing away the tightness. Her composure came back faster this time, practice in the Keaton household, she thought hazily, was bound to make the exercise a success.

"You're divorced?" Richard asked sharply. He didn't like this topic. She'd come here alone, and he liked to think of her that way: as belonging to only him and Andy.

Liz shook her head. "No. Nick died. There was a bank robbery a year ago, one Sunday when we were going to a matinee at the local movie theater. The police arrived and all this gunfire broke out." She smiled a faint, wry smile. "It was just like some scene from a bad Western. Except Nick was the one caught in the crossfire."

Sometimes the memory was so sharp it seemed like yesterday. She was down on the pavement again, all the sirens wailing in her ears. And Nick was sprawled on the ground, blood seeping everywhere. She was crying, but she couldn't feel the tears streaming down her face. She just knew that she had to stop the bleeding, and so her hands raced across Nick's neck and chest, trying desperately to stop the bleeding. But no matter what she did, it kept running right through her hands as if she was no better than a human sieve. And then he was dead.

She twisted the belt of her robe, wringing it with the useless hands that couldn't save her husband's life. Richard watched the motion, feeling the uneasiness grow inside of him. He'd been harsh on her, and now he'd learned she was a widow. Funny, that in some areas he could be so blind. Did he really think he held a monopoly on pain? The expression in her eyes that first day should have been warning enough. He should have handled her more gently, he shouldn't have pushed her so hard.

And yesterday, just yesterday he'd mocked her for not pursuing their kiss. He winced, and hated this feeling of regret. Damn fool, he was a damn fool.

He wondered if he should offer her comfort, but he realized that after all these years, he simply didn't know how.

"Were you married long?" he asked at last, his pale blue eyes expressionless against the firelight.

He could see her take a deep breath, steadying herself. Her hands slowed their agitated motion.

"I loved him all my life," she told him quietly. "From the time we were kids and he would push me on the swings in the playground to the time we went to our high school prom. We were always together. It seemed we always would be."

She said the words with such simple conviction. He hadn't anticipated just how sharply they would pierce him. He could see her with this perfect man all too easily. And all at once, it made him feel empty.

"Then you grew up together?" he asked, his voice giving nothing away.

She nodded. "Maddensfield, North Carolina, isn't that big, and our parents had been friends for a long time. You could say it was classic small-town America. But," she said shrugging, "I liked it."

He gave her an intense, shadowed look. "Then what are you doing here, Liz?" He gestured around the darkened library with its dull leather-bound books and deep walnut wood. "This is a long way from home."

She nodded, and he could see her eyes glitter with suppressed tears. But she took another deep breath, and gave him a watery smile.

"I had to get away. I had to start over. So this is where I am."

He gazed at her, not wanting to push even as the next words burned in his throat. He told himself it didn't matter. He told himself to keep quiet, he didn't care. But it seemed his body was determined to ignore him tonight because he found his lips moving without command.

"Do you like it here?" he whispered intently in the library. "Is it . . . not so bad, after all?"

She hesitated, and he felt the hesitation stab him straight in the chest. Of course she didn't like it here. Who would like living in a mausoleum like this? And he was certainly no better for her. A dark foreboding man that lived in a dark foreboding house. The things he'd said, the way he'd treated her... Certainly he was a far cry from this perfect man she'd loved all her life and married. Not that he cared, he thought savagely.

"Andrew is a great kid," Liz replied finally from the couch. She knew she ought to say more, but no more words would come out. She still didn't know what she thought of this place, she realized suddenly. The child looked like an angel, and probably deep down truly was, but he'd put her through hell before he'd shown it. And the house was intimidating and overwhelming, not to mention downright terrifying at three in the morning when the power was out and branches scratched at bedroom windows. A woman had died here, something Liz was having a hard time forgetting.

Then there was this man beside her, with his wintry blue eyes that never gave anything away. Sometimes she thought he might be a lost soul, like Andy. Sometimes she wasn't so sure he *had* a soul; he had so much control, even when he kissed her. And sometimes she wondered what a man with so much control was capable of....

"Alycia was murdered."

"I doubt we'll ever know who did it."

All at once the library seemed too dark to her. She stole a glance at Richard.

He had turned once more toward the flames, the expression on his face intense, but once again unreadable. He looked like granite, each facet carefully chiseled out, from the high cheekbones to the pitch-black hair. His body echoed the solid strength, the overwhelming control.

In contrast, she thought abruptly, Nick looked young and boyish in her mind. His blue eyes had been open and laughing, not the winter chill of Richard's. And his face, while handsome and strong, had still looked wholesome and untroubled by life. Richard's face, on the other hand, appeared to have been carved from cobalt and was unrelentingly stern.

The two would appear to have little in common.

Except . . .

Richard attracted her, she thought bleakly. She was an idiot to keep denying it. He'd already kissed her twice, dark, dangerous kisses like nothing she'd ever experienced. They had been hard, demanding kisses of a man. Even now, her breath stopped at the thought.

Sitting in this dark and strange library, the past seemed so far away. There was just the haunting sensation of the love she'd once had and that now was gone. In contrast, the man beside her was intensely alive even with his brooding ways. When he looked at her, she felt it all the way to the pit of her stomach.

All this from a man who may have killed his wife.

Her nerves came back full force, and she found herself shifting restlessly on the sofa. Richard didn't seem to notice, his eyes still captured by the flames. Whatever was going on in his mind, his face gave none of it away.

"What about," she began, licking her dry lips, "what about you and your wife?"

He turned to her and, if possible, his face was even darker than before.

"What about her?" he asked coldly.

Her hands once more trembled, but she forced herself to continue. She worked with this man, lived with him. She wanted to know. She *needed* to know.

"Did . . . did you love her at all?"

His eyes returned to the flames. "Once upon a time, isn't that what the storybooks say?" He leaned over to pick up his brandy glass from the table, swirling it.

"But there was no happily-ever-after?"

He nodded, drawing a burning sip of the amber fluid. "You still wonder if I killed her, don't you?" he stated baldly, the words harsh but expressionless in the silence of the library.

She felt suddenly miserable. But she forced herself to keep her chin up. "You said most people suspected you," she said stonily. "And I understand that your marriage wasn't a happy one. . . ." Her voice trailed off, and she found herself shrugging weakly.

"Seventy-five percent of marriages are unhappy ones," Richard said tonelessly. "Fifty percent of marriages end in divorce. But I don't think the remaining twenty-five percent end in murder. Most people just suffer in silence."

From the couch, Liz nodded, but she couldn't help thinking that he still hadn't answered her question. No, he'd simply reverted to quoting safe statistics, so much like Andrew.

"So you didn't kill her?" she found herself asking boldly, though the words were still hushed.

He turned to face her fully, his eyes a cold, pale blue as he looked at her with thinly veiled rage.

"You asked me that same question two nights ago," he reminded her angrily. "Then, you told me you didn't know me well enough to believe my answer. What about now, Liz? You've sat at the dinner table with me, held a midnight vigil, seen my lab."

Kissed me twice.

He didn't say those words out loud, but he didn't have to. They hovered between them, the unspoken desire each was acutely aware of, stirring to life.

Liz turned away.

"I don't want to believe you're capable of murder," she said finally.

It wasn't enough, and they both knew it. She didn't want to believe he was capable of murder, not she didn't believe he had killed his wife. Not she believed in him.

Richard's jaw tightened with barely suppressed bitterness, but he forced himself to do nothing, to say nothing. Even after all these years, the control came at a harsh price.

He stood, swallowing the last of his brandy and setting down the glass on the mantel with a resounding click in the silence.

Against his will, his eyes found her one last time. God, he wanted to hate her, he wanted to keep her shut out of his dark and bitter world. But even now, when his blood simmered with anger and his fists clenched with the effort of control, he found her beautiful.

Even now, he only wanted to drag her into his arms and kiss her until she cried his name in breathless surrender. He wanted to ravage her until she could see nothing but him, think nothing but him. Until his name fell from her lips as a gasp, as a prayer.

And then what, Richard? the voice inside him whispered cynically. *Would she believe in you then?*

"Good night, Miss Guiness," he said abruptly. "And thank you for the conversation."

And then, without giving her another chance to speak, he stalked from the room.

Long after he'd left, Liz remained staring at the doorway. Once more, the intense emotions swirling in the library faded with his absence. Now it was simply herself and the low burn of the forgotten fire.

Sitting there alone, she wished she had the courage to call him back. She wished she understood even a little of this dark man who filled her thoughts and tormented her nights.

And she wondered at the bleakness that seemed to fill her heart.

Chapter 7

Saturday morning dawned bright and brisk. As it was her first day off since starting her new job, Liz pulled on a pair of worn jeans, covering them with an old blue sweater. After brushing her hair briskly, she pulled it back in a casual ponytail. A pair of silver hoops completed the outfit.

Now the question was, what to do?

She needed to go outside, she decided once and for all. A long walk would do her good. Perhaps somewhere along the way her equilibrium would be restored and this nervous feeling would leave her stomach for good. This house...sometimes she swore it had a life of its own, and it seemed determined to suffocate her with its stale memories and ghosts.

She paused in the doorway, and unbidden, thoughts of Alycia filled her mind. There was so much she didn't understand yet, or even know. Maybe this afternoon she would pay a visit to the town library. A small frown furrowed her forehead as she thought about it. Considering how involved she was becoming with the household, going there to conduct a little research would probably be best.

With a short nod of her head, she left her room. Walk first, then town library.

In the foyer, Blaine was standing with Jillian, Parris and Greg. All four looked up as she approached, and she flashed a friendly smile. Except for dinner, she'd hardly seen the group at all. They appeared to keep their own frantic schedule.

As she approached the bottom of the stairs, Blaine whistled at her.

"Hey, nanny, I like the outfit," he gave her an appreciative grin, winking broadly.

Behind him, Jillian frowned slightly.

"It's my day off," Liz informed him, ignoring his suggestive eyes and purposefully keeping her tone light. She didn't know enough about the group of friends to know if Jillian and Blaine were involved, but she had no intention of treading where she clearly wasn't wanted. "I'm planning on going for a nice long walk," she said easily.

"Oh, don't do that," Blaine replied immediately. "Come riding with us instead."

"What a smashing idea!" Parris piped up in his best fake English accent. His hazel eyes swept over her jean-encased legs with as much relish as Blaine had examined them. Liz felt on the verge of blushing, when Greg bailed her out.

"We always ride," he said simply, his tone much more natural than that of the others. "Jillian loves the horses, and Blaine and Richard maintain the best stable. If you join us, we'll be the Gang of Five again."

Jillian stiffened immediately, and Liz instinctively backed off with a wave of her hand. Unfortunately, neither Blaine nor Parris seemed to notice Jillian's discomfort.

"It's settled," Blaine announced grandly. "She's coming."

"No, no," Liz tried. "Really, I just want to walk."

"It's too late for that," Jillian interrupted suddenly, her voice cool while her blue eyes frowned at Blaine. "He has his mind set, so you may as well give in gracefully. In case you haven't noticed, Blaine always gets his way."

The undercurrent in those words made Liz uneasy, but none of the others seemed to notice. They simply took it for granted that she would join their jovial group and it would be a grand time for all.

"What's this?" came a deep voice from above. They all looked up to see Richard standing at the top of the left-hand stairs. Though it was only midmorning, he appeared to be coming down from the tower, rather than heading up. "Or-. ganizing another one of your outings, Blaine?"

Blaine nodded at his older brother. "Yes, we're all going riding. And Liz just agreed to grace us with her beautiful presence."

Richard's eyes swept over to Liz, his gaze emotionless as usual. But his eyes had a way of lingering, a way of smoothing down her figure like a caress. She had to repress the shivers that crept along her spine.

"So you're getting to ride," he said to her, his voice low and soft in the vaulted room.

Liz barely nodded, discovering suddenly that she'd lost her voice.

Richard's eyes returned to the group, speculative and grim.

"Come now, older brother," Blaine goaded. "Why don't you join us, as well? Or will your lab become jealous?"

Liz glanced at Blaine sharply, but his face was empty except for his large, playboy grin. It might have been simple innocent teasing, except the room had suddenly gone thick with tension. Greg began to shift uncomfortably, while Parris had an open scowl of dislike on his face. Jillian appeared as unruffled and cool as ever in her smart Hunter garb, except, of course, when her eyes fell upon Liz. Then her jaw tightened noticeably.

At the top of the stairs, Richard's gaze returned to Liz. She looked as fresh and beautiful as ever. Her pulled-back hair revealed the clean, simple lines of her face, the rosy, healthy glow of her complexion. And she was smiling, that glowing open smile that pulled at his gut. Didn't she know she was supposed to have more reserve? Didn't she know what that smile did to him?

He turned back to Blaine, dear brother Blaine who looked at Liz with wolfish eyes. Richard's voice was clear when he spoke, his eyes betraying nothing.

"All right," he said simply. "I believe I will join you."

Blaine's jaw practically dropped to the floor. "Pardon?"

"I said I'll join you."

"But—"

Whatever he was about to say, Blaine abruptly cut himself off. Instead, he nodded with blue eyes that had suddenly become dark and disturbed. From where she stood, Liz could see the anger settle raw and uncomfortable on his face. He was definitely not happy with his older brother's unexpected answer. Feeling the tension ratchet up yet another notch, Liz smoothly spoke to ease the troubled atmosphere.

"Why don't you meet us at the stable, then," she called up to Richard. "Surely one of us can get your horse ready for you while you change."

"Yes, a groom can see to that."

"Then we'll meet you there," Liz affirmed, starting to usher the group out the door and put an end to the unease.

Above, Richard nodded, watching as the group walked out of the house. He stood there a minute longer, his eyes following Liz's vanishing form through the doorway. When she was out of sight, he finally proceeded down the stairs and journeyed to his room. He probably had riding clothes stashed somewhere, he thought to himself. After all, he'd ridden before.

A very long time ago.

At the stables, Liz found the same pair of boots she'd used earlier in the week. She hung her coat on the peg, knowing she would get warm quickly enough from the riding, then turned around to see Blaine leading a different horse over to her.

"She's beautiful," Liz told him, reaching out a hand to the dark red mare. The horse sniffed Liz's hand with its smoky-colored nose, then nudged Liz for attention. Liz complied by rubbing the horse's nose with a bright smile.

"She's almost as beautiful as you," Blaine told her. Liz was about to chide him, but when she looked up she found that for the first time, his eyes were serious.

"Come on," she said, trying to keep the mood light, "my legs aren't nearly as nice."

There was another intense moment, then Blaine relented with a smile. "Well, nanny," he told her, "I think your legs are absolutely fine. Why don't I help you saddle up?"

"Oh, it's okay," she tried to tell him, but he had already taken out a brush and was grooming the horse's glossy coat. Not wanting to make too big a deal of it, Liz selected a hoof-pick and examined the mare's feet.

Bending down, she could see Jillian behind her, with another horse. The beautiful blonde was watching Blaine, and the look in her eyes was far from happy. Liz finished all four of the hooves, and straightened.

"What's her name?" Liz asked as she picked up the bridle, keeping her voice casual. It was obvious to her that Jillian was interested in Blaine, and in all honesty, Liz wished Blaine would pay more attention to the blonde.

"Honeysuckle," Blaine said, putting away the brush. Liz arched an eyebrow.

"Somehow, I can't see Richard naming anything Honeysuckle."

"He didn't," Blaine replied calmly. "Alycia did."

Liz paused for a moment with the bridle, then forced herself to resume her task. It made sense, she reminded herself as coolly as possible. Alycia, after all, had been married to Richard for two years. Of course she'd done things like select horses and name them.

Still, sometimes it seemed there were reminders of the woman everywhere. How could Richard stand to be surrounded by so many tokens of his dead wife? It was like living in a haunted house.

"So this was Alycia's horse?" she asked, her voice surprisingly level as she selected one of the few available Western saddles.

Blaine shook his head, turning to his own mount. "Alycia rode her once, then decided Honeysuckle's coloring didn't suit her."

"Didn't suit her?"

Blaine flashed her a crooked grin from over his shoulder. "Exactly. See, Alycia was beautiful and knew it. She liked everything around her to reflect that beauty. Basically, life was one big accessory. Sometimes, I wondered if that was why she married Richard. After all, his tall dark looks were the perfect foil for her own china doll image.''

Liz just nodded, not knowing how else to react to such a statement.

"So what horse did she ride?" she asked finally.

Blaine jerked his head toward the horse Jillian was saddling. "The white mare, Lady Godiva."

Liz almost laughed. "Lady Godiva? A horse?"

Blaine shrugged with his golden grin. "She named it, not me."

Liz shook her head, heaving the saddle up and on. She began fastening the girth.

"Looks good," Blaine said, turning to study her work. "Why don't I give you a leg up?"

"No need," came Richard's distinct voice behind them. "I can help her up while you finish your own mount."

Blaine froze. From where she was standing, Liz could see myriad emotions flash across the man's face: anger, frustration, and finally, resignation.

"He always did have the most damnable timing," Blaine muttered. He straightened and gave Richard a curt nod.

"Goliath is waiting over there," Blaine informed his older brother, pointing to a large black horse that sported its own Western saddle. "The groom took care of him."

Richard nodded, his pale eyes unreadable as he watched Blaine walk away. He turned his scrutiny back to Liz.

"Shall I help you up?" he asked coolly.

Liz looked at him, trying hard not to stare. This was the first time she'd seen him in anything other than slacks. She'd half expected him to come out in the full Hunter regalia the other riders were wearing. Instead, he was wearing an old pair of jeans that clung to his lean hips. His long legs were half encased in fine leather boots, and he was wearing a beautiful wool sweater. This close, she could catch the faint hint of spicy cologne, mingling with the scent of leather and horses.

The effect wreaked havoc on her senses. All of a sudden, she wanted desperately to lean just a little closer. Or maybe reach out, and touch the light stubble on his finely carved cheek. Or rest her head on his strong, broad shoulder, close her eyes and inhale until the scent of him drowned out all other sensations.

He moved forward, and she caught her breath in a quiet gasp. But he simply braced his hands together and offered them to her as a step for mounting the horse. Shaking her own silly thoughts from her mind, she gripped the pommel of the saddle and prepared to hoist herself up.

He propelled her up and onto the saddle easily, his shoulder brushing her leg as he helped her gain her balance. Then she was settled, sitting back low and easy in the saddle.

He remained there, looking at her with his steady blue eyes that revealed nothing, but tormented her, anyway.

"All set?"

"Yes," she managed to reply, her nervousness making her Carolina accent thicker so the word came out sounding heavy and sweet.

His eyes darkened, resting for a minute on the curve of her leg, outlined snugly by her faded jeans. Wordlessly, he turned and walked away. Unbidden, her gaze followed him as he gathered the reins to the giant mount, and easily swung himself into the saddle.

All the riders were ready now, so he directed his horse to the front, leading them to one of the many trails that wound through the six acres of land. It had been a long time since he'd been in the saddle. He hadn't taken up riding until Alycia had come into his life. Then, he'd discovered an inherent joy for the sport: the smell of the horses, the freedom of the wind, the feeling of strength and stamina beneath him.

But as with most things he'd enjoyed, Alycia had found a way to taint it. Eventually, trips to the stable had him over-hearing unseemly giggles and the rustle of hastily adjusted clothing. He spared a cold glance for Parris, riding a couple lengths back. If Parris hadn't been part of Blaine's gang, Richard never would have allowed him back in the house. Then again, if he turned away all of Alycia's old lovers, he'd never have a visitor again.

Not even his own brother.

He spared a sharp glance to where Blaine rode beside Liz, and even as the sight of it made his jaw clench, Richard tried to block the knowledge out. He didn't care if Blaine was interested in Liz, he reminded himself. She was just the nanny.

His face, however, remained grim as he rode.

Liz could still feel the tension coiling off the dark man in front of her. Even on this bright, beautiful day, his features remained dark, his control impenetrable. Perhaps it was just the contrast, but her attention remained drawn to him even as Blaine said something light and funny in her ear.

"I'm sorry?" she found herself saying yet again, trying to focus her attention back on the man at her side.

"I'm glad you decided to come," he repeated gallantly. "It really wouldn't have been the same without you."

Liz didn't have to look at her to know that Jillian's features were frosting over even more at the words. Liz wished she could tell the woman she had nothing to worry about. Blaine was beautiful in his own playboy-type way. And he was funny, too, with all his flirtations and teasing. But despite his best intentions, he reminded Liz more of a mischievous boy than a possible lover.

Richard, on the other hand . . .

"I think I'm going to move up and ride with Greg and Parris," she informed Blaine casually. "I haven't really spoken to them much yet. Why don't you ride with Jillian?"

Blaine gave her a sideways glance. "Leaving me so soon?"

She gave him a careless shrug, then winked with mischievous spirit, herself. "Well, you know, why ride with one good-looking man when I can ride with two?"

He laughed at that, a light golden sound that drifted through the group. He leaned forward slightly in his saddle, lowering his voice to a conspiratorial whisper. "I hate to tell you," he said softly, "but don't fall too hard for Parris, as handsome as he is."

Actually, Liz hadn't paid much attention, one way or the other, to how Parris looked, but she nodded. "Why?" she whispered back.

"Well, he's impotent, you know."

Liz's eyes opened so wide with shock, Blaine promptly began laughing again.

"You really are something else," he told her, grinning hugely until she wasn't sure if he was joking or not.

"You're making that up," she accused.

Blaine simply shrugged. "You never know."

Shaking her head, Liz urged her horse forward until she caught up with Greg and Parris. Sure enough, after a moment or two, Jillian's horse picked up the pace to come alongside Blaine's. That ought to keep them both occupied, Liz thought wryly.

Liz chattered briefly with Greg and Parris, but her eyes had a way of wandering. Even as she nodded or smiled at their casual banter, her eyes kept falling on the man not far ahead of her now. He sat back, comfortable and easy in his saddle, looking at home on his large black mount.

Strange that he'd told her he wasn't good with horses, Liz thought, because he certainly seemed at home on one. Indeed, with his worn jeans and fine boots, he blended in perfectly.

Who was this man who could look so professional and restrained in a lab, yet so comfortable on an outdoor horseback ride? she wondered. And why did just looking at him make her cheeks flush?

She shifted slightly in the saddle, realizing that the nervousness and restlessness was back. Suddenly, walking along placidly wasn't enough. She wanted to run, she wanted to ride hard and fast and feel the brisk fall wind burn her cheeks. She wanted to see the landscape fly by, the rolling hills, the flame-colored trees. She wanted to feel free.

"If you'll excuse me," she found herself saying, "I actually think I'll ride ahead for a bit. Is that okay?"

Greg and Parris exchanged startled glances.

"I guess," Greg said finally. "We've been on these trails before and they're tame enough. You should be fine."

She nodded, thanking them. Then, before she could question the impulse that was guiding her, she nudged her horse into a brisk trot.

She didn't look at Richard as her horse trotted past him, though she could feel his gaze slide over her. Instead, she focused her attention on the rhythm of the horse beneath her, relaxing into the trot with rusty muscles. But it still wasn't what she wanted, she realized. After all these days, she needed to run.

With a small touch of her foot, she moved the horse to canter, and then to run.

And it was great, she thought with exhilaration, feeling the horse bunch beneath her, then leap forward. The brisk wind rasped against her rosy cheeks, the green hills rushed by. Around the gentle corners, and over the small bumps, through the sloping valley—

Vaguely, she heard the sound of hoofbeats behind her. But rather than slow her down, they urged her forward. Faster, she urged her horse, faster.

But the sound of the hoofbeats grew.

She could feel the rhythm in her pulse, feel the excitement of the chase. Now she was the wind and wild and free and she wasn't ready to stop yet. Months' worth of tension and strain was in her blood. She wanted to exorcise it all, feel it pound out with each crashing thud of her own horse's hooves. She leaned forward, and urged her horse even faster.

Then, from the corner of her eye, she could see the other horse gaining on her, a black blur approaching on her left. Not giving it another thought, she veered her mount off the trail altogether, racing across the short crisp grass.

But still the black horse gained.

Of course, Goliath.

In earnest now, Liz leaned forward, whispering notes of clicking encouragement to Honeysuckle. If Richard wanted to chase her, she'd give him a race.

All of a sudden, she was fifteen again, racing away from her brothers in childish glee. Except her brothers had never ridden powerful mounts named Goliath.

She could feel Honeysuckle laboring, the horse's breath coming out in heaving gasps. There wasn't much run left in her. Still, there was one last fleeting moment of the thrill, the wind racing through her hair, the sunlight on her face.

And then, like lightning, Goliath appeared on her left. Having been caught, Liz wordlessly reined her mount to a trot, and then to a walk. Richard did the same.

"What the hell where you doing?" he demanded the minute the horses had slowed.

"Running," she said simply. "And God, was it beautiful."

Her face was flushed, her cheeks rosy in the morning sun, while her eyes glowed a beautiful exhilarating blue that pierced him deep in his chest. Damn it, he hadn't known what was going on when she'd suddenly raced away like that. He'd followed, thinking that perhaps her horse was out of control. But then he'd seen her lean over, seen how gracefully she moved with the horse as they'd raced away from him like a streaking arrow.

The challenge had been too much, and he'd sent Goliath in hot pursuit. Damn, she hadn't been easy to catch. And now, having caught her, he wasn't so sure what to do.

Just looking at her, glowing and exhilarated, he felt the ache hammer its intensity all over again.

He stopped his mount, abruptly, instinctively. She stopped hers as well, but in confusion. Instinct and the restless need pounding through his blood guided his arm, reaching across the distance. And anger, too, he understood vaguely. Anger at her for making him want her, anger at how she and Blaine had ridden together, laughing like a pair of lovers while he'd ridden ahead, all alone.

He grabbed her arms and pulled her onto his mount.

He saw her eyes grow wide with shock. If she'd cried out then, he might have come to his senses. But instead, her gaze fell helplessly to his lips, and he saw the midnight depths grow even darker.

He didn't need any other sign.

He wasn't gentle when he took her lips with his own. He wasn't a man asking, nor a man coaxing. He was a man possessed by hundreds of sleepless nights, a man driven by raging demons seeking reprieve.

He plundered her lips, his tongue plunging into the moist recesses of her mouth, relishing the softness of her lips against his own. She opened her mouth to him willingly, arching against him as his hands wrapped around her ponytail, pulling her closer. She tasted of October sun and wild exhilaration. He could feel the softness of her breasts crushed against his chest, smell the beguiling scent of flowers, and horses, and heat. Beneath them, Goliath shifted impatiently, but Richard simply tightened his legs for control.

He'd dreamed of this moment too long, damn it, to have it end abruptly.

Liz sighed beneath him, her hands tangling up through his thick dark hair. They wandered around, stroking through the wonderful rasp of his morning whiskers as she slanted her mouth across his. She could feel the heat on all sides, from his mouth, from his firmly muscled body, and from the powerful mount beneath them. She could smell sweat and leather and horseflesh, and it made her press against him harder. Her breasts were swollen against his chest, his cheeks rough against her fingers. His tongue, wrapped around her own, exciting her unbearably.

Goliath shifted again. With a groan, Richard pulled back, steadying both of them on the horse.

His eyes were dark, and for once he didn't try to hide the expression on his face.

"I want you," he said thickly, the passion still thundering through his veins. He'd never wanted anyone as badly as he wanted her right now. And by God, he would have her. Only then would the hunger leave him, he was sure. He would take her, take her with fire and fury. Then the restlessness would finally be gone.

And he would be able at last to return to his lab and his work. Back to the isolation.

Back to the loneliness.

She shivered against him, her eyes falling helplessly on his lips. Never had she felt her pulse race so fast, until her heart practically pounded in her ears. Her face was fiery with heat and desire. She wanted him, too. It was at once that simple, and that complicated.

She stiffened in his arms.

He bit off a low growl of frustration as he felt the change come over her. His body was on fire, and once more she was withdrawing from him. He wanted to curse her to hell and back. He wanted to pull her closer and kiss all that reluctance away.

Instead, his eyes glittering with frustration, he simply let her go. He'd been called a bastard in his time, he'd been called the devil's own spawn. But he'd never pushed a woman, and he wouldn't now.

The muscle in his jaw clenched, but he forced his hands to relax. Pure physical desire, he reminded himself. Lust was a simple hunger. Sooner or later, she would realize that, too.

Liz slid down from the horse, knowing from the sudden looseness of his grip he would let her go. She staggered away from the horse, embracing the early-fall chill against her flaming cheeks as she collected her composure. She wrapped her arms around her middle, and once more that gesture struck him as surely as a physical blow.

She was protecting herself from him. Again.

"I'm sorry," she said finally. "I didn't mean for things to get that far."

"Then just what did you mean?" he asked curtly, feeling an abrupt sense of desolation fill him. His face turned to granite, and he retreated behind the stone wall of his incredible self-control.

"I . . . I don't know." Liz said weakly. He was looking at her with his cold blue eyes, as if, now the kiss had ended, he had no use for her anymore. Again, she realized just how dangerous such a man was for her. He knew how to kiss, how to touch, how to arouse without ever losing anything of himself. She only knew how to love, how to give her entire heart, trust and soul. She didn't want to go through that kind of pain again. The memory, as always, came unbidden and sharp.

Kneeling on a sidewalk, trying to hold on to her love as he died in her arms—

She turned away, pushing the memory back and staring at the bright, blue sky.

"We should return to the others," she said finally.

Richard nodded, not saying anything, his wintery eyes once more impenetrable.

He wheeled his horse around.

After a small moment, she mounted her own horse and followed.

Chapter 8

Liz and Richard were careful to remain apart for the rest of the day. They rode to the stables only to find the rest of the party had already returned. In silence, they walked back to the house, each lost in their own thoughts.

Liz, for one, was very confused by her reactions to this dark and volatile man. Her whole life she'd loved only Nick. He had been her friend, her husband and her lover. She had thought it would always be so.

But now those warm childhood days seemed so far away. Maddensfield loomed in her mind almost like a fairy-tale kingdom where all had been magical. Except for one Sunday afternoon of course, when the fair prince had died in her arms and the fairy tale had ended.

Now she was Liz the woman, living in a dark and gloomy house, trying to help a dark and gloomy child. And there was Richard the man, no fair prince, to be sure. Yet she was drawn to him in a way she had never been drawn to anyone. It was not the easy, simple love of her childhood. It was something more complex, something that tied her stomach in knots and left her breathless in his mere presence.

She liked his kisses. Very much.

But who was this dark man that drew her in? This house had too many secrets, and even as Maddensfield slipped away in her mind, Liz missed those golden days. In this new environment of morbid statistics and midnight vigils, she didn't know her way around. A woman had died here. Liz slept in Alycia's room, rode the horse named by her, cared for her child. But what had happened to Alycia? Who had pushed her from the tower?

Was it Richard?

She wanted to ignore such a thought. She wanted to push all doubt from her mind. Because she had liked his kiss, because she would sell her soul for another. But Richard seemed so distant at times, and his blue eyes were so often cold. He had secrets, too, secrets known only to him as he swirled his glass before the midnight flames.

In the dark of the night, she still didn't know what went on behind those pale blue eyes of his. Nor how much it could cost her.

The doubt tore at her. She was accustomed to people who talked, people who shared. She'd fallen in love with a man who'd returned her passion as purely as she'd given it, until she'd seen his love in his eyes, his smile, the casual touch of his hand.

Attraction was a physical thing, entirely different from love. It wouldn't last, especially with a man like Richard. He was too good at control. It would be easy for him to rouse her into flames while keeping his own heart untouched. And when he was done, when the passion at last was slaked, he would simply walk away.

But she would remain behind, and she would feel the pain. She only knew one way to love: absolutely, wholeheartedly and for forever.

She didn't want the pain of parting again.

She went straight to her room when they entered the house, Richard disappearing without a word toward his tower. Halfway down the hall, however, she paused.

Her bedroom door was closed. Odd, she thought she had left it open. Puzzled, she turned the knob slowly. And maybe it was the mood of the house, or the strain of the past few days, but she opened the door with great care.

Cautiously, she peered around the doorframe. Nothing. She probed deeper into the shadows. Still nothing.

Then she turned, and found the note on the bed.

She picked it up carefully, noting the delicate feel of the feminine paper. She relaxed, catching the faint hint of dried wildflowers, and admired the lavender trim. Already beginning to tug at her sweater, she unfolded the paper.

What's mine is mine. Go away, little nanny.

Alycia

The paper dropped to her bed from suddenly nerveless fingers, and once more her eyes darted around the freshly renovated room. But nothing in the room stirred, not even a light breeze.

She stared back down at the beautiful stationery with its cold words. It was a long time before she stopped shaking.

When the grandfather clock began to ring its eleven o'clock chimes, she found herself opening her bedroom door, her stomach still tied in knots. Her feet directed her down the stairs, moving silent and cautious over the hardwood floor. She needed to take her mind off things, she thought vaguely. She needed to think about anything other than that note.

She came to the library.

He was already there, his broad back to her as he sat before the low-burning fire. He was still wearing his worn jeans and the pale woolen sweater, the familiar brandy glass in his hands. He looked right in front of the fire, a part of a cozy winter scene. Outside, the fall wind probably blew, but in here, the heat flickered still.

She stepped into the room.

He turned at her approach, his pale eyes taking in her lithe figure as she neared the sofa. Her steps faltered, the nervousness compounding in her stomach under his scrutiny. She took another deep breath and sat down on the sofa as if doing so was the most natural thing in the world.

As if she didn't spend her mornings kissing a dark and fore-boding man, and her afternoons receiving notes from a dead woman.

"I didn't think you'd come here tonight," Richard said gruffly, his eyes back on the fire. His fingers resumed their methodical twirling of the crystal glass. He still wasn't sure why he'd come. Logic dictated that he work in his lab, not stare at the fire like a fool.

"I—I needed a break," she said at last.

He turned enough to arch his eyebrow. A break? It was her day off. He would have thought she'd go out someplace and celebrate her freedom. But then he noticed for the first time how pale her face was, how luminous her midnight eyes suddenly appeared.

"Everything all right?" he asked, his eyes abruptly penetrating as they swept over her features. His fingers stopped their turning of the glass as all his attention focused upon her.

Once more, she hesitated, then her chin shot up. "Should anything be wrong?" she asked carefully.

He frowned, not liking the game they were playing at all. First she kissed him, then she pushed him away and now she was suddenly probing him for something. He was beginning to remember why he spent so much time in his lab.

"You tell me," he retorted at last, turning away from her completely.

For no reason at all, that movement hurt her. Once more he was the dark and remote man. And right now, with all the doubts haunting her mind, she needed him to be something more. She needed to be able to trust him.

On its own, her hand reached up, as if to touch his shoulder. But at the last moment, she looked at his chiseled features, and her hand fell back. She stared at the flames bleakly, feeling the knots tie her stomach ever tighter.

She should tell him about the note. But for all she knew, it was just some childish prank. Maybe Andy had decided the statistics weren't working well enough. Someone had scared away the third nanny when she'd started to make progress. Liz didn't want to be the fourth to desert. Then again, she didn't know what to think anymore, what to feel.

What was this man capable of? Why, after all these weeks, didn't she know?

Richard turned abruptly, not being able to stand the intense feel of her eyes on his face anymore. He caught the look of need in her eyes, the look of doubt, and he swore low and dark. He didn't need an interpreter to know her thoughts. The fact that she, of all people, could still wonder if he'd murdered his own wife filled him with rage.

"Ask it," he demanded harshly.

Her eyes flew open with genuine shock. "Ask what?"

"Stop it!" he growled. "Stop pretending. Just say the words, Liz. Say the words burning on the tip of your tongue. Did I kill Alycia? That's what you want to know, right? What you're still struggling to figure out?"

She tried to shake her head but the movement was ineffectual.

He threw his brandy glass into the flames, the sound of shattering crystal making her jump. The flames flared with the impact of the alcohol, but they didn't begin to compare to the power of the man rising before them. He looked down at her, his jaw clenched, his eyes hooded. Then abruptly, he reached down and dragged her up out of the chair.

She came crashing against his chest, but there was no time to even gasp before his lips captured hers. They were bruising, fierce and demanding. He did not wait, but thrust his tongue between her lips, delving into the moist recesses of her mouth.

He jerked away just as fast.

"Is that how a killer kisses?" he asked with glittering eyes. "Or maybe it's more like this."

His lips came down once more, but whereas last time they had crushed hers, this time they were barely a caress. He teased her mouth with light exploration, reveling in the fullness of her lips, nipping in at the corners. It was gentle and tender, and all the more horrible because she knew he felt none of it. His tongue eased between her lips, seeking and gaining access like a long-lost lover. She felt the first of the tears prick her eyes as her arms wound around his neck.

He deepened the kiss, and even as she knew he was mocking her, she tilted her head in acquiescence. Suddenly his hands were burying themselves in her hair, gliding through the long, luxurious strands until she wanted to purr like a cat. One large palm smoothed up her back, arching her against his chest. Then it slid back down to cup her buttocks and pull her closer. She complied, and the feel of his rigid length against her sent new sparks of awareness through her.

Maybe he wasn't in as much control as he thought.

Her hands became demanding on his neck, kneading the corded muscles as she opened herself fuller to him. She rubbed her breasts against his chest, and was rewarded by the sudden raggedness of his breath. Her tongue dueled with his, no longer the passive recipient but suddenly an aggressor. Her senses were already beginning to reel as his palm slid abruptly under her sweater to capture her breast.

She moaned at the first touch, feeling the heat of his fingers through the thin lace of her bra. He brushed a callused thumb over her nipple, and she sighed with the wicked voluptuousness of the sensation. Her left leg came up, and rubbed against his hip. She wanted his hands on her body—the texture, the heat of him full against her. She wanted to feel soft and desirable. She wanted anything but the dark doubt hovering at the corners of her mind.

He unfastened the back of her bra, his breathing no longer steady as he trailed kisses down her jaw to her ear. He caught her earlobe with his teeth as he rolled her nipple with his fingers. She shivered, and he groaned his encouragement in her ear.

She was soft and sweet and so, so passionate. He tore off her sweater, and dipped his head to her breast, capturing one of her nipples. He suckled delicately, and she buried her hands in his hair, arching her back and whimpering her need.

He didn't care anymore that she didn't trust him. He didn't care about the past, the future. He was a man consumed by the moment, and the passion raging like a fire in his blood. He needed her. He wanted her. He would have her. Now.

He pulled her down to the floor.

At the first contact of the Oriental rug against her bare skin, Liz stiffened. But his lips were back on hers, swallowing any protest she could have made. His hands were gliding down her hips, moving closer and closer to where she wanted, needed him to touch. She kissed him harder and tugged on his own sweater.

It drifted to the floor without protest, leaving his chest bare to her gaze and her touch. He had a mat of springy black hair that thinned to a small line disappearing into his jeans. She followed that line with her forefinger, and was rewarded by the sharp contraction of his stomach muscles. Momentarily, she became fascinated by the washboard ripples. Apparently, he was putting those weights in his lab to good use. Her finger drifted back up, and she found herself captured by the burning intensity of his gaze.

For just one moment she hesitated, her finger stilled on his chest, her midnight eyes caught by his own wintry fire.

She'd never done anything like this, rolled on the floor with a man she barely knew. Would she really be able to give just her body, or would she give him her heart, too? And how badly would it hurt when he finally turned away?

"Why?" she whispered. "Why do you want me so much?"

And the minute she saw the tightening of his jaw, she knew.

"That should be clear," he said harshly. "It's obvious how much we desire each other."

She nodded, not refuting that statement, but inside, she felt a tiny spark die. Maybe she'd been hoping, after all, hoping beyond hope that he would talk of something other than desire, like caring. Suddenly she felt cold and exposed.

She reached for her sweater wordlessly. Watching, he cursed once more.

"How many times," he said tightly, "are we going to go through this scenario before you finally admit to the passion between us? You look at me, and your eyes fall to my lips. I look at you, and all I can think of is the way you taste, the way you feel beneath me. We are attracted to each other, Liz. It's the most basic, natural, elemental force there is. And sooner or later, you won't be able to pull away."

"It's not enough," she said at last, pulling her sweater over her head. She couldn't meet his gaze; instead, her gaze fell almost wistfully upon the flames. "Desire is easy to come by. I want more."

He stiffened beside her, and abruptly reached for his own sweater. "I won't put a ring on your finger," he said bluntly. "I won't fall for that again."

She shook her head, impatient now with his suspicions. "I'm not talking about marriage," she told him seriously, risking a glance at his granite face. "I'm talking about love, compassion, caring. I'm talking about knowing someone so well, loving them so much, that when they touch you it reaches your soul."

He looked at her with iron eyes. "You really are naive," he said dispassionately. "Love is hardly necessary for passion, that's merely a fairy tale to keep little girls protected. Passion is a basic biological function, and sex is as much a need as anything else. When you're hungry, don't you eat? Well, let me tell you, I am hungry."

The way he said the words caused a slow blush to heat her face, and her gaze skittered back to the fire. But despite the pulsing race of her blood, she plunged on stubbornly.

"That's sex," she managed to say, the words prim but angry, at him, at herself. "And sex may fill your 'hunger' but it's about as lasting as a snack." She paused for a moment, her voice growing softer. "I've never had sex," she whispered. "My first time, I waited for marriage. I think, maybe, it's worth it to wait again."

His face grew dangerously darker. He didn't want to hear what she said, didn't want to believe in anything more than the physical. He'd been a fool enough to believe those lines once before.

"That's fairy-tale foolishness," he told her harshly, rising off the floor and severing the intimate scene once and for all. "You think sex is merely superficial? You think it means nothing? Let me tell you, Liz, even sex can make your head spin. Shall I demonstrate it to you once more?"

She gasped, swallowing hard as her face paled. The anticipation still simmered in her blood, but she didn't think she could take two of these lessons in one night.

He laughed mockingly at the look on her face, and strode angrily to the bar. He went to pour himself another glass of brandy, then saw the way his hand shook. With an oath, he slammed the decanter down. Brandy wouldn't do a thing for the ache in his stomach now.

"Sooner or later," he said without turning around. "Sooner or later, Liz, you'll understand what I mean. You can't fight nature."

She stood up slowly behind him, grateful for the distance even as she hated it. Would she ever get through to him? Would she ever see anything other than the darkness in him? Yet again, she was painfully aware of the fact that he'd never answered his own question. *Did you kill Alycia?* Funny, he had yet to say no.

She shook her head, and felt the beginnings of a headache throb at her temples. Tomorrow she would make it to the town library. She swore it. She turned, and, not knowing anything else to say, she simply walked out of the room.

Richard felt her leave, and his fists clenched on the bar until the knuckles turned white. He didn't believe in love, damn it, or any of the rest of her naive drivel. Love was a fool's fantasy, some ridiculous fairy tale invented by people who wanted to romanticize the baser instincts of life.

There was no such thing.

He would not be led down that path again. He'd learned his lessons, he'd been to the altar of disbelief.

Then his tensed muscles relaxed and a new thought entered his head. He would have to find another tack. He'd handled things too harshly this time. But surely there was another way.

Because God knows, he had to put out this fire raging in his blood. Somehow, some way, he vowed before the silenced library, he would seduce her.

How else was he ever going to forget her?

She was avoiding him. There was no other way of stating it, Liz thought two days later. She was quite simply going out of her way to avoid the man. Sunday, she'd tried to go into town, only to learn from a dismal Blaine that everything there was closed on Sundays. Rather than try to keep up appearances in front of his gang, she'd sneaked back to her room and hid out like some bandit. And even when the grandfather clock rang out the hour of midnight, she had not, absolutely would not, go anywhere near the library.

By the time Monday arrived and she could once again immerse herself in Andy and their activities together, she was grateful for the distraction.

The truth of the matter was, she didn't trust herself around Richard. He did things to her senses no man should be allowed to do. She'd thought she was a strong person, firm in her convictions, but somehow, when he looked at her with those smoldering blue eyes... She wasn't sure she wanted to test that theory.

At least Andy didn't leave much time for thinking. After two days of Mrs. Pram's supervision, he was sullen and whiny. Liz had suggested they go outside. Andy had informed her that due to the deterioration of the ozone layer, more than seven hundred thousand cases of non-melanoma skin cancer were diagnosed each year in the U.S. as being sun-related. Therefore, he couldn't possibly go outside.

Too floored to even begin arguing, Liz had simply nodded. When was she ever going to get through to this child? Just to prove her point, however, she'd devised several in-house games for them to play. Andy had looked suspicious, but he hadn't come up with any great statistics to get out of them. God knows, he would probably research the matter tonight and in the morning report the number of people who had died of respiratory diseases caused from household dust. Until then, she had him involved in a game of hide-and-seek.

Andy, being Andy, had never played hide-and-seek. The simplistic rules had caused a sneer from him. How could counting to fifty possibly be a challenge? He thought they should change it to counting to four hundred, calling out only prime numbers. Liz had informed him he was welcome to use whatever method he desired; she was counting to fifty.

Given the size of the house, they'd restricted themselves to hiding only in the main structure. That range was further limited by the fact that half the main structure, namely the two grand ballrooms and a formal study/smoking room, had been shut up. That left them with the kitchen, the foyer, the formal dining room, and of course, the library. Liz had hidden first, settling for the pantry in the kitchen. Andy had found her within five minutes, claiming the pantry was the most logical place for her to have chosen, given her affinity for snacking.

Liz had scowled, but couldn't see any way around his logic. After all, the main reason she'd selected the pantry *had* been the fact that she was hungry. She'd declared a truce with Andy over two small bowls of strawberry ice cream. To her satisfaction, Andy was coming along nicely in his new appreciation for such simple pleasures as ice cream. His mechanical bites were slowly giving way to something closer to enthusiasm. And this time, he even went so far as to scrape his bowl.

There might be hope for the child yet.

Now it was Liz's turn, so she stood in the foyer, counting out fifty in her soft lilting voice. At first, she could hear the faint scurrying and scraping sounds of Andy trying to find a good place to hide. Then, there was only the silence.

She finished counting, and raised her head. The last noise she'd heard had been in the direction of the library, so she headed there. She took a first, skimming inventory, looking behind all the furniture. No Andy. Next, she went to the kitchen, where she also conducted a quick search. No Andy there, either. She moved on to the dining room.

But Andy wasn't in the dining room or the foyer. Growing perplexed now, she started back to the library. Andy was a remarkably bright child, to say the least, what hiding place might he have come up with? Racking her brains, Liz tried to remember all the tricks she'd employed in her own youth. This time her search was much more thorough. She checked behind curtains, under desks. She checked all cabinets, and all nooks and crannies within nooks and crannies.

But after half an hour, all she'd found was more silence. And the worry within her slowly turned to dread.

Where was Andy?

Concerned now, she turned her mind to the problem with earnest. Maybe he'd forgotten their rules and hidden in the shut-up rooms. It was a thin strand of hope, given the fact that Andy never forgot anything, but looking for him there was worth a try.

Liz stepped over the velvet rope that draped across the hallway, and journeyed toward the two ballrooms. The air in the hallway was much colder here, and smelled musty with disuse. Despite herself, Liz shivered. She should have brought a flashlight, she realized. The hallway was growing darker as she moved away from the foyer. Trying to keep her uneasiness down, she put her hand along the cold stone of the wall, and began feeling for a light switch as she walked along.

"Andy?" she called out softly. But there was no reply.

Surely he wouldn't have gone down this way. Given his tight nerves and skittish demeanor, she couldn't see the child willingly walking along this dark, damp passageway. Still, he had to be around someplace. Swallowing grimly, she kept walking, her footsteps echoing down the long, dusty hall.

Finally, when her nerves were strung so tight she was afraid the slightest noise would make her snap, her hand came to a light switch. She gratefully snapped it on.

There was a small flicker, then the entire hallway filled with soft, dim light. She should have felt relief, even comfort. But she couldn't, because for the first time, she could finally see what was around her.

Along both sides of the wall loomed the dark, somber oil portraits of past Keatons. Beneath each one, she could see their names carved in a small brass plate. So it went, all the way down, father, mother, sons, wives, sons, until you reached the end. And at the end sat one lone portrait. An oil portrait that wasn't sitting so neat and nice on the wall. Instead, the frame hung at a drunken angle, while the painting itself appeared to have been torn out. Now, it littered the broad hallway in little bits of meticulously cut canvas. Liz felt her feet moving of their own accord, drawing her to the destruction. But she didn't have to journey all the way there to know what the little brass plate would say.

Alycia Wynston Keaton.

There was no trace of the beautiful blonde anymore. The pieces were slashed so tiny, reconstruction would be impossible. Liz could only stare at the ragged pieces with growing horror. It was as if the person who had done this had been trying to obliterate her completely, to stamp her out beyond repair.

The destruction was so total, the anger so complete, that Liz felt it.

Cold shudders raced through her uncontrollably. Instinctively she sensed the truth. The person who had murdered Alycia was still out there, the rage still burning dark and bitter in the musty halls. Who else could have done such a thing as what she saw before her?

And unbidden, his picture rose to her mind. *Richard.* Richard sitting in the library with his cold, controlled eyes. Richard twirling his brandy glass while his eyes darkened with unholy secrets.

Could the man who touched her with such passion be capable of such violence? Her fingers rose to tentatively touch her lips, as if searching for some proof in the memory that would tell her irrevocably, no, Richard was not such a man. But the truth was, she didn't know. She had seen him cold, and she had seen him angry. And she didn't know just what he was capable of.

Had Alycia?

There were no answers in the dark hallway, only the drafts of an old cold wind that chilled her soul. After all these years, this house still clutched its secrets. And in these long dusty hallways, it kept the anger, as well.

She moved back down the hall in earnest.

Andy, she had to find Andy. Where was the child, where could he have gone?

And once again, the terror was back. She had to find Andy, and she had to find him now. He couldn't be in the ballrooms, there hadn't been footprints in the dust, she realized belatedly. Therefore, he could only be in the study, or perhaps he had been in the first rooms and she just hadn't realized it. Nodding to herself to keep calm, she turned back, calling out his name as she went.

"Game's over, Andy," she said, trying to keep the tremor out of her voice as her panic grew. "You can come out now. You win."

But still there was only silence.

She searched the study. She searched the library, the kitchen, the foyer and the dining room. She went from room to room, crying out his name, and at long last, begging him to come out.

But still there was no sign of the little boy.

Completely panicked now, she went up to the rooms. The hour was growing late, darkness falling with steady swiftness, but she couldn't find a trace of anyone—Blaine, Jillian, Parris, Greg. They were all gone, and so was Andy. The house appeared to be completely deserted.

Except, of course, for the left-hand tower.

She had to tell Richard, she thought instantly. She couldn't find Andy anywhere, and he knew the old house much better than she did. He would know where a child might disappear or become trapped. She had to believe that, had to believe that Andy was somewhere in this old mansion and in a matter of minutes, they would figure out where.

Her midnight eyes tight with the strain, she fairly ran up the left-tower steps. She didn't even pause at the top, but pounded on the thick wooden door with fierce determination.

It was opened immediately.

"What do you want?" Richard demanded. But his voice trailed off as he saw her face. It was completely ashen, her blue eyes huge and bright with panic. Something was wrong, horribly wrong.

"What happened?" he asked, a thousand and one emotions racing through him before he had a chance to feel even one. The dread settled hard, and suddenly he knew. "It's Andy," he whispered.

She could only nod, fighting her way through the knot of panic in her stomach. She had to remain in control. If she could just keep her thoughts clear, they would figure this all out. It would be okay. It had to be.

"We were playing hide-and-seek," she managed to get out. "He was supposed to hide only in the main structure, in the open rooms. But I've looked and looked and looked, and I can't find him anywhere. I'm sorry. I'm so terribly sorry." She had failed, failed miserably. Andy and Richard had both trusted her, and she had failed them both.

Richard frowned, some of the tightness leaving his chest. "He's probably just in his room," he said.

She shook her head. "I looked there a moment ago. He wasn't in."

"Well, did you call for him, tell him that the game had ended? You know how clever he is, he probably just came up with a really good spot so that you missed him."

"I called," she whispered. "I told him the game was over. He never appeared."

Richard's face froze, the tightness returning to his chest. He could feel the beginnings of an uncommon emotion, and he fought against it: worry. The child was somewhere in the house, he repeated to himself, clinging fast to his rational mind. They simply needed to deduce where.

"Well, then," Richard said briskly. "We'll both look for him. I'm sure if we conduct a thorough search, going methodically from room to room, he will turn up. He's probably just being stubborn, you know, trying to get more attention."

Liz simply nodded. She hoped that was the case, she really did. Wordlessly, she went with Richard to the bottom of the stairs.

They did as Richard suggested, going from room to room to room. In their need for thoroughness, they even looked under sofa cushions, as if the small boy was simply waiting somewhere for their careful eyes. But in each room, they only found the emptiness, and the echoing cries of their own voices, calling out his name.

They never spoke about it, but as they went from room to room, their faces grew paler, their eyes more strained. To all intents and purposes, Andy had disappeared.

Richard was having to focus hard as they reached the last room. Emotions and pictures seemed to be assaulting him from all sides, and he didn't want any of them. He could remember the fragile weight of baby Andrew, sleeping so soundly in his arms as Richard rocked back and forth in the rocking chair. He could remember the smell of baby powder, Andrew's toothless grin when Richard bent down to pick him up. He could remember the sound of baby laughter as he tossed Andrew up and down in the air. He could even remember the simple responsibility of changing diapers.

It seemed so long ago. So long since he'd looked at this tiny baby and felt only the love that gripped his heart so fiercely. It was nothing like the pain and betrayal that would come later. The time when he would look at the boy, and feel only the raw wound in his chest. Everything about the boy practically screamed Alycia.

He'd wanted the child to leave, all those years ago. Thought he wouldn't be able to stand to have a reminder so close. Even now, he wanted to keep his distance from the boy. It was for the best, he'd told himself time and time again. For both of them, it was for the best.

But the thin logic didn't prepare him for the concern that gripped him now. He could feel the weight of the worry in the unbearable tightness in his chest. He didn't want to feel this panic. He didn't want to care, damn it. He'd been tricked into caring once before, and the betrayal had practically ripped him apart.

He didn't want to feel anything.

But for once, the control was beyond even his reach. Andrew was missing, and he could only feel the fear freezing his veins.

What had happened to the baby who would look at him and smile his innocent grin? What had happened to the child that had once slept so trustingly in his arms?

And then in a cold rush of certain dread, he knew.

Chapter 9

Richard turned, his entire face frozen into a grim expression.

"Come on," he said. Liz looked at him with confusion, but he wasn't waiting to see if she followed. Instead, he was already heading toward the right-hand stairs. Liz felt the sudden rush of coldness like ice water in her blood.

He was going to the right-hand tower.

The place where Alycia had been pushed. Liz felt the goose bumps prickle along her spine.

Surely Andy never would have gone there. But then, all of a sudden, she wasn't so sure. She'd never broached the subject of his mother's death after that first evening. She had no idea what Andrew did or did not know about Alycia's murder. Perhaps, innocently unaware, he'd deduced that the right-hand tower was a new and clever place to hide. It sounded like an Andy thing to do.

So why did her heart still pound in her chest?

Her fear increasing tenfold, she followed Richard up the increasingly narrow and winding stone staircase. As they neared the top, the air became colder, the spiraling stairs even darker. Liz had to put her hand against the solid stone wall for support, but Richard continued without ever faltering. Perhaps it was only her imagination, Liz tried to tell herself, but it seemed so unnaturally dark, so unnaturally cold there. As if something else was there.

Something dark and bitter and, even after five years, filled with rage.

She shook her head and continued. Even then, she found herself falling back slightly as they neared the door at the top.

Richard didn't, of course. Cold controlled Richard went right up to the door without a single hesitant footstep, as if a woman had never been murdered in this room, as if that woman hadn't been his wife.

And for one long desperate moment, Liz would have given anything just to be able to see his eyes. Surely there was some emotion there. Surely something other than the cold measured beat of his feet on the last two steps was reflected in his eyes. But he never turned around, and whatever thoughts were running through his brilliant mind, he never gave them away. His hand came up, and easily pushed open the solid wooden door.

At once, she could feel the draft. Strong and bone-chilling.

"Andrew?" Richard called, his voice deep and without a tremor. "Andrew, are you here?"

Liz came up behind Richard, now, trying to peer over his shoulder through the dim light. He pushed open the door all the way, exposing the whole room. The round stone expanse slowly appeared, curves falling into dark shadows while dim rays of moonlight broke through the tall glass windows.

There, in the middle of the dusty stone floor stood Andrew.

"Andy," Liz breathed. She was so glad to have finally found the child, she forgot her own fears and pushed past Richard to get to the boy. Without another thought, she bent down and wrapped the child in her arms, feeling the tremors of his shaking little body. "Oh, Andrew, are you all right?"

Against her shoulder, she could feel his head nod, and the relief washed through her in waves. Tentatively, then fiercely, Andy's own arms wrapped themselves around her neck.

From the doorway, Richard watched it all, his face growing dark. Once again, the emotions were back, racing uncontrollably across his chest. Seeing the child here, finally safe and sound, he could feel the relief even as he felt the corresponding anger.

He didn't want to feel worry, fear, relief. Damn it, he was supposed to remain uncaring. Yet here he stood in the doorway of this horrid room with its cold drafts swirling around him like an icy rage, feeling, feeling, feeling.

What if Andy had been hurt? What if something awful had happened to the boy? What if he'd rushed in to find the tall windows pushed open once more, as he had five years ago? What if he'd found this tiny, trusting little body lifeless on the cold ground below?

The relief in his chest exploded resolutely into rage.

"What are you doing here?" he demanded out loud, his voice tight. Liz pulled away from Andrew long enough to look the boy in the eyes. Andy was still shaking, his blue eyes wide in fear. He looked up at the dark face of his father, and his shoulders quivered slightly more.

"I thought I heard her," Andy said in a shaking voice.

"Who?" Richard punctuated coldly.

Andrew's bottom lip began to tremble. *"Her."*

Richard took two steps forward, his face ominous. Damn it, the boy had scared them all nearly half out of their minds. And now all he could say was "her"?

"You have until the count of three to explain yourself," Richard said darkly. "One, two—"

"I heard a noise, I heard her, I heard her," Andy cried out wildly. "I didn't have a choice, I had to come."

Liz reached out, and put a stabilizing hand on the boy's shoulders. It was obvious Andrew was deeply upset, and it was even more obvious Richard was only making matters worse. She spoke in her calmest voice, determined to take control of the situation.

"Why don't you tell us who she is, Andy," Liz said soothingly, her Carolina accent as comforting as velvet. "We were very worried about you when we couldn't find you, you know."

Andrew's eyes darted at once to his father, as if seeking some sign the tall dark stranger might have cared. Richard, however, was still silent and glowering.

"Alycia." Andrew said simply. "I heard Alycia."

Liz felt her face pale at the words and dared not look at Richard. Surely Andy must be mistaken. Most likely he'd heard one of Blaine's friends banging around. Except, she realized faintly, she'd already learned no one else had been home.

"Alycia's dead," Richard said flatly. "Now, tell us the truth."

Liz turned enough to shoot Richard a level glare as Andy once more began to tremble. "Andrew's had a rough day," she stated loudly, keeping her shoulders straight. "I think some rest would do him good. We can discuss this matter more later on."

Richard's face grew tight, but he remained silent. Damn it, he wanted to move forward with his life. But here was this child, this child he'd sworn he would keep away from, and yet he'd been so worried when they hadn't been able to find him. He didn't like feeling worried, he didn't like feeling vulnerable.

And he refused to be told he had been feeling all these things because of a ghost.

Once more the anger spiraled. He could feel the rage and the frustration blending easily with the remnants of worry and fear, until he was clenching his fists at his side. And still the anger grew.

It could not be Alycia. Alycia was dead. *And he wanted to move on with his life, with his damn solitary life!*

He didn't trust himself anymore. Nodding coldly to the golden-haired child who twisted his gut, and the mahogany-haired woman who haunted his dreams, he turned on his heels and stormed out of the room.

Alone now with Andrew, Liz took the little boy by the hand. She could see his gaze peering into the darkness where his father had so abruptly disappeared.

"He just needs some time to calm down," she told the boy soothingly. "He was very worried when we couldn't find you. Honest, Andy."

Andy looked up, and she could once more feel the tremors in his tiny hand, clutching her own so tightly.

Solemnly the little boy nodded his head, but Liz could see the disappointment in his eyes. Taking one last look at the round tower with its huge windows, she led Andy to the stairs. But even when she closed the door behind them, she could still feel the chill from that room.

Coming down the stairs into the foyer, they were just in time to see the front door opening. Andy immediately tightened his grip on her hand, but the open door only revealed the Gang of Four and Mrs. Pram walking in. Both Mrs. Pram and Blaine appeared to be carrying grocery bags, with Parris carelessly dangling two jugs of milk. Jillian, on the other hand, sported a fine collection of nicely decorated shopping bags, while Greg followed with a garment bag swung over his shoulder.

"Oh, no," Blaine said upon seeing Liz and Andrew. "I think we've been caught carrying groceries." He immediately turned to the stony-faced Mrs. Pram. "She made us!" he said in his best theatrics. "We tried to resist, but she ran us down in the driveway and forced bags of food into our hands."

"Absolutely," Parris concurred.

Jillian flashed them both annoyed looks, while Greg simply smiled lazily.

"Trust me," he said. "We didn't actually do anything as helpful as grocery shopping. Just the carrying of the bags." He indicated his and Jillian's loads. "The trip to Saks was much more our style."

Jillian seemed to give Liz's dusty garb a pointed look, and in spite of herself, Liz felt self-conscious. Andy tugged at her hand, clearly wanting to be on the way, while Mrs. Pram breezed by with stern efficiency.

She was about to follow Andy, when another thought caught her. "You've been out shopping all day?" she asked, hoping her voice sounded casual.

"But of course," Blaine assured her. "Jillian doesn't take shopping lightly." He shot the lounging Parris a meaningful glance. "Especially with someone else's credit cards."

Parris just shrugged. "She's a blonde. I have a weakness."

Jillian, however, was flushing a dark shade of infuriated red. The look she gave Blaine shot daggers.

Liz looked at them all again, and wondered why the more she got to know the group, the less she understood them. This time she did follow the prodding of Andrew's grip. With a few parting exchanges, she followed him up to his room.

She tucked him immediately into bed. She figured as traumatic as the day had been, he could use the rest. But she'd no sooner settled into her own room, when he was knocking at their adjoining door. With a small sigh, she let him in.

Andy was wearing his navy blue satin pajamas, looking like a little gentleman with his thick glasses and solemn eyes. He no longer looked scared, she decided, but he was definitely nervous.

"Will you," he began then paused. "Will you read me a story?"

Slightly shocked, Liz stared at the child. She'd offered to read him stories before, only to be curtly informed that he was perfectly capable of reading to himself. After that, she'd stopped offering. Still, she wasn't going to turn away from the child now. Today's episode certainly must have rattled him.

"Of course I'll read you a story," Liz told him, reaching down to affectionately rumple his hair. "What would you like?"

She led him into his room and watched as he considered the matter. He climbed onto the bed and she pulled the covers back over him. "Well?" she prompted.

"When you were six," Andy asked with an intense look, "what stories were read to you?"

Liz was somewhat taken aback by the question, but she gave it careful consideration. "Fairy tales, mostly," she said after a bit. "You know, 'Cinderella', 'Sleeping Beauty'. And things like Dr. Seuss, *Winnie-the-Pooh*. The usual."

Andrew looked at her solemnly. "I don't know those stories," he said seriously. "I've never read them."

"What kind of stories would you like?" she asked tactfully, sitting on the edge of the bed beside him. It was obvious Andy knew how different he was from other kids. And while most of the time he was very defensive or disdainful about that fact, nights like tonight, he could be painfully vulnerable.

"I read *A Brief History of Time* by Stephen Hawking," he volunteered. "I liked it. And *Cosmos* by Carl Sagan. I liked *Cosmos*, too."

Liz nodded. "I hear those are very good books. Maybe you'd like to read to me instead."

But instantly, Andy shook his head, the intensely shy look on his face appearing once more. "I want *you* to read *me* a story. *Winnie-the-Pooh*, okay? Read me *Winnie-the-Pooh*."

"I don't have the book here," Liz said. "But I think I might remember enough to tell you the story."

Andy nodded, the intense look becoming satisfied. Looking at him, Liz felt herself smile softly. He really was such a great kid, once you got underneath all his defenses. He was definitely a child prodigy, no doubt twenty times smarter than herself. But he was also just a kid, and sometimes, he needed to be a kid as much as the next child. Only, given his genius, it was that much harder to accomplish.

Starting out in her soft Carolina voice, Liz began with her memory of Winnie-the-Pooh and the sticky honey pot. Slowly she wove a gentle spell of Eeyore, Piglet, and Tigger, too, until at long last Andy's eyes grew heavy with sleep and he drifted off into safe slumber.

She whispered the last of the story, easing off the bed and shutting off the light. Quietly she turned to her own room.

"Sweet dreams," she whispered, and closed the door.

Alone now in her own room, she put on her nightshirt and robe, trying to collect her thoughts. But as she stared out her window at the deep fall night, certain pictures wouldn't leave her mind.

Richard, staring at the fire in the library, swirling his brandy glass with long, lean fingers. The scented stationery note with its round, feminine scrawl and cold, threatening words. Richard, peering down at her with concern as she wavered in the hall, reaching out a hand to steady herself. Alycia's portrait, shredded into hundreds of irretrievable fragments in the dark dusty hallway. Richard, his eyes grim with worry as they went from room to room, searching for Andrew. The right-hand tower, cold and musty with past rage and haunting chills.

Richard, his eyes like blue steel, piercing her with impenetrable control. Richard, his lips like a fiery brand upon her own—

With a small cry, she turned away from the window, pacing the room in her agitation. Oh, she'd wanted to get away from Maddensfield, all right. And she certainly had. Now she was staying in a dark house with a dark man and a troubled child. Not to mention the golden younger brother and a host of his friends she didn't understand. How had she gotten herself into such a mess?

And where would it all end?

In such a dark, cold place, who did you trust?

"Alycia was murdered."

"I doubt we'll ever know who did it."

And then all at once, she became aware of another sound. A movement. Down the hall? No, closer. Much closer. Perhaps the other side of the wall. Yes, there it was again. The telltale sound of someone scratching.

The chill returned to her spine, and she felt the first tremor. She repressed it with determination. Someone was on the other side of the wall, the wall opposite Andrew's room. Who? What was next to her room? She didn't know.

Determined now, and unwilling to be frightened yet again, she strode determinedly to the doorway, throwing open her door.

Nothing. Just the long, empty expanse of the hall. Puzzled, she went out, turning to her left. There was another doorway just one down from her own. Feeling the slight prickliness of fear, she forced herself toward it. She did not believe in ghosts. The things that happened were caused by someone with a purpose. Well, she had a purpose, too, and that purpose was to help Andrew.

Tightening her robe around her waist, she padded softly to the open doorway of the room next to hers and, reaching in, she abruptly snapped on the light.

It was a small room, a sitting room perhaps. To the left, the wall that joined with her room, there was a long mahogany coffee table with two plush blue chairs sitting at either end of it. An elaborate desk sat against the back wall, but it was obvious that it was more for show than use. Judging from the new decor of the room, Liz guessed it had been redone when the master suite she and Andy occupied had been redone. In fact, it might have been part of the original suite, given that many master bedrooms had once contained sitting rooms. Intrigued, she went over to explore the wall, forgetting her fear as her curiosity kicked in. Sure enough, the left wall was just plain Sheetrock, a far cry from the thick stone structure of the rest of the house. So this room had once been part of her own.

But what would anyone be doing, searching around here? And who? Mentally, she ran down the list of people currently staying in the house: Blaine, Parris, Greg, Jillian, Mrs. Pram, Dodd, Richard, Andy and herself. Of course, Dodd often left after dinner, so that would leave eight people. She sat down abruptly on one of the blue chairs, trying to approach this rationally, as Richard and Andy might do. If she assumed someone was indeed searching this room because it had been part of the original master bedroom suite, who would know that? She wasn't sure. Blaine, Richard and Mrs. Pram, definitely. But she didn't know how well Blaine's friends knew the house. It sounded as if they popped by a few times a year, but if this occasion was anything to go by, they certainly didn't spend much time in the house. Still, they'd known Blaine for a long time...

With a small sigh, Liz rubbed her temples. She wasn't cut out for these kinds of things. But then she dropped her hands with a small glint of stubbornness. She didn't believe in ghosts, but she knew for a fact this house was haunted by unfinished business. Something had happened to Alycia five years ago, and the event was far from over with. Andy was already a morbid child, these kinds of influences were very damaging for him. So she would just have to do something about it.

But then abruptly, she remembered the tiny shredded bits of Alycia's painting, and felt the small tremors in her spine.

Such violence, such anger. What did a small-town girl from Maddensfield, North Carolina, know of such things? Well, she was about to find out.

She rose to her feet, peering at the wall once more. She couldn't answer the question of who, but maybe she could figure out what. Bending down, she peered at the bottom of the wall as if it would reveal to her all the mysteries of the universe. Instead, she simply saw white plaster. She frowned, looking closer.

Still nothing. She decided the lighting was her problem, so she moved over to grab a lamp off the desk, dragging it as far over as the cord would permit. Armed now with a brighter light, she examined the wall once more. It took her a few minutes to find it, but it was there. The telltale signs of someone's scratching at the floorboards. Someone wanted to get under the floorboards. But why?

Then she noticed something else, as well. The hardwood flooring next to the wall was darker. Using the lamp for better light, she could make out the faint outline of where a piece of furniture must have sat on the floor, protecting it from fading like the rest of the boards. But the outline wasn't complete, running under the wall.

Without any hesitation, she replaced the lamp and ran to her own room, estimating where the desk was on the other side in relation to her half of the wall. Then she closed the door behind her, not questioning the instinct, but turning once more to her wall. The pine armoire stood in her way, but she pushed it aside with a great effort. Bending down, she was rewarded for her exertions. There on the floor was the other half of the outline. She didn't stop to think anymore, instead she rummaged around her room for a suitable tool. She finally settled on a metal file and a wire hanger. With another light perched next to her for guidance, she attacked her half of the floor.

In the end, she discovered the tools weren't necessary. It was only a matter of hitting the right board in the right place. Upon doing so, a floorboard popped straight up, revealing the gaping black hole of a small hiding place. She paused for a moment, feeling a small shiver as the import of her discovery hit her. Something was hidden here, something someone was looking for. But what? Suddenly she remembered Blaine's comment about Alycia's diary.

With shaking hands, she reached inside the darkness. Carefully, her fingers felt out the cubbyhole. First the left-hand upper corner, then the lower corner. Her hand moved slowly to the right, stumbling upon its find: the soft, square shape of something solid. Holding her breath, she drew the object out.

It was a book, a small leather-bound book covered by disintegrating dust. Lightly, feeling the frailty of her find, she blew on the cover. One, faintly gold-gilded word appeared: Diary.

She'd found Alycia's diary!

She paused, almost afraid of what she might find between the soft leather covers.

How many people had looked for this over the years? Richard, the police, maybe. Blaine. And yet she'd found it almost by accident. She frowned, suddenly unsure. She didn't like to believe in things like fate or luck.

But then, the secret compartment had been in the heart of the outlined piece of furniture. Perhaps people had searched what she assumed had been a desk, and maybe the floor around the desk, without moving the desk itself. When Richard had the renovations done, just recently, that had finally carried the furniture away.

And someone else must have realized the new opportunities, she thought suddenly with widening eyes. Someone who had come back to continue searching for the book....

She looked at the leather volume once more, and saw it tremble in her hands. She opened it to a front section and began to read.

August 18
  Blaine Keaton asked me to marry him today. Of course I said no. Everyone knows the real money belongs to Richard. I have given it a great deal of thought and Richard it will be. Richard controls the bulk of the estate, and he's so caught up in his work he won't interfere with me at all.
  Then the matter of Blaine ... Perhaps I shall sleep with Blaine. He is a beautiful man, quite unlike Richard. I shall have the money, and the brother. What fools men are.

January 8
  Today was my wedding day. I wore white, of course, a beautiful Christian Dior gown that cost $10,499. Mama told me I looked like a princess in my dress. Of course I looked like a princess, I have always looked like a princess.
  Blaine attended the wedding. He'd said he wouldn't because he didn't think he could bear the sight of me marrying his brother. I told him to stop such nonsense, of

course he must attend. So he did, kissing me on the cheek all prim and proper like a perfect brother-in-law. Do men know nothing at all?

Richard said nothing, of course. He doesn't like Blaine. I wonder if he knows Blaine asked me to marry him. It's so hard to tell what goes on under those eyes of his. I will have to be more careful of that. At least in the beginning.

Tonight's my wedding night. I wonder... Richard is such a large man, and so dark-looking. Not my type at all, really, but I suppose I can make do. Men may have muscle, but they're also fools. He looks at me with such affection, thinking we're so close when he knows nothing about me at all.

I like it that way. Odd, how easy it is to hide ourselves. There are times, I don't think any of them know me at all. Not Blaine, or Parris, or Greg.

If you bury something deep enough, ignore it long enough, do you suppose after a while, it never happened at all?

Liz flipped more pages, skimming the large flowing handwriting as she was drawn into this dark, teaming world. So Blaine had tried to marry Alycia. He must never have told anyone. At least, he'd refused to admit it to her when she'd asked. Was he trying to protect his brother's feelings? Or himself?

She turned to the middle of the diary.

November 10

My back hurts all the time and I'm only six months pregnant. Mama keeps telling me it's the burden women must bear. To hell with the burdens women must bear. I'm bloated and fat and miserable. This wasn't part of the plan and it's all Richard's fault.

He tries to take care of me, offering to rub my back, giving me his arm. As if that helps at all. At least now I don't have to put up with his attentions anymore. Last week when he reached for me, I told him it hurt to have sex. He looked at me with his blue eyes, of course, those damn all-knowing eyes. But he didn't admit that he knew the truth. He simply said that if it would make me comfortable, he would sleep in another room. I was sure to look disappointed, but I certainly agreed. There's no point to angering him now, when I'm as big as a boat and no one would want me.

Oh, why didn't I see this coming? I should have just gone to the doctor again. I swear I should have!

March 15

I hate this dreadful house. I used to think it was impressive, my own castle for entertaining. But now I know better.

The stone walls press in on you until you can barely breathe. I haven't been out in seven months, and now that the baby's born, there's no reason why I shouldn't. Richard loves the brat, always holding him, rocking him, changing him. He gave me a string of pink pearls as a gift for bearing his child. They're a beautiful strand, but even for them, I don't think I'd go through that experience again.

Richard has his heir. That will be enough. I have my figure back, and I have things to do.

I wonder what Blaine is up to these days . . .

April 20

We had another fight today. Not just a typical fight, but a big one. Richard had the audacity to tell me I should spend more time with Andrew. Really, who does he think I am? He wanted a child, I gave him a child. It was a fair exchange. He got his heir, now I want my freedom.

I don't understand him. I can wear my prettiest dress, brush out my hair until it glistens like gold, and still he looks at me with those penetrating eyes. Last night I made the effort. I went to the damn library and sat and simpered while he talked of work. I asked all the right silly questions about his silly little inventions, and I looked at him with my big blue eyes. I told Mama I didn't squander all my time at that finishing school—a woman has few enough weapons not to hone them all she can.

For a while, Richard even relaxed. But then I simply mentioned there was a party tonight that of course I was going to and instantly, his eyes turned that chilly, chilly blue.

I don't like it when he looks at me like that. As if he knows exactly what I'm doing. And his face turns grim while his jaw tightens and his fists clench. Sometimes, I am afraid of him. . . .

This state of affairs simply can't continue.

I know, I will tell Blaine that Richard scares me. Blaine will vow to protect me. His eyes aren't nearly so cold. And neither are they so all-knowing.

April 15

Richard came into my room tonight, dressed in his dark satin robe, as if he had every right to be here. I told him I had a headache, but his eyes merely hardened. He told me that it seemed I was perfectly healthy for other men.

I suppose I should have pretended not to understand, but after more than a year, I'm tired of the games. I told him the other men were none of his business. I would lead my life any way I chose.

I admit, it was a bold approach, but Richard doesn't fall for the normal simpering. I have three-fourths of the male population wrapped around my finger, but my own damn husband doesn't so much as blink when I flutter my china blue eyes. Damn dark bastard. I fear I might have made a miscalculation.

Perhaps I should have married Blaine. He had less money, but at least Blaine I could have controlled...I can control.

Richard, on the other hand... You could see the anger in his eyes as he stood in my doorway, see the fierce clenching of his jaw. Then all of a sudden, he took two steps into the room, his eyes grim with dark determinat—

A knock sounded on the door, breaking Liz's concentration. Scrambling like a guilty child, she closed the diary hastily, and tucked it between her mattresses. Her eyes turned to the newly moved armoire and the gaping black hole of the hiding place in the floor.

The knock came again.

Liz rushed to the cubbyhole, replacing the boards with shaking fingers. She didn't question her need to keep her discovery secret, just as she'd kept the note and slashed portrait a secret. She already knew why. In this house, the only one she could definitely trust was herself. She went to push the armoire back, but the knocking sounded again, louder and more persistent this time.

"Liz?" came Richard's distinctly low voice. "Liz, open the damn door."

To hell with the armoire, Liz decided, tightening her robe around her waist. She'd just have to think of some excuse. Smoothing back her hair with a nervous hand, she approached the door. Taking one more deep breath, she opened it with a pounding heart.

There stood Richard, dark and intense in the doorway. He must have gotten ready for bed himself, because he was wearing a deep, burgundy terry-cloth robe, belted at his waist. But even then, she could see the exposed expanse of his chest as the robe formed a V to his waist.

She licked her lips nervously, her pulse rate increasing even as she searched for the appearance of normalcy.

"Good evening," she said, the words coming out stilted and formal. Richard frowned, his steely eyes peering into her. Unbidden, the words from the diary came back to her. *Those damn all-knowing eyes. . . .*

"What were you doing? Why did it take you so long to answer the door?" Richard demanded, automatically trying to look past her. He'd heard the sounds of someone scurrying around the minute he knocked. Coupled with the heightened color of her face, her eyes avoiding his own told him something was going on. For a moment, he felt a small flicker of dark panic. Blaine. So help him God, if Blaine was in her room, he'd kill the bastard.

But Liz was moving aside slightly, gesturing emptily to the room with her shaking hand. "Oh," she tried to say casually, "I was just moving around the furniture some. Couldn't sleep, you know?"

Richard peered at her once more, then swept his keen eyes across the room. Could he tell? Liz wondered frantically. Could he see the floorboard that had just been raised? Spot the outline of the piece of furniture on the old floor?

But as she'd moved the lamp back, the whole area had fallen into dim lighting, helping her cause. After a long, breathless moment, Richard's gaze swept back to her, faintly satisfied. He still didn't believe her story, but at least Blaine wasn't involved. Dear, brother Blaine.

"I came to apologize," he said abruptly, having the faint pleasure of seeing her eyes go round with shock. "I behaved badly in the tower today," he continued curtly. "I should have had more control."

In an instant, Liz knew what he was talking about. He was sorry for how he'd acted with Andrew. And in that moment, she forgot all about the dark writings of the diary, and could only see Richard, *her* Richard, in front of her.

"It's okay," she told him honestly. "It's a natural reaction to go from fear to anger. Ask any parent."

He simply nodded, studying her eyes while she spoke. The nervous shadows were now gone, her midnight blue eyes softening with sincerity as she spoke in her beautiful Carolina voice. She looked relaxed, her hair loose around her shoulders and tumbling like thick molasses down her back, her cheeks still lightly flushed but glowing with health and vitality. Looking at her, he sometimes wondered how he could ever have found Alycia to be so beautiful. In hindsight, he saw her as only a brittle, porcelain centerpiece.

Whereas this woman before him, she was real flesh-and-blood vitality. Her eyes glowed with understanding, while her voice whispered of fresh-cut hay and warm summer days. She knew how to smile, how to laugh. She knew how to make Andy relax, and gain the little boy's trust. She even knew how to penetrate his own grim control. Then again, perhaps she didn't know that yet.

And he had every intention of keeping it that way.

If only just looking at her didn't make him remember the feel of her skin, the taste of her breasts.

"Still . . ." He tried to maintain his purpose, but the word came out huskily. "I shouldn't have been so harsh."

"Perhaps you could talk to Andrew in the morning," Liz suggested. He was looking at her quite differently, she recognized. His eyes were no longer so piercing, but had warmed to pale velvet, caressing her cheeks. She licked her lips once more, trying to keep her concentration. It was no use.

"Liz, sweetheart," she heard him whisper. "Let me do this." And then he was bending down, capturing her lips with his own. This time, he did not demand. This time, it was a gentle plunder, a warm exploration of her soft lips as she sighed and answered his age-old request by moving closer. Her hands seemed to move of their own volition, entwining themselves up and around his neck. She could feel the softness of his robe, and the warm silk of his black hair. Seizing his shoulders, she pulled him closer as the kiss deepened.

He reveled in the softness, the sound of her surrendering sigh against his lips, the feel of her arms wrapping around him. It made his blood pound hot, but he ignored the fiery beat. Too often, he'd simply claimed. Now, he wanted to gently cajole, to feel every acquiescent movement of her body. Lightly, he traced the outline of her lips with his tongue, asking, not taking. She responded by meeting his tongue with her own, slanting her head back for greater access.

He complied, and felt the answering shiver in her body. Entranced now, he journeyed away from her mouth, tracing light kisses to the graceful curve of her neck. She arched back, and his lips found the soft nub of her earlobe. Her hands clutched at his back for support, the blood in her veins turning to molten lava that melted her willpower. She found herself playing with the collar of his robe, one hand slipping under it to feel the fiery heat of his naked skin against her palm. She could trace the firm outline of his muscled chest, feel the pounding rhythm of his heart against her palm. She wanted to follow that touch with her lips, wanted to press herself against the hard rippling contours of his body.

She wanted to lose herself to the magic of his touch, as his lips explored the sensitive curve of her neck. She could feel his hands, lightly tracing her shoulders, then moving down to gently outline the curve of her breasts through her robe. She felt the lava in her veins burst into fire.

This time it was she who pulled his head up, finding his lips with her own, overwhelming his control with a fierce hunger that demanded satiation. The gentleness was gone, and new primal instincts took its place. His hands didn't ask anymore. They went directly to the belt of her robe and tore it aside, seeking and finding the warm shape of her curves, protected now by only a thin T-shirt. His broad palm cupped her breast, his thumb rubbing across the nipple as her own hands traced down to the outline of his boxer shorts.

The building sparks of the past few days caught, turning into an unexpected inferno. She knew she had reasons not to get involved, she knew she ought to have doubts about this man. But suddenly, she was no longer thinking, just feeling, his lips, his body, his hands. She pressed against him, and her body shivered with the intensity. If only she could tear off his robe. If only he would sweep her away to the bed and satisfy them both by plunging so sweetly and fiercely into her.

If only...

With a savage cry, she tore herself away. Richard, his eyes dark with burning desire, watched her. His jaw set, and for a moment, despite his best intentions, his hands clutched at her. Brutally, he clenched them back under control at his sides.

She could see the muscles cord on his neck with the effort.

She had to close her eyes and turn around, and even then she just wanted to cry. Her body shouted out for release, begged her to give in. She was young and healthy, and it had been so long since she'd been touched, since she'd felt desirable and passionate.

Her head bowed, and she took deep, gulping breaths of air. It didn't help. Nothing helped.

Slowly, with trembling hands, she managed to belt her robe once more.

"I'm sorry," she said at last, the words shaky. "I didn't mean...I never meant for it to get that..." She gave up on the words completely. He could fill in his own.

"Then just what did you mean?" Richard growled darkly, his eyes watching her intensely. His pulse was racing so fast, he could practically feel the ringing in his ears. Never had he wanted a woman the way he wanted her. One minute so sweet and willing in his arms, the next pulling away like a nervous virgin. He would swear she was a witch.

"I think you should go now," Liz managed to say. She didn't trust herself enough to turn around.

"What if I don't want to go?" he threatened softly.

"You will," she told him. She took another deep breath, willing sanity even as her body cried out for satisfaction. "I know I let things go too far, but I meant what I said last night. I'm not a one-night stand kind of woman, Richard. I'm...I'm just not."

"Sweetheart," he drawled thickly. "I think it would take more than one night to get enough of you."

She whirled, the passion suddenly replaced by fury. "That's not what I mean and you know it. One night, one week, it doesn't matter. It's all temporary and it's all merely physical. I want more. I want something more out of life."

Richard's jaw clenched, and for a minute, he had to restrain himself from reaching out and shaking her. Damn her and her hang-ups with emotion. Didn't she realize love was as fickle as desire? Hunger was pure in its own way, giving exactly what it promised each and every time.

But he could see from the look in her eyes, she was beyond yielding to him. And he'd made a fool of himself too many times before to do it again. Instead, he drew himself up, the control at last falling icy and clean across his features.

"Very well," he said dispassionately. "Have it your way."

He moved to the door, pausing as he was about to close it behind him. "Sweet dreams, Liz," he said, and even she could hear the mockery in his voice.

The door closed behind him abruptly, leaving her alone in the shadows of her room. Too overwhelmed by the conflicting desires of heart and body, she sat down on the edge of her solitary bed, and wept.

Chapter 10

Liz fell into a dark, tumbled sleep filled with chaotic images. The dusty emptiness of the shut-up ballrooms. The long dark hallway, shadowed and cold. Andrew standing at the very end, his eyes wide with fear as he held out his six-year-old hands and cried her name. But the more she walked toward him, the longer the hallway became, until it was twisting and turning as she stumbled through.

Then she turned the sharpest corner, holding out her hands to find Andrew, but running into Richard instead. He took her in his arms with his dark shuttered eyes, kissing her while an icy rage swept around them. And even as the bitter chill cut through her clothes, his kiss kept her warm. So she clung to him, pushing herself closer, wanting more....

Liz sat up in bed with a jerk, her heart pounding in her chest from the nightmares. All around her, the sheets and blankets were twisted into complete disarray, a waking testimony to her unconscious turbulence. Already she could feel the dull throb of a burgeoning headache. She shook her head slightly, willing the images away once and for all.

The strain of the past few days was getting to her. She could feel it in everything from the headache to the faint trembles in her hand.

But with determination, she pushed herself out of bed, walking over to the window to throw the curtains back. The revealed sky was a sharp blue, contrasting nicely with the crisp fields of grass. The only trees around the mansion were cypress and fir trees, but she imagined somewhere down the road, the maple and birch trees were turning a fiery golden-red.

She contemplated the view a little longer before the idea came to her. Of course, a picnic. An early October picnic. It would do them all good to get out of the house. But then, another thought tightened her stomach. She should ask Richard to attend, to help get him and Andy closer together. Given his regrets for yesterday's behavior, she could probably get him to agree. But that, of course, meant she would have to seek him out. And assuming he agreed, that meant they would have to spend the afternoon together, sitting so quaint and cozy on a picnic blanket.

She could see him in a thick, wool-knit sweater, his eyes matching the cool sky as he poured them steaming cups of hot chocolate from a brown thermos. Would he smile when he offered her the cup? Did he ever smile? How would he look, those dark, stern features broken up by something as simple as a smile? She was willing to bet he had a dimple. A beautiful, sexy dimple.

Abruptly, she shook the thought away. Andrew needed to get out more, and Andrew needed his father. Which meant she needed to get over her brief infatuation with Richard now. She'd come here to take care of Andrew, and she would not forsake that duty. It was that simple.

With determination, she quickly showered and threw on jeans and a red-and-blue-plaid shirt. Humming softly to herself, she brushed out her long hair and tucked it behind her ears with a simple hair band. Her hair was still wet, but by the time she was done running around this morning, it would be dry enough for her to go outside. Satisfied, she left her room.

Only to find Blaine lounging negligently in the hall outside her door. She paused, and unconsciously, felt the wariness set in. Why hadn't he told her he'd proposed to Alycia? Who was he trying to protect? She stiffened slightly, but didn't say anything. Instinct already told her the diary should be her own little secret. At least until she had time to read all of it.

For now, she pasted a smile on her face and tried to appear casual.

"Good morning," she said. "Isn't this a little early for you?"

Blaine glanced down at his Rolex. "Eight o'clock. Sure enough, I don't remember the last time I got up at this hour. Going to bed at this hour...now, that's another thing."

She nodded, looking at him intently. Was it her imagination, or was he having a problem meeting her eyes?

"So what's the special occasion?" she tried again.

Blaine sighed, giving her his best woeful look. "Jillian. She has this thing for early-morning walks. Who could have known?"

In spite of her suspicions, Liz found herself smiling. It looked as if Jillian was finally making progress. Perhaps that would warm the blonde's chilly face. "The things we do for love," Liz teased.

Blaine gave her a distinctly wolfish grin. "I don't know if I'd call it love, but you're right, the things we'll do for it."

Liz didn't have to ask for explanation. Given the conversations she'd been having lately with Richard, she caught Blaine's connotation all too easily. What was it with the men in this family?

She was saved from further comment, however, by a door opening several doors down. Jillian appeared, looking sharp and attractive in a blue and green silk jogging suit. The minute the blonde looked up, though, and saw Liz and Blaine standing together, her features froze. Her blue eyes darted from one to the other, but she said nothing.

Immediately, Liz understood the impression it must make, her and Blaine talking so cozily together. Not wanting to create problems, Liz greeted Jillian with a warm smile.

"Blaine was just telling me how excited he is to walk with you this morning," Liz attempted to explain, her voice light.

Jillian arched a delicate eyebrow. "Excited?" she quizzed dryly.

Liz smiled. "All right, my choice of words, not his. But I'm sure you'll both have a great time."

Jillian's expression still didn't relent, though Liz was getting the distinct impression Blaine was enjoying the byplay very much. Wanting to untangle herself from the mess once and for all, Liz hastily made her goodbyes.

At the bottom of the stairs, however, Liz's footsteps began to drag. She moved forward into the foyer, her eyes sweeping up to the left-hand tower stairs. Better now than never.

She didn't question the fact that Richard would be in the tower at this early hour. Near as she could tell, he was always in his lab, keeping ungodly hours. Sure enough, with the first knock, the door swung open.

"What do you want?" Richard asked bluntly, his eyes dark. Liz swallowed, seeking her voice as her eyes swept over him. If it was any consolation, he didn't appear to have slept much, either. His hair was rumpled, his cheeks littered with a twenty-four-hour shadow. His slacks were slightly wrinkled, and his shirtsleeves had been rolled up to reveal strong forearms. As if he could sense her taking a mental inventory, he straightened before her, his hand raking back his hair into its usual smooth black waves.

"Are you playing more games of hide-and-seek?" he prodded curtly. "Or did you merely get lost on your way to the kitchen?"

Flushing slightly, Liz pulled herself up for the encounter. "Actually," she began primly, "I came to invite you on a picnic this afternoon."

"Picnic?" Richard frowned. "Do you have any idea how brisk it is out there?"

She nodded, her face unperturbed. "Yes, we're going to have a fall picnic, complete with soup and hot chocolate. It really is a beautiful day out. Did you notice how bright the sun is in the sky?"

He scowled. She would notice such things. How bright the sun was in the sky. What did he care? He was a scientist, he had work to do, mysteries to unravel, data to calculate. Last night he'd decided he'd already lost way too much time thinking about the woman in front of him. He'd let her lead him astray, all that wild mahogany hair, those deep, midnight eyes. Well, not anymore. He'd been happy as a workaholic, he'd be happy again.

So why in the world did just looking at her make his chest hurt?

"I've got too much to do," he said tersely, already beginning to shut the door.

Her eyes opening in shock, Liz automatically stuck her foot in the way.

"Wait!" she said hastily, her face unconsciously cajoling. "Really, I think this is a great opportunity for you to spend more time with Andrew. You know I'm trying to get him outside more, and I think he'd agree to go on the picnic if you came, too. And well, after yesterday, it would be a chance for you to make amends with him."

The words were seductive, he could feel the soft Carolina accent wrapping around him like velvet. Go on a picnic, Richard. Sit on a bright blanket next to this beautiful woman, Richard. Talk to Andrew about dielectrics and pretend, if just for a few hours, that life is warm and normal, Richard.

He shook his head against the spell.

"I have a lot of work to do," he reiterated.

With a deep breath, Liz straightened her spine, and willed herself to look in his eyes. "If this is because of last night," she began, "well, I think it's best if we left that behind us."

It was the wrong thing to say, because immediately his eyes darkened, raking over her with unconcealed desire.

"Oh, of course," he drawled darkly, "let's just forget about last night. The way you melted against me, the soft sighs and your kisses. Even the way your breasts felt, heavy and full, in my hands."

Liz had to take another deep breath, feeling the impact of the words all the way to the pit of her stomach. Her knees were suddenly weak, and she had the overwhelming desire to step forward until she could feel the solid strength of his muscles, firm and hot against her. With grim determination, she willed the thoughts away. She was not some weak-kneed virgin. She was a grown woman with a job to do.

Even then, her voice sounded raspy to her own ears. "Exactly," she said. "We have to forget all that."

His eyebrow raised in mockery. "By all means then, consider it forgotten."

She should have been grateful, but the way he said the words made them cut through her instead. She steeled herself against the pain. She had no right to feel hurt, she was the one denying them both. It was her decision and he was going along with it. She should be grateful.

But still . . .

One last steadying breath. She composed her face into a calm, professional demeanor.

"Then you'll come today?" she persisted.

His mind still told him it was a bad idea. He really should be working, he'd slacked off these past couple of days. But her deep blue eyes were so beguiling. Damn it, just looking at her made him ache with the sharp pangs of desire all over again. Then he was filled with another quite unholy thought. He leaned against the doorframe, suddenly deceptively relaxed.

"I'll come," he said smoothly, "on one condition."

She nodded, looking visibly relieved. It was very important to her plan that he come. "And what is your condition?" she asked easily.

"That you kiss me."

There was silence for a moment, his request catching her completely off guard.

She looked at him warily, shifting from foot to foot. "I thought we agreed that was behind us."

He nodded, watching the play of emotions shift across her face. "I agreed to forget," he said calmly, "which means I forsake the past. Since I can't have the past, well then, I'd like a future moment or two."

She swore softly under her breath, seeing his trap too late. And for the first time, she saw him grin. A deep, easy grin of amusement as he, too, recognized that he'd caught her. And damn if the man didn't have dimples.

"This is blackmail," she told him. But despite her words, she could feel the anticipation wash through her. She remembered last night too vividly. The way he made her feel, beautiful and desirable and passionate. She'd never realized just how lonely the past year had been until his lips had found her own.

Still, she wavered.

Richard's face darkened slightly. Suddenly, the possibility she might refuse loomed in his mind. The grin was gone, his face suddenly completely controlled.

"Those are the terms," he said curtly. "Take it or leave it."

She nodded abruptly. "All right. I accept."

He relaxed, but only for an instant. Because then, her midnight blue eyes swept up to meet his own, and the blatant desire he saw there rocked him clear to his toes. Just as he was drawing in a badly needed lungful of air, she was rising and entwining her arms languorously around his neck.

"I kiss you, right?" she whispered against his lips, her voice trembling only slightly. "So you can't kiss me. I have to kiss you."

Feeling like a drowning man, he found himself nodding.

"Good," she whispered. She pulled herself closer, until he could feel her soft breasts against his chest, her warm hips against his own. Her lips were so tantalizingly close, he could feel every whisper of her breath on his lips. But she still didn't kiss him.

Instead, she turned her head slightly, landing the first touch on the square sternness of his jaw. Her lips felt like butterfly wings on his skin, light and sweet. Abruptly, her tongue came out to lick the spot, and the desire stabbed through him like a lightning rod. She moved, but not coming closer to his lips. Instead, her lips trailed to his ear, and the next thing he knew, she'd taken his earlobe between her lips and bitten him tenderly. He had to consciously fight back his groan.

His overwound nerves leaped to life, and he could feel the passion so sharp it was almost painful. She seemed aware of it also, shifting slightly to cradle his growing hardness in the soft embrace of her pelvis. It was everything he could do not to grab her arms and crush her against him. He wanted her, soft and sweet and willing. He wanted to lose himself in her embrace, her taste, her touch. He wanted to be reborn in her arms, her name torn like a cry from his lips.

He trembled, his eyes closing, but he kept his end of the deal.

Her lips trailed back along his whisker-roughened cheek, nearing his lips. She reached the corner of his mouth, and her tongue tantalized the spot. Then slowly, ever so slowly, she dipped her tongue between his lips. She tasted him, reveling in the feel of his stubble against her cheeks, the flavor of his mouth on her tongue.

She sighed softly, and kissed him with a slow tenderness that revealed more of her heart than she was willing to face. He'd always let her have control, she realized suddenly. He'd always let her pull back, no matter how fiery the burn of the passion. And now that he'd agreed it was her kiss, he let her have that, even as she felt his biceps bunch with the effort at restraint.

She deepened the kiss, slanting her lips across his, dueling slow and elegant with his tongue as she thanked him for his gift, and wondered at the tightness slowly squeezing her chest.

Such a dark, brooding man. Cold and controlled. But strong and protective, as well, with his own brand of caring. She'd seen it when Andrew had disappeared. And sometimes, by the midnight fires, she had seen him look at her with a slight shift in the depths of his eyes. He had so much to give, and yet he would never give any of it because he was so determined to keep it all locked inside. He didn't believe in love.

Her hands trembling on his shoulders, her eyes squeezed against the pain, she softly, reluctantly, pulled away.

Instinctively, his hands came up to pull her back, but after a long, frozen moment, they dropped back to his sides. When she opened her eyes at last, she saw something in his face that might have been pain. Then abruptly, harshly, his features froze over once more.

"This picnic had better be good," he muttered softly, "because the price is getting to be high."

She could only nod, not trusting herself enough to speak. She should never have gone along with his game, she knew. Except that she'd wanted to. Even now, she wanted to crawl back into his arms and find his lips once more. He was so warm and hard and masculine—strong and rough and dark, and she liked his touch, *needed* his touch.

When had Nick gone so far from her mind? When had she begun kissing this man, without thinking of Nick at all? She didn't know anymore.

More and more, it was Richard who filled her thoughts, Richard who made her breathless with anticipation. Except Richard didn't believe in the softer emotions. He just knew lust, and she couldn't seem to convince him otherwise.

She shook her head unconsciously, wondering at herself more than him, and the fool she seemed to have become. Then before he could ask any questions, she simply turned and walked down the stairs on unsteady legs.

One of these days, she was going to have to learn his control.

Andy wasn't Andy today, and it was beginning to worry her. His round blue eyes were nervous behind his thick glasses, and he was practically glued to her side all morning, seeming anxious to be near her. He was too agreeable, as well. She'd told him about the picnic, and he'd simply nodded. No statistics on the number of people who died of pneumonia each year, no thoughts on the number of colds inflicted on little boys forced to go outside by their dreadful nannies. Nothing.

She'd even asked him to change from his suit into jeans and a warm sweater, and he'd simply nodded. His only condition had been that she come help him pick it out. Liz figured that request had more to do with the fact he couldn't stand for her to be out of his sight. She'd asked him several times if he was all right, but each time, he would nod while his eyes darted around the room with renewed nervousness. Yesterday had clearly spooked him, and she was beginning to miss the old Andy.

At twelve-thirty, he helped her pack the picnic basket with the soup, sandwiches and hot chocolate. Liz had even gotten old Dodd to throw in some rich homemade shortbread for dessert. Already, the anticipation of the picnic was making her feel better. She hummed a little as she and Andy tucked in the last of the silverware.

Then, abruptly, she felt Andrew fit his hand into hers. She looked over to smile at the child, only to see his eyes riveted to the doorway. She turned, and sure enough, Richard was standing there.

He'd also changed to a pair of jeans, coupled with a dark gray flannel shirt and wool coat. He even had hiking boots on his feet. From scientist to outdoorsman in thirty seconds or less, Liz thought dryly. But the thought didn't stop her pulse from pounding at her throat.

She swallowed heavily, and willed an easy smile on her face. "You look ready to go," she said casually, hoping her own easygoing smile would transmit to Andrew. Ever so slightly, she felt the child relax.

Richard was looking from Liz to Andrew, his eyes at last settling on the bright blond hair of the little boy. Richard frowned. The child looked downright spooked, as if he were looking at a monster. On the heels of that thought, came the guilt. He'd wanted to keep himself distant from the child, hadn't wanted to hurt the boy. But it seemed he was failing miserably at both. He forced himself to appear more relaxed.

"Is there anything you need me to do?" he asked in a low voice.

Liz shook her head. "No, I'd say we're just about done. Oh, wait, we need a blanket. Preferably something very warm in case the wind blows up."

Richard nodded, then paused. "What if we built a fire?" he asked casually.

Liz looked at him, genuinely impressed. "A bonfire. Of course, why didn't I think of that? How completely perfect. What do you think, Andy?" she asked, looking down at the little boy who was still clutching her hand.

Slowly, his eyes never leaving the huge presence of his father, he nodded. "And marshmallows," Liz thought out loud. "If we have a fire, we definitely need marshmallows."

The decision made, Liz untangled herself from Andy to search for marshmallows, while Richard went to steal a pile of wood from the library. Andy followed Liz into the pantry. Ten minutes later, they were ready to go.

They walked out for about a half mile, trudging along the grass while their cheeks reddened from the crisp fall breeze. They stopped at the top of a low rolling hill and declared it the official picnic site. From that location, they could look around to the rolling hills of the rest of the kept grounds. Just beyond the grass, to the left, there was the tall fringe of a field and the thick pines of a forest were on the right. It was beautiful.

Humming softly to herself, Liz laid the blanket down while Richard went about building a fire. Andy remained with his eyes fixed on his father in total concentration.

After a moment, Richard looked up, noticing the child's eyes on him. "Would you like to help?" Richard asked softly. Andy paused, the nervousness in his eyes warring with worship. Abruptly, he nodded. Richard handed the boy some of the smaller twigs for kindling, and explained how to arrange them all in the center. With serious eyes, Andy set about the task. Liz watched as discreetly as possible under her lashes, trying to keep the self-satisfied smile off her face. Perfect, it was all going so perfect.

Perhaps that should have been her first warning of the trouble to come.

Once the fire was going merrily, Liz dished out the tomato soup in the coffee mugs she'd brought along. They drank the soup in silence, but it wasn't an unpleasant one. Liz was letting the bright sun beat out all the tenseness of the past few days, while Richard was content to watch the warm smile that spread across her face. Picnics and outings suited her. She was at home outside, and at home with Andy.

In short, she was everything Alycia had never been—warm, vivacious and compassionate. He found the combination unsettling. How much easier to believe in the darkness, than in the light.

He looked over to see Andrew watching him with his solemn blue eyes. God, the child looked so much like Alycia, sometimes it hurt to see him. And sometimes, when the child gazed at him with a look so somber and ancient, the pain in Richard's chest had nothing at all to do with his past wife.

He looked away, not knowing how to confront the child after all the years and not understanding the fierceness of the emotions ripping through him. Instead, he passed out the tuna fish sandwiches, grateful for something to do.

Presently, as Liz was prone to do, she engaged them all in conversation. Having learned her lessons from the past, she didn't even try small talk, but went straight to asking Richard about his work. Richard automatically began telling them about his newest experiments, mixing the mica with cyanide to see what kind of dielectric the combination would yield. Andrew sat and listened with enraptured eyes, occasionally throwing in a fact or two that revealed *Winnie-the-Pooh* wasn't his sole bedtime reading. Liz brought out the marshmallows.

"All right," she declared, "time to roast marshmallows. We'll need three twigs."

Andrew looked shocked, his blue eyes blinking. "What for?"

"To put the marshmallows on, of course."

"But twigs have germs!" the child exclaimed. Liz smiled, the real Andrew was back. Funny how she had missed his academic prudishness.

"We'll brush off the twigs," she assured him, already looking through the remnants of the woodpile to find suitable candidates. Andrew turned to his father. Surely this brilliant man wouldn't let him down, the boy's look said.

"Wood has dirt," Andrew reiterated to Richard. To his relief, his father nodded.

"It does," Richard agreed easily. "But I'll show you some tricks to take care of that." Immediately, Andrew sat up straighter, obviously intrigued. His father was going to show him some tricks. So Richard did, teaching Andy how to peel back the bark to reveal the raw wood beneath.

"But it's still wood," Andy said, his eyes visibly disappointed at this revelation. Richard nodded again, beginning to fully understand Liz's point on Andrew's needing to get out more. The child clearly had a one-dimensional understanding of life.

"Once the bark has been pulled away," Richard explained patiently, "the wood beneath is completely clean. Did you know that in earlier times, this would be used as a toothpick or a toothbrush?"

Apparently more interested now, Andrew shook his head. "For that matter," Richard continued, "the bark of some trees can be boiled into teas, like some Native Americans use to cure illnesses and aid healing."

Andrew looked at the remnants of the bark on the ground, his small face frowning as he was apparently trying to imagine this. "Have you ever done that?" the child demanded.

Serious, Richard shook his head. "No, but I wouldn't mind having the opportunity to try. There's more about plants and animals that we don't know, than we do know."

Andy was clearly hooked. "Where did you read this?"

Richard shrugged, already knowing the reasoning behind the question. "You can find some of it in *National Geographic,* or in various books on herbal remedies. Not to mention the studies and stories on Native American culture."

Andy nodded vigorously, and Liz could see him making the mental list. "Great," she told Richard. "Now you're going to have to expand both your magazine and book collection to satisfy his curiosity."

Richard looked at her, feeling suddenly self-conscious. "It's not a bad thing," he said, "to want to read and learn like this."

"No," she said softly, "it's not." She smiled at him, but he had to look away, not quite able to handle such warmth. He busied himself with putting a marshmallow on the end of his stick. Andrew watched intently, then followed suit. Andy, however, looked at the results with a more skeptical eye.

"Now what do we do?" Andrew asked, holding up his dubious creation.

"You put it in the fire," Liz said promptly. "To roast it."

"When is it done?"

"Whenever you want it to be."

Andrew frowned, trying to translate this vague recipe into more concrete terms. Watching him, Richard could almost see himself at that age. So serious and intense, wanting to know everything, but never quite mastering an understanding of all the adults who populated his world.

"Watch this," Richard found himself saying, plunging his marshmallow into the merry flames. "I like mine nicely toasted all the way around, so I keep the stick toward the outer flames and rotate it." He nodded toward Liz. "Or you can try the burn-to-a-crisp approach."

Andy looked over to see Liz pulling out a flaming torch from the fire.

"Your marshmallow's on fire," Andrew exclaimed, clearly alarmed. But Liz simply blew it out with a smile in his direction.

"Exactly," she told him. "None of that evenly toasted stuff for me. Marshmallows are serious business. And everyone—" she gave Richard an arched look "—*everyone* knows that marshmallows are best all burnt on the outside and gooey on the inside."

Andrew stared at the blue flame surrounding her marshmallow as she blew it out. "The sugar," he said abruptly, earning a nod from Richard and a puzzled glance from Liz. "The sugar in the marshmallow burns hotter than the wood, giving off a blue flame and melting the marshmallow." He nodded his head intently, as if he'd just puzzled out the origin of the cosmos.

"It tastes better," Liz reiterated promptly.

Both Richard and Andrew gave her such skeptical looks at the comment, she had to laugh. They didn't even know how much alike they were, she realized. She waved her marshmallow at them both. "Don't knock it until you try it," she told them sweetly, then promptly devoured her burnt masterpiece with a look of complete satisfaction on her face.

Richard felt the impact of that look in the unexpected tightness of his jeans. Shifting slightly, he tried to appear relaxed. Did everything about this woman have to turn him on? Looking for a diversion, he turned back to the marshmallows. He looked at Andrew.

"What do you say?" he asked the boy. "She seems to be the expert."

Andrew gave in with a skeptical nod. Closing his eyes, he thrust his stick deep into the flames. He managed to peel one eye open enough to watch. Sure enough, his marshmallow burst into flame.

"Not yet," Liz exclaimed when he pulled the stick back. "You want it to get nice and melted on the inside. Takes a minute."

Nodding solemnly, Andrew complied, watching his experiment with serious eyes. Liz could practically hear him counting off sixty seconds in his mind. Sure enough, exactly one minute later he pulled out his blazing marshmallow, blowing on it with timid little gasps. Finally giving up, Andrew held up the marshmallow to Richard, who promptly complied by blowing out the flames. Then Andrew held up the puffy, blackened remnants of his marshmallow with clear suspicion.

"I agree with you," Richard told him. "It certainly doesn't look edible to me." They both turned to Liz, their serious blue eyes once more in sync. Liz rose from the blanket, shaking her head as she sought to get more comfortable.

But as she rose, Richard saw something else move. A glint of the afternoon sun off metal, coming from behind, in the woods. Metal where no metal should have been.

He didn't think, he just moved, throwing himself powerfully forward even as he heard the distant boom. In slow motion, he could see Liz's face turn to shocked alarm, but then he was on top of her, dragging her to the ground as he threw an arm over Andy, as well.

And the gunshots echoed through the deep autumn sky.

Chapter 11

Embers flew as a burning branch of the fire exploded, the bullet plowing into flames. Before Richard could think of a good area for cover, another shot rifled overhead. Underneath him, he could feel Andy's shaking form, but the child was silent. Under his right arm was the still form of Liz, but there was no time to see if she was hurt. Above, as he tensed with the waiting, the chilled October air was silent.

Seconds grew into agonizing minutes, the silence unbroken but for the crackling of the injured bonfire. Finally, muscles bunching for action, Richard raised his head. Silence reigned.

He waited one moment longer, sharp eyes scanning pine trees for any sign of attack. But whatever—whoever—had come, seemed long gone by now. Richard looked down to see Andrew gazing at him with solemn blue eyes. His glasses had fallen off when Richard had pushed the child down. Now, Andrew reached down to pick up his thick lenses from the crushed grass. In unison, both father and son turned to Liz.

She was still half under Richard, and he pushed himself completely away, looking at her intently for signs of injury. He couldn't find any sign of even a scratch, but her midnight eyes were glazed over with shock.

Concerned, Richard reached over to touch her shoulder.

"Liz," he said quietly, his eyes intense. "It's over, sweetheart."

But her eyes wouldn't focus, turning to him only with an opalescent mix of anguish and fear and shock. Belatedly, he remembered what she'd told him of her husband. He'd been shot down. Even more worried, Richard shook her shoulder lightly.

"Snap out of it," he ordered this time, keeping his voice firm and low to penetrate her fog. He was rewarded by a distant nod, as if some corner of her mind was with him.

"There's so much blood," she whispered. "I can't stop all the blood. I can't, I can't, I can't." Her head had dropped to look at her hands with unseeing eyes, the past mixing with the present. She could swear there was pavement beneath her, the sound of cars screeching to a halt. The screams of pedestrians, the wail of sirens. It was all there again. And Nick's head on her lap, the blood pouring, pouring, pouring....

"What's wrong with her?" came the distant sound of a child's voice.

"She's in shock," a low male voice replied. "She'll be all right. She just needs a minute. Liz. Come on now, Liz."

She shook her head at the voices, her eyes falling once more to the golden head on her lap. This was Nick, Nick, needed her. She had to keep him alive. It was up to her. But the blood kept flowing through her fingers, his blue eyes peering up through the haze of pain to find her. She wasn't going to be able to do it. She wasn't going to be able to stop the blood, after all. Nick, oh, Nick.

But then abruptly the blue eyes weren't Nick's anymore; instead, she was peering into the intent gaze of a solemn little boy.

"Liz?" Andy said, his voice tight with worry. "Are you okay?"

She nodded, her eyes swinging over to find Richard, who was sitting just a foot away. She could still feel the pain like a knife in her gut. She'd loved Nick so much, he'd been her life, her future. They were going to grow old together. So many dreams lost on a Sunday afternoon. And there had been nothing at all she could do but hold his head on her lap and cry on his golden hair.

Why couldn't she have done something?

Richard could feel her blue eyes pleading with his, and the pain he saw there was more than he could stand. Without another thought, he reached out and drew her into his arms. "Shh," he whispered against her head, stroking her long hair with a gentle hand as she trembled against him. "It's all over now, Liz. It's all behind you. Now you're here with Andy and me, and a couple of hunters who couldn't hit the broad side of barn. It's all okay now."

Behind her, Andy nodded his vigorous agreement. His face was still tight with worry, but the look he gave his father was filled with trust. Something bad had happened, but Richard would fix it, the look said.

Richard held Liz a little tighter, and wondered how a lost man like himself had ever garnered the trust of two such people, and why the thought filled his chest with such fierceness.

His hand kept smoothing through her hair, reveling in the silky feel of the long, mahogany strands. He could feel her soft and vulnerable against him, the gentle brush of her shaky breath against his shoulder. Her hands wrapped around him, pulling herself closer to his strength, as if in his arms, she truly found comfort. As if she needed him. She shuddered, the last of the tension leaving her body as her head relaxed against his shoulder. It touched him far deeper than any of their intense kisses ever had, and in that instant, he wouldn't have let her go for all the supercapacitors in the world.

Minute turned into minute, and slowly Liz collected herself. It was so nice in his arms, warm and solid and safe. She'd always thought he could be tender, and now she knew the truth. She wanted to stay just like this, and the intensity of the need frightened her a little. What if the shots had been a little closer? What if he hadn't gotten them down in time?

She didn't want to go through another Sunday afternoon. She would never be able to bear that kind of pain again.

Once more she was conscious of Andy's eyes upon her. Richard gently let her go, and she forced herself back into functioning, not wanting to disturb the already troubled little

boy. She gave Andy a weak but determined smile to let him
know she was all right.

"I guess we should be packing up," she said, her voice only
lightly trembling. "Richard will need to check in on who was
hunting, so such things won't happen again."

She drew in the last sentence as much to comfort Andy as
herself. But after the darkness of the past few days, she found
she couldn't quite believe her own words.

She shivered slightly and turned to the picnic basket.

"Come on, Andy," she said, forcing herself to sound brisk
and calm. "Help me pack up."

Andrew still looked at her with troubled blue eyes, but then
wordlessly, he began to help.

It was a silent group that returned to the house. All wanting
to think it was an accident, but not all quite willing to believe
in such coincidences. Liz had thought she would never welcome the sight of the dark, sprawling mansion. This cold afternoon, however, she discovered she was wrong.

Andrew was the most troubled by the incident, as she found
out later that night when she tucked him into bed. He'd been
silent for the rest of the afternoon, watching her with dark and
worried eyes. She'd tried to distract him by playing dominoes,
but his mechanical movements had revealed his mind wasn't
really on the game.

He made her tell him another bedtime story as she tucked
him in. This time she went through the story of Peter Pan and
Never-Never Land. She even got him to clap for Tinkerbell. But
in the end, as she went to turn out the light, his true thoughts
surfaced.

"Liz?" he called out softly as she stood in the doorway.
"Liz, my mom's dead."

Liz stood there, not sure what to say. This was a different
tactic from the one he had used that very first day, when he'd
announced his mother had been murdered to try to frighten and
scare her. Now, his young voice was solemn, with just a small
quiver in his lips.

Finally, she nodded. "Yes, sweetheart," she said. "Alycia is
dead."

He paused, the uncertainty clear on his six-year-old face.

"Did—" He seemed to have a problem with the words, but finally they came rushing out, "Did my father kill her?"

Taken aback, Liz was slow to react. But resolutely, she drew herself up. She would not have this little boy tortured by such thoughts. Whoever had told him his mother had been murdered had been cruel enough. It was time to put his young doubts to rest, once and for all.

"Of course not," she said firmly. "Your father would never have done such a thing."

For one moment, she could see the fierce relief on his face, then Andy nodded solemnly. Her word was clearly good enough for him. The absoluteness of that trust staggered her.

"Good night, Liz," he said softly. She nodded, turning once more to leave.

"I won't let anything bad happen to you," Andy said suddenly, the words determined. "I won't, Liz."

She glanced back, meeting his solemn oath with her own serious expression. Andrew was just a six-year-old boy. For all his brilliance, he did not yet know of life's monsters and tragedies. Like holding your husband's head on a bright Sunday afternoon as he bled to death in your arms. Like shredded portraits in long, abandoned hallways. But she knew what an intense little boy Andy was, and she would not wound him by treating his promise lightly.

"Of course," she told him. "And I'm going to take care of you, too. Promise."

Andy raised his small hand. "Promise," he returned.

She turned out the light, blanketing the room in darkness.

Outside in the hall, however, she could feel the dull throbbing of her head. She had spoken to Andy with conviction, but there was no conviction in her heart. This house held dark stirrings and five-year-old hatreds.

She needed to get back to the diary, she thought abruptly. Perhaps it held the key. But first, she decided, she was going to find Richard. This situation with Andrew had gone on long enough. The child was scared, he needed to be able to believe in his father. And there was no reason that he shouldn't be able to.

She stormed her way to the library without giving it much thought. She knew he would be there. Of course, he would be there.

And he was.

This time, Richard wasn't sitting. Instead, he was standing before the crackling flames of a newly made fire, one hand resting on the fireplace's mantel while his other hand held his nightly glass of brandy. He didn't turn around when she entered, but she knew he was aware of her nonetheless.

"I want to talk to you," she said straight out, coming to a halt just inside the doorway. The words seemed to echo across the distance as a challenge, and already she could feel the faint humming in her blood.

Slowly, he turned enough to see her.

"About this afternoon?" he asked softly. In his own mind, he'd seen the scene time and time again—the faint glint of metal in the trees, followed by the cracking sound of a rifle shot. He'd gone through the forest after they'd returned to the house. All he'd found were two spent shells from a .22 rifle. And there was no way in hell he believed some hunter had shot into a bonfire by mistake. Certainly not twice and not on private land. He would have gone to the police, but his relations with the local law enforcement were not the best. Besides, whoever had done this had been far too clever, leaving nothing behind that was traceable. Involving the police, with no evidence—and considering the source—would be seen as a case of the boy who cried wolf.

"Partly," Liz said. Her chin was up, her cheeks flushing with adrenaline. She looked beautiful, Richard thought. Beautiful and vital and much too young to be shot at. He could feel the bitterness eating up his gut, more potent than even the brandy. He could still remember her trembling in his arms, and he hated to know he'd helped cause that pain. Inwardly he cursed. His life swirled with darkness, tainting everything around him. Even a fresh, wholesome woman like Liz.

He lifted the glass, willing the brandy to burn away all the confusion. But Liz remained clear and strong before him.

"I'm worried about Andrew," she said abruptly. She didn't move toward him, instinctively wanting the distance between them. But even from here, she could sense the turmoil surrounding him as thickly as a fog. His face was grimmer tonight, the lines etched more firmly in his face than ever before. His eyes, however, were no longer a steely blue. Instead, they had darkened to something much more dangerous, and much more compelling.

"What about Andrew?" he asked, his voice deep and low. "Is he still upset about this afternoon?"

For the first time, Liz hesitated. Then she forced herself to get it all out. "It's more than just the afternoon," she said boldly. "It's the knowledge that his mother was murdered. It's living in a house that's too dark and foreboding for a normal child. It's having a father who seems intent on ignoring him."

Richard's eyes narrowed, his look becoming even more guarded. He didn't want to hear any of this, not with his emotions already so raw. "I warned you before," he said tautly, "that Andrew's and my relationship is no concern of yours."

"And *I* told *you* before," Liz countered fiercely, "that it is." She took a step forward. "For God's sake, Richard, even you can see what a serious and morbid child he can be. He needs a stable, giving household. He needs to feel that being a genius doesn't mean being a freak. He needs you, Richard."

There was silence as her words echoed away, a silence broken only by the crackling pop of a burning log. Slowly, Richard's eyes never left hers as he deliberately raised his glass for another sip.

"I'm sending the child to boarding school soon," he said silkily, though for the first time, doubt about that decision clouded his mind. "That ought to take care of the problem."

Liz looked at him incredulously from across the room. "Have you heard anything I've said?" she asked intently. "He does not need boarding school. He needs a *father*. Do you know what he asked me tonight? Do you know what he said?" She crossed the library with determined strides until she was only inches away from him. "He asked me if you murdered Alycia. He wanted to know if his father had murdered his mother!"

Richard didn't say anything, only the tightening of his hand on the glass giving him away. Inside, however, he felt the unwanted emotions rip through him once more, her words slamming into his gut one by one until he had to call upon all his iron control to even breathe.

He didn't want to care about the boy. He didn't want to feel anything. But even now, he felt pain, fierce and burning, tighten his chest.

Andrew wanted to know if he'd murdered Alycia. Even Andrew. And who could have been so cruel as to tell a little boy such things? It wasn't his concern, Richard tried telling himself, but the emotions continued to war within him. Andrew was brilliant and, yes, he was morbid. No one would look at him and think of him as a normal, happy child. And despite his best intentions, that realization filled Richard with guilt.

He could see Andy looking at him with trust as he thrust his marshmallow into the bonfire. He could see Andy eyeing him with worship as they talked of dielectrics. And he could see Andy turning to him when Liz didn't get up from the ground, clearly expecting him to make things all right.

The boy looked up to him.

So maybe . . .

Fiercely, Richard rejected the idea. Alycia had taught him too well the price of weakness. He wouldn't become soft now and believe in things that could only lead to bitterness and pain. He had survived for years with his iron control, keeping himself untouched by everything. He would survive many more.

He turned back to the fire, clearly dismissing Liz. She however, refused to let the matter drop. If anything, his coldness only made her more determined.

"I'm not leaving this room," she warned clearly. "I've already overstepped my bounds, so I might as well take it all the way. Damn it, Richard," she tried again, placing her hand on his arm to command his attention. "I care for Andy. He's come a long way in the past three weeks. I've gotten him to play some games, I've gotten him to go outside. I'm trying very hard to teach him that there's more to life than statistics and books. But there's only so much I can do. When push comes to shove, I'm only his nanny. He needs *family*. How can you deny him that? Not even you can be that cruel."

She must have struck a nerve, for his head pivoted sharply. His eyes had turned an icy blue, his jaw clenched so tight she felt a minute of deep fear. His chilling gaze fell to the hand on his arm, and, despite her best intentions, she pulled her hand away. When he spoke, his voice was deceptively soft.

"You know nothing of what I'm capable of," he said slowly. "And it's none of your business."

His words sent a tremor through her, and with soul-wrenching clarity her mind replayed what she'd read in Alycia's diary. When Richard looked this cold, this grim, he truly scared her, as he must have frightened his wife. For a long moment, she couldn't say anything at all. Then she forced herself to remember this afternoon, the way he'd held her in his arms. He could be harsh, but there was tenderness in there somewhere.

"You're not omnipotent, Richard," she said fiercely, her eyes never leaving his face. "I know a thing or two about people, and I saw what you were like when we couldn't find Andy yesterday. You were worried, genuinely worried. And you hated it."

His face darkened fully, his mind reeling away from just how close to home her words struck. The unbridled emotions welled up once more. He didn't want to feel this guilt and regret. He didn't want to wonder, to hope, when he'd sworn off such petty emotions long ago. Damn it, he'd learned his lessons five years ago. He'd learned them well.

"I don't wish Andrew any harm," he said coldly. "The boarding school will be an excellent opportunity for him." Once again, however, doubt nagged at the back of his mind. Andy really wasn't like other boys, and he'd already improved so much with Liz's presence. Maybe he could spend more time with the little genius.... He forced the thought back down harshly. He couldn't weaken. Not now.

Liz's eyes narrowed, her face becoming set as she peered at him intently. "No, you won't," she said clearly, crossing her arms in front of her with a stubborn expression.

He laughed mirthlessly, but her level gaze was beginning to unnerve him. She couldn't know what he was thinking, she couldn't know just how dangerously close Andrew was getting to all the walls Richard had built around himself. And he had no intention of telling her.

He drew himself up to his full height until he towered above her. Almost negligently, he swirled the brandy in his glass. "I'm afraid you're mistaken," he said softly, his tone as unrelenting as the expression on his face.

Another shiver rippled along Liz's spine, and the tension made her want to run. But she knew she was right, knew it deep in her heart. She would not back down. Damn it, she'd built up backbone living with four older brothers, she was going to stand up to this man, come hell or high water.

"I don't believe you," she said shortly, her chin lifting another notch with her defiance. "You mentioned sending Andy to a boarding school well over a week ago, but you've never mentioned it since. Not even yesterday, after he disappeared. And you're not one of those people who lets things hang. Unless, of course, you're not convinced it's the best solution."

"Of course it's the best solution," he said tautly, frowning at her persistence. In his eyes, the shadows around them grew and shifted as unnamed emotions floated by. How had she ever gotten so close? How had she come to see things he hadn't even wanted to face? When had he started giving so much away?

"I want you to leave," he said harshly. "Right now."

"I can't," she whispered, her body trembling as his eyes turned dangerous. Hesitantly, she reached out a hand and placed it delicately on his arm. His eyes shot warning daggers, but this time, she didn't pull back. "Tell me," she said softly, her voice giving away the smallest tremor. "Tell me why you turn away from Andy."

"I don't turn away," Richard said flatly, his fists clenching by his side from raw anger and scathing bitterness. "I provide the boy with shelter, food and clothes. I will see to his education, and I will give him all the financial support he ever needs. I think that's more than generous."

Liz's eyes widened with shock, her face paling. She'd never heard anyone talk about their child so callously.

"You can't really believe that," she managed to say, her eyes stark and pleading. She leaned forward slightly, needing him to take the words back, begging him to give her some sign of the man she wanted to believe lived within him. "Surely you understand a son needs more from his father than financial support. Surely you believe he needs love and comfort, as well."

"As you said," Richard stated coldly, his gaze raking over her dispassionately, even as her pleading eyes cut him to the quick, "that's what a son needs from his father. But Andrew isn't my son."

He stated the last words emotionlessly, throwing them out into the silence of the room, his eyes daring her to react.

"You can't be serious," Liz said at last, leaning back as her forehead creased over this unexpected statement. Anyone could see how alike Andrew and Richard were. "What makes you think that?"

"My dear departed wife told me, of course. Alycia never was bashful about her life-style. I don't even think I can count the number of liaisons she had. She used to tell me, once she produced an heir—Andrew—that what she did with her life was her business. But then just a week before she died, she confessed that not even Andrew was mine. She'd been fooling around long before then."

He could still remember the scene. How Alycia had looked when she'd told him, her porcelain face all twisted into mockery. How she'd laughed at the shocked look on his face, how she'd called him a fool. *"Of course Andrew isn't yours, darling. Did you ever think such a pitiful brute as yourself could create something so beautiful?"*

He'd hated her at that instant, felt the last of his misguided affection die a bitter death deep inside. And so help him God, at that moment he'd wanted to wrap his hands around her lovely pale neck, and silence her taunting laughter forever. In the course of two years, she'd broken every illusion he'd ever had about women and relationships. Then she'd stolen his son.

Unconsciously, one hand reached up to clench the mantel, the grip so tight his knuckles turned white. His jaw muscle jumped, his body trembling with the dark fury sweeping through him. Five years, and he could still almost taste the hatred.

Watching him, Liz swallowed thickly as his face contorted. She felt a moment of breathlessness, too frightened to even move. Suddenly she knew without a shadow of a doubt that it was true. This man, Andrew's father and her employer, the one man who attracted her as no other ever had before—*This man was indeed capable of murder.*

Abruptly, his grip on the mantel eased and his eyes focused upon her with grim control. Her hand slowly slid off his arm, her muscles nerveless and limp.

"So, as you can see," he finished emotionlessly, "the child really would be better off at a boarding school."

Slowly, she shook her head. "I think," she said levelly, as his words turned around in her mind, "that you've been had."

His eyes flashed dangerously, but she held up a quick hand before his anger could explode.

"Andrew must be your son," she said, leaning toward him with a clear, earnest face. "He may not look like you, but in everything he does, every way he acts, he *is* you all over again. You can see it in his brilliance and in his mannerisms. He even *blinks* like you do."

Richard raised a dark, mocking eyebrow. "Blinking, Liz?"

"Look," she persisted, feeling as if she were taking her life in her hands, but knowing she had to try to get through to him for Andy's sake, "in the course of your marriage, didn't Alycia lie to you? Didn't she do things to deliberately hurt you?" Liz didn't need to see his faint nod, she'd read and heard enough about his marriage to know the answers for herself. "And what better way to hurt you than to tell you that your own son was somebody else's? Can't you see how well it's worked? Here is this perfect child, a six-year-old version of you, and you're denying yourself any relationship with him. You've let her win, Richard. You've let her take your son from you."

Her words were sincere. But rather than show him the light, they only brought him more confusion. All these years, in his heart of all hearts, he had wanted to believe that perhaps Alycia had lied. In the beginning, he had refused to fully accept her accusation. But he'd looked at Andy time and time again, searching for some trace of himself. And all he'd ever seen was Alycia staring back at him.

Liz could see the doubt growing on Richard's face. Deep inside, she felt a burst of intense anger at the blond bitch who'd been his first wife. What kind of woman destroyed her husband and child? What kind of woman could torture a man even five years after her death?

"Let's think about this," Liz said, determined to conquer the ghost once and for all. "Did Alycia tell you who the father was?"

Silently, his eyes still grim, Richard shook his head.

"Do you have an idea?" she prodded.

Richard's jaw tightened, but he didn't say anything. In that instant, Liz knew exactly what he was thinking. Blaine. He thought it was Blaine, and God knows Andy's blond looks hardly contradicted the suspicion. No wonder there was such animosity between the two. Seven years ago, they had pursued the same woman. And even now, it was hard to know who had won.

"You should simply have Andy tested," Liz said quietly. She didn't tell him she knew what he was thinking, because then she would have to explain how she knew of Blaine's interest in Alycia. And she wasn't ready to surrender the diary yet. Instinct still told her to keep it a secret at least until she'd read all of it. Maybe by its end, she would have a better idea of who to trust.

Richard turned away, looking into the flames. Absently, his hand began to once more swirl the last of his brandy. Liz could almost feel the heaviness of his thoughts. She wanted to reach out to him so badly, to tell him she understood, but she was too afraid he would look at her with that ice in his eyes again.

"You're afraid," she said softly, her eyes steady on his face although he didn't look up. "You're afraid the test might prove once and for all that he's not your son, and then you won't be able to torture yourself with the faint hope that he is."

Slowly, his gaze came up to find hers, keen blue eyes shadowed by the weight of past demons. Her chest contracted until she could barely stand the pain.

"It's better to know," she said finally. "It would be better for you and Andrew."

His eyes went back to the flames and she didn't push it. It was hardly the kind of decision to be made overnight. Instead, she moved slightly closer, wanting to offer what comfort she could. Then another thought struck her.

"Is that why you cut up her picture?" she asked. "Because you were angry about what she'd done to you and Andrew?"

Richard's head jerked up, finding her eyes just inches from his own. Suddenly his face was no longer grim, but sharp with an alertness that was almost as intimidating.

"What picture?" he demanded at once.

Liz faltered, unnerved by his blue eyes boring into her own. "When I was looking for Andy," she began, "yesterday. I went down the hallway leading to the ballrooms. Alycia's picture had been torn from the wall. It had been cut to shreds."

Richard's eyes narrowed. "And you thought I did it?"

Slowly, pinned by his gaze, she nodded. The next thought, though never spoken, welled up between them as sure as a steel barrier.

And do you think I killed her, Liz? Do you think that, too?

But he never voiced it. Instead, as surely and physically as if he'd stepped away, he pulled away from her. She could see it in the sudden closure of his face, the way all the lines became smooth, his eyes that wintry blue, betraying nothing.

He was the dark, grim-faced man again. Something within Liz seemed to wilt. Despite her earlier thought, she had told Andrew that Richard would never do such a thing as murder—and she had believed it. But once again, when she saw him like this, she realized, she wasn't so sure.

He could get so angry, and Alycia had given him so much to be angry about. What if, one afternoon, the anger and hatred had simply become too much?

She took a small step back, and his eyes grew colder.

"Go to bed, Liz," he said harshly. "You've been a good little nanny and argued Andrew's case. Now, just go to bed and leave me the hell alone."

She opened her mouth as if to argue, then abruptly realized she didn't know what to say. The diary, she thought suddenly. She needed to get back to the diary. Maybe it, at long last, would bring them the truth.

She nearly fled from the room.

Chapter 12

She didn't find what she was looking for until she reached the last section of the diary.

August 8

Somebody knows. I don't know how, and I don't know who, but an unsigned note was delivered to the house. I have to put five thousand dollars in small bills in a suitcase and leave it out in the stables. If I try to watch, they'll tell Richard immediately.

Damn, damn, damn. Why is this happening now? I swore never to remember that day. I swore it!

If I ever find out who's doing this to me, I'll make the person wish they were never born. They will never know such pain as what I can create for them. Damn them to hell!

I have no choice, at least not yet. Richard is reaching the end of his rope. This may be all the excuse he needs to demand a divorce, and knowing how cold Richard can be, he'd leave me without a penny by the time he was through. I can't risk it.

I'll use my allowance. No one ever has to know.

September 9
   Another note, this one left on my bed, and this time wanting ten thousand. I have to figure out who is doing this to me. It must be someone close, someone with access to the house. Who can I trust? Who could have possibly found out the truth?
   I don't have that kind of cash on hand. I already had to forgo a trip to Monte Carlo with the gang because of the last time. Who can I get that kind of cash from? Who won't ask questions? Who can I trust?
   I can't believe this is happening. I mustn't lose control. There has to be a way out of this. I told no one of that day, no one at all. If I think back, if I'm very clever, I will solve this riddle.
   And so help me God, I'll kill the bastard!

November 15
   I'm close now, so very close. Better yet, I've found a way out of everything—the blackmail, my marriage, everything. Just as well. I don't think I could take one more year with Richard. The dark, brooding bastard. And those eyes. I swear he watches me like a hawk.
   It's almost as if he knows something is wrong....
   It doesn't matter anymore. Parris will play the dupe. This time, I'll be free... and rich.

Four more entries followed, none of them any more enlightening. Liz closed the book with an overflowing mind and exhausted eyes. Obviously, someone had been blackmailing Alycia, but who? And with what information?

Had the blackmailer killed her when she'd try to execute her master plan? Or had Parris tired of playing the dupe? What about Richard? What if he'd found out the truth—whatever it was—and in a fit of rage had killed her?

The thoughts swirled in her mind, until she could barely stand the confusion. She tucked the diary under the bed, and with her forehead creased, finally fell asleep.

In the morning, however, nothing was clearer. She wanted to know what was going on, but only felt further from the truth. Halfway through getting dressed, a small inspiration hit her and she dug out the lavender-edged note from beneath her socks in the dresser drawer. Comparing its scrawled handwriting to that of the diary's, she determined it was a poor imitation.

It at least proved there were no such things as ghosts. But someone still wanted her to leave. She remembered the shots fired at the picnic, and shivered. Hastily, she pulled on a sweater. Was someone really trying to kill her? Or were they after Richard and Andrew?

She sat down once more on the bed, and realized her thoughts were only leading her in circles. Finally, she called downstairs to Mrs. Pram, and pleaded a headache for the day. Mrs. Pram would watch over Andy, Liz was going out on a ride to clear her head. Perhaps on horseback, in the crisp fall air, the pieces would click into place.

No one was out at the stables as she led Honeysuckle from her stall and quickly brushed and saddled the horse. In less than twenty minutes, she was following the winding paths on the property, lost in her own thoughts.

Alycia had been an unhappy woman. It appeared she'd been married to Richard, yet had had affairs with Blaine and probably Parris, as well. In a jealous rage, either of the three men could have killed her. But what about now, five years later? Richard had looked honestly shocked when she'd mentioned the oil portrait—and he had been present when the rifle was fired at the picnic.

She frowned, and urged Honeysuckle into a trot, sitting deep in the saddle as the hill bounced by. Maybe, with all his money, Richard had paid someone to fire at them? She shook her head. She couldn't believe that. She could possibly accept Richard pushing Alycia in a moment of rage, but she couldn't see him cold-bloodedly plotting to hurt her or Andy. Especially Andy. She believed what she'd said last night—Richard honestly cared for the child.

Which meant, she thought after a minute, that she could probably eliminate Richard as a suspect as he couldn't have been responsible for what had happened since.

Her head cleared a fraction, and she felt the beginnings of relief. She could trust Richard. She would give him the diary, she decided resolutely, and show him the note. Maybe he could make more sense of it, knowing Alycia better than herself. Together, they would get to the bottom of this thing.

Nodding to herself, she leaned forward and urged Honeysuckle into a canter. The grass rushed by as the horse slid into the smoother gait, the last of Liz's nerves easing with the steady rhythm. She could trust Richard. She could tell him everything.

She smiled, and clicked Honeysuckle into a full gallop.

The horse had just leaned forward, when the saddle began to slide. Startled, Liz threw her weight to the right, but it wasn't enough to halt the progress. Honeysuckle kicked up wildly, unsettled by the unbalanced weight on her back. The motion jolted Liz out of the gallop's rhythm, and she lost control completely. Panicked, she kicked free of the stirrups and threw herself forward onto the horse's neck, exchanging the loose reins for thick handfuls of mane. It was too little too late. The leather saddle fell to bang against the horse's hooves, and Honeysuckle gave another startled kick. Already off balance, Liz hurtled over the horse's neck and through the air.

Her last thought was to duck and roll. Then she only saw blackness.

"Liz! Liz, sweetheart, can you hear me? Damn it, open your eyes, Liz! Open your eyes!"

Slowly, with a low groan, she complied with the insistent voice. Her heavy lids fluttered open, making out the blurry image of Richard's face. His eyes were intent, his face stark with worry. She tried to move, and instantly winced.

"Lie still!" he ordered immediately, an order she was only too happy to obey. This time, more carefully, she tested out each limb. Fingers wiggled, toes wiggled. She seemed to be all here.

"What the hell happened?" Richard demanded curtly, his hands still running along her neck and shoulders for signs of serious injury.

"I'm fine," she managed to get out, sitting up slowly. Her vision swam, then cleared. Wincing, she rolled her neck. She hadn't taken a tumble that good for a long time, and she'd bounced more as a child. "What are you doing here?"

"Running after you. And it looks like I came just in time," he finished curtly. Damn it, he'd lost twenty years off his life when he'd come out to the stables looking for her, only to find Honeysuckle trotting back in half-unsaddled. Mrs. Pram had said that Liz had headed out toward the stables, allowing him to put two and two together. When he'd first seen her crumpled form on the ground, his blood had run cold.

He searched her face for signs of further injury. Then carefully, his hands came up and brushed through her long hair, probing the back of her head. His fingers were strong but gentle as they searched for a lump. He found one tender area, earning another wince from her. Frowning, his fingers eased more carefully, finally coming down to knead the tension out of her neck.

God, he'd hated seeing her on the ground like that, knowing once more that something bad had happened and it was probably all his fault. His hands rested on her shoulders as he fought the urge to sweep her into his arms and just hold her, hold her until all the darkness went away once and for all.

Her midnight eyes met his, and the intensity of his gaze made her breathless.

She could see the harsh remnants of guilt in his eyes and it tore at her. She wanted to tell him fiercely that she knew it wasn't his fault. He could be cold, he could be harsh, but he wasn't a killer. He was the man who wanted to believe in his son once more. The man who scorned all things soft, then held her with amazing tenderness.

She understood that. She understood everything about him from all those midnight conversations.

She loved him.

She caught her breath, and very slowly, her hand came up to cup his cheek. She could feel the faint roughness of his morning beard, feel the scouring intensity of his unreadable gaze. He'd come out looking for her because he cared, and even now, he searched for signs of her well-being because he cared.

How could she have been so blind to it all? The nervousness when she was around him, the need to see him, the need to touch him. She had never met anyone like the dark beguiling Richard Keaton. He was the antithesis to her whole upbringing, her approach to life. And yet, he'd chased the last of the tragedy from her life. He'd filled her thoughts, and allowed her to finally leave Nick behind. He'd challenged her to stand up and be strong, and he'd held her when the pain had been too much.

And he needed her, in a way she wasn't sure she'd ever been needed by anyone.

"I'm really all right now," she said at last. She smiled at him, a small luminous smile, and wondered if her heart shone in her eyes. Her gaze fell languorously to his lips.

Richard's stomach clenched at the movement, his eyes darkening with desire at the unconscious invitation. He should help her to her feet now, and get her back to the house so she could relax fully. But he couldn't seem to move. Instead, his eyes remained on her face while images of her crumpled body washed through his mind.

What if she'd been seriously harmed? What if he hadn't come looking for her? His insides churned, his jaw tightening with the raging intensity of the emotions warring inside of him. He should move, but he didn't want to let her go. Hell, he didn't know what he wanted. He didn't know what he needed.

Or maybe he did, and that was what scared him so much.

He stopped thinking, leaning forward instead. He didn't give her a chance to say yes or no. He simply pulled her to him, and with his lips began to show her all the things his heart could never say.

He kissed her, slowly and sweetly, yearning. She didn't fight him. No, she melted against him like the sweet molasses of her voice, until he could feel her body meld with his own. He pulled her closer, even as her arms entwined themselves around his neck. She smelled like horses and fresh fall air, the scent tantalizing and seductive in its own way.

Slowly, he eased them down fully onto the ground, until she lay half across him, her breasts firm against his chest. He stroked her hair, kissing her deeper as he pressed closer. His hands slid under her sweater and found the smooth curve of her naked skin. She was so soft to the touch, soft and warm and vital.

He kissed her harder, deeper, demanding more and reveling in each heady response. He could feel her gasp against his lips, feel the rapid beating of her heart against his own chest, feel her breasts swell with desire. One hand came up, and he cupped her cotton-covered breast with his warm palm.

She shivered, arching against him, and he felt the fire in his groin. He wanted to make her cry against him, wanted to hear the whispered plea of his name upon her lips. He wanted to consume her as she had consumed him. Until she could taste only him, feel only him, want only him.

Until she would never leave.

The kiss became more urgent, his lips demanding her total surrender. And she gave it to him. With a murmured sigh of submission, she turned herself over to the raging fires he was building in her blood. She gave herself up to the magic of his touch, the brand of his lips. She knew this man, his temper, his control and his pain.

And she loved him. God help her, she loved him.

He rolled over abruptly, cushioning her head with one arm as he plundered her mouth fiercely with his tongue. Her hands raked down his back in response, urging him on. He found the edge of her sweater, and together they tugged it off. The fall air chilled her skin, but she only pressed closer to him for warmth. Her bra floated down, to be followed by his coat, then his shirt. Each item was practically ripped off and then thrown carelessly on the ground to form a wanton testimony to their desire. And then at last was the electric feel of his callused hands on her soft skin, of her breasts against the rippling heat of his muscular chest. Her hands splayed across the naked expanse of his pectorals, exploring and discovering. She could feel the powerful thundering of his heart against her palm. She ran her hands through the crisp black curls of a light smattering of chest hair, then she traced the hairs down as they formed a thinner line, running into his slacks. Her hands lingered there, and she was rewarded by his low groan.

Then suddenly, he had her hands above her head, capturing her mouth in a raging kiss, blazing a burning trail down the graceful curve of her neck to the soft promise of her breasts. His mouth found her right nipple, rolling it luxuriantly in his mouth while she arched against him. Helplessly, her hips shifted against his, seeking the relief that would put out the flames. In response, he ground his hips against hers, pressing his burning hardness into her welcoming curves.

"I want you now," he said thickly. "I have to have you."

She nodded, her eyes closed against the quivering sensations flooding her body. Every nerve felt on fire, every fiber of her being screaming for his touch. She wanted him, too, needed him, too. She wanted to feel him, hot and slick, sliding into her. She wanted to hear her name torn raggedly from his lips. She wanted the furious pounding, the building heat, the crashing release.

His hands were already unfastening her jeans, and she didn't stop him. She wanted him too much. She would give herself over to him at last, follow the will of her heart. And...

The thought penetrated like a painful chill in her oversensitized mind. And would he love her? This man that claimed there was only lust? This man that even after all those burning kisses, could look at her with eyes so cold she thought she didn't know him at all? He wouldn't love her. He would take her now to slake his hunger, and turn away the minute he was satiated.

He had the control. And she would just be the foolish woman that had given her body and heart, while ignoring her mind.

She closed her eyes, willing herself to have the strength to pull away. But when she opened them again, it was to find his eyes burning into hers with raw, ragged need.

And she knew then, as the first of the tears stung her eyes, that this time she wouldn't pull away. Because she only knew one kind of love, and that was to give all of herself. So she put her body and her heart in his hands, and hoped she had the strength to handle a second loss.

Slowly, she drew his head to her with her hands, and found his tongue with her own. He groaned against her mouth, delving into the moist recesses and sucking on her tongue as her hips arched against his. He didn't need the hint. With impatience, he pulled off her jeans, cupping her mound with his palm while his tongue explored her mouth.

With his fingers, he slowly outlined the rim of her panties, then dipped one finger beneath the cotton to find her warm, moist folds. She gasped, moving against his hand, feeling the tension twist voluptuously inside her.

His first finger penetrated, sliding in slow and languorously while she shuddered against him. It had been so long, so very long. Her body cried out against the abstinence, longing to be filled, to be loved. He pushed deeper, and she cried out his name.

Her panties disappeared and then she pulled him back down, embracing the warmth of his chest against her breasts as her hands found the front of his jeans. With one finger she outlined his rigid form, shivering with anticipation. In a matter of minutes, they'd wrestled off his jeans, freeing him to her touch.

She sighed, enjoying the heavy weight of him in her hands. Raising her hips, she guided him into her.

He gritted his teeth at the first penetration, the muscles on his neck cording with the effort at control. She was so tight and delicate, he didn't want to hurt her. But she was gasping beneath him, arching up against him while her legs wrapped securely around his waist. He sank in deeply, and felt her teeth sink into his shoulder with her passion.

He thrust again, creating a smooth, demanding rhythm that made her cry out his name. Deeper, faster, he plunged into her. He felt her hips arch one final time, her body trembling like a fine wire, then abruptly she collapsed beneath him, her body convulsing around him. With a dim roar, he let his own control go, and poured himself into her as his head fell against the curve of her neck.

She held him tight, her hands warm and sure on his back. The first of the tears escaped from her lashes to mingle with sweat on her cheeks, but she didn't say a word. She just held him, and wondered how long it would last.

The brisk air forced them to recover their clothing sooner than either would have liked. In silence, they pulled on their jeans and sweaters, not quite meeting each other's eyes. And suddenly, one arm through her sweater, Liz knew she had to tell him about the note and the diary.

For the first time, she wondered how he would take it. She hadn't told him in the beginning because she hadn't trusted him. Of course, she trusted him now. But would she be able to make *him* realize that?

"Richard," she began hesitantly, pulling the sweater down over her head. "Richard, what would you say if I told you that I'd found the diary?"

Richard froze in the motion of pulling on his coat. *"What?"*

Liz took a deep breath, and forced herself to stand tall. "I found Alycia's diary," she said levelly. "It was hidden in the floor of my room—or I guess, Alycia's room."

"When?"

She paused, then swallowed. "A few days ago."

He didn't say anything, but a muscle suddenly twitched in his jaw. "Anything else?" he asked quietly, too quietly.

"There was a note," she whispered. "A note from Alycia that appeared on my bed. It said I should leave. I compared the handwriting with the handwriting in the diary. It wasn't really from her."

"How reassuring," he drawled darkly. His eyes landed upon her face, the depths suddenly icy steel. He didn't have to ask why she hadn't told him. She hadn't trusted him.

She, of all people, had believed she couldn't tell him... because he'd killed his wife. The realization hurt more than he'd ever expected. He felt as if daggers had been stabbed into his chest and he had to grit his jaw just to breathe.

"Richard—"

"Don't bother," he said curtly, cutting her off. "I understand completely. After all, half this town thinks I killed Alycia, you might as well think it, too." And then, because he was hurt and he hated the pain, he gestured casually to the ground, where minutes before they'd lain. "And don't think you have to explain on account of what just happened. Lust is lust. It needs no more explanation than that."

She winced, her head falling to hide the stricken look on her face. She'd known that was coming, known what he thought about what had just happened, but it was harder than she'd ever imagined to hear it from his lips when her body was still warm from his touch.

She'd hurt him, but his repayment was more than adequate.

"We should go back to the stables," she whispered woodenly. "I need to see to the horse."

Richard just nodded, his face closed off and grim. Goliath was tied nearby, so they rode the horse double, trying not to touch too much even as the horse's gait threw them together. Liz was grateful when it came time to finally slide down off the beast.

It turned out that the groom had already taken care of Honeysuckle. Richard, however, walked over to the discarded saddle with a frown on his face. The groom had thrown the girth aside, as it was now in two pieces. But Richard ran a finger over the separated ends, noting that three-fourths of the leather wasn't ragged and frayed, but clean-cut, as if sliced. He looked up sharply to find Liz staring at him with bleak eyes.

Someone had obviously tampered with the saddle, and there were only two people who rode Western: Richard and Liz.

Chapter 13

Richard remained glacierlike on the way back to the house. He was still hurt, and the pain infuriated him. She should not have been able to hurt him; he'd sworn never to be that vulnerable again. Lust was lust. He'd had her, now he would move on.

But he didn't feel finished as he stormed behind her into her room. He felt tightly strung, deeply wounded. And looking at the fresh renovations of the room, the fury washed over him once more. Someone had come into this room, under his roof, and placed an intimidating note on her bed. Someone had shot at her on his property, someone had tampered with her saddle in his stables. That he'd been so remiss only fueled his anger higher.

He took the diary without a word, not even muttering a single syllable as she offered a brief recap of its contents. He merely waited for her to finish, then whirled with the small volume in his hand. Refusing to notice Liz's look of hurt and regret, he thundered down the hall.

He had only one destination in mind.

He didn't bother with the preliminaries of knocking as he bore down on Blaine's room in the upper level of the house.

Instead, he slammed the door open with all the force of a five-year-old rage. He had a moment of grim satisfaction, seeing the way Blaine bolted upright in bed in the shadowed room, with shock and fear rippling across his playboy face. Then Blaine's face settled into the wariness Richard knew so well as Richard stepped fully into the room.

"What the hell do you think you're doing," Blaine demanded, "barging into my room like this?"

"You thought you could get away with it again, didn't you?" Richard growled low and dark, taking another menacing step toward the bed. "You thought I'd simply stand back and let you."

"I don't know what you're talking about," Blaine replied tersely, throwing back the covers and reaching for his robe while his own jaw set. "And at ten in the morning, I don't really feel like playing games, Richard."

Richard didn't reply, his sharp eyes skimming around the room.

"Liz is still alive, you know," he mentioned almost casually. "Too bad she's such a good rider, isn't it?" He moved closer to the bed.

Blaine's eyes narrowed with shock and confusion. "Something happened to Liz?" Blaine asked sharply, quickly belting his dark green robe.

Richard nodded, his keen eyes unconvinced by the display in front of him. "You can stop the pretense," he stated coolly. "I'm not buying the act. Five years ago, I didn't question you, Blaine. Five years ago, I stopped pursuing the truth. I thought it was better to leave the matter in peace. But it's not five years ago anymore, and it's not Alycia we're talking about now. It's Liz. And so help me God, Blaine—" he moved closer, towering over Blaine as his voice sunk to a menacingly velvet whisper "—if you so much as touch her again, *I will kill you myself.*"

Blaine's face paled, but he didn't back down. He stood there firmly, his own blue eyes sparking with rage.

"You and I have never gotten along," he began, earning a sarcastic laugh from Richard, "but I'm telling you now, I never tried to harm Liz. For God's sake, she's the best thing to ever happen to this household. You think I don't know that?''

Richard opened his mouth to reply, but Blaine didn't let him.

"Furthermore," the younger brother stated, drawing himself up straight, "I did not kill Alycia. I don't know what you think, and I don't know what you believe, but I'm not the one who killed her, Richard. And you of all people ought to know that."

Richard's face darkened at the accusation, his hands balling into fists at his sides. Far from retreating, Blaine's own muscles tensed, his eyes daring his brother to go through with it.

And Richard wanted to. At that moment in time, nothing would have given him more pleasure than to slam his fists through his younger brother's golden face.

For a long tense moment, they glared at each other and let the room fill with the tension. Abruptly, Richard thrust the leather-bound diary between them.

"I know you were blackmailing Alycia," he growled, throwing out a wild card. "The diary says it all."

Blaine looked at the book with shock, but Richard's statement appeared to receive equal bewilderment. "What the hell are you talking about?" Blaine snapped. "And why the hell would I blackmail Alycia? If anything, she could have blackmailed me."

For a moment, Richard stiffened, and felt the dagger of pain once more. He knew what Blaine was talking about. Andrew, of course. Alycia could have made a mockery of them both over that. Abruptly, his gaze narrowed and his jaw clenched with fierceness. Andrew was his. His! He wouldn't give up the boy now. Damn it, after the past five years, the least he deserved was his son.

"Andrew's mine," he said coldly, his eyes like unsheathed steel. "You had Alycia. That ought to have been enough."

The words were so brittle, so laced with venom that Blaine winced. "Damn it," he retorted vehemently. "I've never tried to interfere with Andrew. I've never even suggested a paternity suit. You only have to watch the kid to know he's you all over again. Hell, Richard, I remember how you acted when you were six . . ." He trailed off, raking his hand through his hair, and then it appeared he just couldn't take any more.

"I loved her, Richard. Do you even know that?" he demanded bitterly, his blue eyes stark. "She's the only woman I ever loved, and she was a total bitch. Oh, yes, Richard, I realize that, as well. I asked her to marry me, but she had to have you, she had to have the real money. When I came to your wedding, I thought someone might as well skin me alive and salt the wound. I tried to be happy for you, brother. I tried to stand back, but I really loved her. Even when she used us both and played us for fools, I still loved her. I suppose it just goes to show you truly did get all the brains in the family." He paused and looked at Richard stonily, his eyes level. "And I never forgave you for what you did to her."

Richard stared at his brother for a long moment, struggling to accept the truth laid out so baldly before them for the first time. He swore, and realized suddenly that he hated the fact that his brother didn't believe in him. Damn it, they'd been brothers once. Blaine would get into trouble, Richard would think of a way out. They'd grown apart, but they hadn't been enemies—not until Alycia had come, and they'd both fallen in love and learned of hatred all at once.

"I didn't kill her," Richard said stiffly. He could see the disbelief on Blaine's face, and it needled the pain a little deeper. "I swear to you, Blaine, I was in my lab that day. I'm not saying I didn't hate her. I'm not saying there weren't times she drove me to such rages, I could almost feel my hands around her neck. But I never so much as bruised her pinkie. I swear it."

Blaine sighed heavily and turned away. He took two steps, and dragged his hands through his rumpled blond hair once more. He laughed harshly, and swore at the same time. "So, if you didn't kill her, Richard, and I didn't kill her, who did? And why didn't we ever think of this sooner?"

But they both knew why. Liz Guiness had never arrived as the nanny before, and forced them to look at things a different way.

"I don't know who," Richard said darkly. He frowned, and this time his fists knotted with frustration. He began to pace the room, long restless strides that didn't begin to ease the knot inside his chest. He had to figure this out. He had to get to the bottom of this. Liz's life depended upon it. He slapped at the diary with one hand, deeming it a hateful thing. "Damn useless book," he muttered. He turned sharply, pinning Blaine with his gaze as a new thought struck him. "Did you cut up the oil painting?"

In reply, Blaine lowered his head. "I was angry," he said quietly. "I loved her, and she'd basically fed on my heart. I hated her for that. But, Richard, I cut up the painting nearly three years ago."

Richard could understand his brother's rage only too well, and once more he began to pace as he digested this piece of news. "Did you leave a note on Liz's bed signed from Alycia?" he prodded. Blaine looked startled, and Richard took that as a no. "What about the blackmail? Did Alycia ever talk about that?"

"I didn't know. Every now and then she'd ask me for money or wheedle me into buying her something. I didn't think much of it. Except for Jillian, we're all rather loose with that sort of thing."

"And Parris?"

Blaine shifted uncomfortably, and once more his jaw set. "So you know about him, as well."

Richard looked at him darkly. "Alycia liked to tell me things."

Blaine laughed, that bitter, humorless sound. "Oh, we did pick a winner with her. An absolute prize."

"But you still associate with Parris."

Blaine shrugged. "How could I condemn him for my own crime? Besides, Alycia had already scorned me by then. She told me I didn't have enough backbone." He looked Richard in the eye, leaving no doubt who she'd compared him to. "Parris, though—" Blaine frowned and looked at Richard intently "—he hates you, you know. He thought he was going to save Alycia from you, and then one week later she was dead. He never could see the truth about her. In his mind, she was the angel, and you were the brute who killed her."

"Does he hate me enough to go after Liz?" Richard asked. "Could he think it's revenge?"

Once again, Blaine looked uncomfortable. "He's my friend, Richard, I've known him since college. But then . . . I don't know. Alycia did strange things to him. She did strange things to us all."

"And Greg?"

Blaine looked more relaxed. "Greg's the only man I've ever met who wasn't affected by her. He used to give Parris and I both a bad time for falling for her so hard. Alycia never cared for him much. They used to engage in the most intense verbal sparring, but I was never sure who won."

"And Jillian?" Richard finished, making mental notes of everything. The culprit had to be someone staying in the house, which would include Jillian, Parris, Greg, Mrs. Pram and Dodd. Dodd was ruled out, as he'd only started as cook three years ago. But that left Blaine's three friends and Mrs. Pram. None of whom he was willing to dismiss offhand.

"I don't know," Blaine said at last. He shook his head, and began his own restless pacing. "For crying out loud, Richard, these are my friends we're talking about. We've all been together for ten years now. Hell, Parris and I survived Alycia. Greg is surviving Jillian's interest in me. You know how we became the gang, Richard? It was one night in Princeton, when we all went out with our dorm and got roaring drunk. The five of us sat outside in the hall and sang 'Ninety-nine Bottles of Beer On the Wall' until four in the morning.

"At five, Greg told us about walking into his parents' bathroom and finding his father hanging from the shower head. I talked about the day the cops came to tell us Mom and Dad were dead and Mrs. Pram looked at us and said we should have been better boys. Then, Jillian confessed her father had declared bankruptcy, and her mother had sold her diamonds to pay her tuition. Her father thought if they could just hold out a little longer, her sickly grandparents would finally die and they'd be all set. Parris talked about coming home to find his mom passed out on the sofa from the alcohol and the drugs— she overdosed our junior year. Finally, Alycia had this real touching story of how she was actually adopted. Her real parents had been nobility who'd been viciously murdered in a coup d'état." Blaine looked at Richard flatly. "That, of course, was a lie. Then again, she said that night she'd always thought she would die young. I think sometimes that was the only true statement she ever uttered. It doesn't matter." Blaine shook his head, looking at Richard with intense eyes.

"At the end of that night, Richard," he said quietly, "we swore to be friends forever. Through ten years, we've stuck to that. It's the only decent commitment I've ever made."

"Someone's trying to kill Liz," Richard said just as quietly, his own eyes unrelenting. His anger had disappeared, though, his pacing stopped, his fists unclenching. He'd never learned so much about his brother as he had now. He'd never realized that not only had they shared a love for the same woman, but a loneliness, as well. Blaine had found his friends, Richard had found his work. Odd, when they could have at least recognized each other.

Now Blaine hung his head and sighed deeply. "I'll keep tabs on them," he said finally. "I'll keep my ears open."

Richard nodded curtly. "That leaves just Mrs. Pram."

Blaine raised an eyebrow. "Hell, Richard, Mrs. Pram hates everyone. If she could murder, I think she would have killed us all."

"But she particularly disliked Alycia."

"True enough."

And, Richard thought to himself, Mrs. Pram seemed none too happy with Liz. He glanced down at his watch. It was now nearly eleven, midday approaching. He had a lot of work to get done, he realized, if he wanted everything in place by nightfall.

He trusted Blaine to keep an eye on his friends, but Richard had no intention of leaving anything to chance. First, he would remove Liz and Andrew to safety, and then he would put his genius to work. He hefted the diary in his hand, and nodded thoughtfully to himself.

Tonight. Five years had already been long enough.

He nodded at Blaine curtly, then, already lost in his own thoughts, disappeared down the hall.

Back in her room, Liz stepped out of the shower and tried to shake the uneasiness away. A glance at the clock revealed it was only ten-thirty, but the room seemed to be growing darker. She glanced out the window, only to find storm clouds moving in.

Great, just great. Now the sky matched the mood of the house. She shivered, and unconsciously pulled on her thickest sweater, as if that could somehow protect her from the encroaching storm.

If only Richard would come to his senses and realize she truly believed in him. If only he would calm down enough so she could talk to him once more. Her nerves were on edge, muscles jumpy from a tension she didn't fully understand yet. She just knew that at the moment, she would give anything to be back in his arms.

And all of a sudden, pulling on her worn jeans, she missed Maddensfield and her family. She missed those golden days when everything had seemed so simple and sure, when dreams had lived and lovers had loved, when it had seemed everyone would grow old, laughing. The days when she could run with her brothers through tall fields, chasing summer's exhilaration with coltish legs, brace-filled teeth, and—

Abruptly the phone rang, scattering her hazy memories. The childhood day was suddenly gone and she was back to being the adult Liz again, sitting in a darkened room with shadowed corners. Puzzled, she picked up the phone next to the bed.

"Hello?" she asked, sitting down tentatively on the edge of the bed.

"A Mr. Guiness for you," came the distinctly disapproving voice of Mrs. Pram. Then, before Liz had time to reply, there was the sharp click of Mrs. Pram hanging up.

"Liz?" came a deep male voice Liz would have recognized anywhere. "Liz, are you all right?"

She couldn't help herself, a smile broke out across her face even as the tears welled up in her eyes. The past and the present, the sunshine and shadows merged suddenly, all with the sound of his voice. It was Mitch, her dear, oldest brother, who always knew exactly when to call and exactly what to say.

"Of course I'm all right," she replied, though her voice came out choked and tear-soaked. "How are you?"

"Fine, fine," Mitch said, his voice dismissive. "You're sure you're all right?"

Liz nodded into the phone, suddenly understanding completely. "You had one of your spells, didn't you?" she asked calmly. Mitch never liked to talk about it, but every now and then, he got these intuitions, very strong intuitions. Like the one that had him on a plane back to Maddensfield even as Nick was being shot. The one that had led him to the hospital first, so he could hold her in his big strong arms while she cried out all her shock and grief and horror.

"Yeah," Mitch agreed gruffly. "I did. Now, are you going to tell your big brother what's going on?"

It was tempting, Liz thought. Tempting just to tell him everything. From the time she was born, she'd been convinced there was nothing Mitch couldn't do, and over the years, he'd never disappointed her. The eldest of her four brothers, he was the most responsible one. He had been the one to bring home all sorts of stray animals, quietly and thoroughly caring for each one, much as he had looked after his four younger siblings. He worked for the FBI now, and though he didn't talk about his job much, Liz knew all she had to do was tell him everything, and he would take care of her.

But, as she tucked the receiver against her ear, Liz knew she wouldn't tell him about Richard's bitter past or the looming present dangers. Because she'd come here to grow, to build a new life away from Maddensfield. And that meant standing on her own two feet. That meant fighting her own wars and slaying her own dragons.

"There was just a small accident," she said at last. "But no one was hurt. Honest."

There was silence on the other end as Mitch was apparently considering this information. And in that silence, she could hear his disbelief.

"Is the family treating you all right?" Mitch asked finally.

Liz didn't know whether to laugh or cry. "They're not exactly what I was expecting," she admitted. "But Mitch, the little boy here, he needs me so much. And I know I can help him. It's just going to take time and a miracle or two."

"If anyone can work a miracle," Mitch told her assuredly, "you can."

She felt another tear well up, streaking down her face. God, it was so good to hear his voice, to hear one person make it all seem so simple again. And for an instant, she almost gave in and told him everything. But then her resolution came back to her, and she stiffened her spine.

"Learn any good magic tricks lately?" she asked instead, switching the topic altogether. In her mind, she could see his answering smile.

"None as good as the disappearing act you pulled," he told her lightly.

"What about women?" she teased, beginning to regain her composure now. "Any good blondes to break your heart?"

"Now, you know, little sis, you'll be the only woman capable of breaking my heart."

She laughed, the sound still wobbly, but getting better. Then she sobered.

"Things really are all right," she told him, serious now. "I'm glad I did this, Mitch. I'm glad I came here. It was the right thing to do."

There was another small moment of silence, then at last she could hear the pent-up sigh in his voice.

"Listen," Mitch said, his voice as serious as her own, "I've got to go away for a couple of weeks. You know the drill. But if you need me, Liz, if you need anything at all, you let me know, okay? Contact the number in D.C. I'll get there as soon as I can."

"I know," she told him, "but honestly, Mitch, I can handle this. Your little sister is growing up, you know?"

"I know, I know," he said, but his voice said he didn't find the idea comforting. "Well, I'd better let you get your beauty rest. Take care, Liz. And, well—" his voice grew a little gruff "—I'm proud of you. And I love you."

She smiled, feeling the tears threaten again. She took a steadying breath. "I love you, too, big brother. And Mitch, be careful."

He agreed as he always did, and then he was gone, just the dial tone ringing in her ear. She set the receiver down slowly, willing the tightness in her chest to leave her. It was good to talk to Mitch, good to hear his voice. When Nick had died, she might have fallen apart completely if it hadn't been for Mitch. He'd been the shoulder she'd cried on. And when she'd started to heal, he'd been the one she'd laughed with as he teased her with his magic tricks.

But those days were gone now. Nick had died, her life had moved on and she'd grown up a lot in the past year, she'd gained strength. Enough to stare down the darkest man she'd ever met.

Enough to fall in love.

She rested her chin on her knees, and wondered how long it would be before Richard calmed down enough to talk.

She shivered, and for no good reason at all, felt afraid.

She must have fallen asleep, but the next thing she knew there was a tentative knock at her door. Opening her eyes groggily, she called for the person to come in. Obediently the door opened, and Andy peered in at her with solemn eyes behind his thick lenses.

"Are you feeling better, yet?" he asked quietly.

She nodded, trying to sit up on the bed and wincing as she discovered new aches and pains. Andrew's sharp eyes missed nothing.

"Why are you wincing? Do you want some aspirin?" he demanded.

She held up a hand in a silent plea for mercy, offering him a faint smile. "Honest, sweetheart, I'm fine, but thanks for asking. I just had a bit of a riding accident when I was trying to cure my headache, that's all."

Andy's eyes narrowed shrewdly. "Was it anything like the hunting accident?" he demanded suspiciously. He walked into the room, examining her with careful eyes, as if he needed proof of her well-being.

Once again, she was amazed by his perceptiveness, and a little lost at how to put him back at ease. "I fell off Honeysuckle," she said briskly. "There's nothing dangerous about that except my own stupidity. Now, what did you do all day?"

He simply looked at her. "I read," he said finally. Then abruptly, he frowned petulantly. "I don't like Mrs. Pram.

Don't leave me with her anymore. You have to stay with me forever. I demand it!''

She managed to raise an eyebrow at his tone of voice. "You demand it, huh?"

He nodded vigorously, and she didn't know whether to scold him or commiserate with his sudden insecurity. She settled for rumpling his hair. "I like being with you, too, Andy," she said simply. "Want to read me a story for a change? You can cheer me up."

"What's this?" came Richard's voice from the doorway. "I thought you were resting."

Andy immediately stood straighter, his tiny face rigid. "I was helping Liz feel better," he chirped out quickly, looking at his father with big eyes. "She said I could come in."

Richard looked at the boy, recognizing the tension in the young face and immediately hating himself for having caused it. Why couldn't he have treated the child better in the beginning? He was just a six-year-old boy, too smart for his own good, lost in a world where he was neither child nor adult, but simply genius.

Unconsciously, Richard's face relaxed, and Andrew allowed himself a little breath. Richard walked forward and placed a casual hand on Andrew's shoulder. Immediately, the boy stiffened, but Richard just remained standing there as if it was the most natural thing in the world. It would take time, he reminded himself. Time for both of them to adjust.

"How are you feeling?" he asked Liz, his voice carefully neutral.

"Like I've fallen off a horse," Liz replied. Briefly, her eyes searched his face, but once again, his face was expressionless. At least he appeared less angry than when he'd left.

"I thought the three of us might go out to dinner tonight," he announced. Both Andrew and Liz looked at him in amazement, but he plunged on, as if it were nothing out of the ordinary. "There's a new restaurant downtown I've heard is excellent. I thought we might give it a try. Does six o'clock sound good?"

Blankly, Liz and Andrew nodded, though in fact, six o'clock was early compared to the usual time they had dinner.

"Perhaps we can catch a movie afterward," Richard continued, filling in the missing pieces. "Andrew, why don't you and Liz pick something you'd like to see?"

This time, Andrew couldn't keep the shock off his young face. His blue eyes looked like saucers, and his mouth hung open as he stared from his father to Liz to his father again. Abruptly, he snapped his mouth shut and nodded vigorously. Liz didn't say anything at all.

"I think it will be a late night," Richard thought out loud in the silence. "Perhaps you should take a nap, Andrew." Then he frowned, as if something new had just occurred to him. "Actually, it might be better if you spent time with Liz. Helped her feel better, you know. Why don't you go down to the library together. Didn't I hear you were going to read her a story? Yes, you can do it there."

That seemed to satisfy him, for he nodded to himself. Liz, however, was narrowing her eyes shrewdly. He was up to something, all right. And whatever it was, he wanted her and Andrew out of the way. Tonight. Once more, a frisson of tension raced along her spine. But for Andrew's sake, she did her best to appear calm. She would wait until Andrew left, then she would grill Richard.

Richard, however, seemed hell-bent on not giving her the chance. He suddenly pivoted, and his message delivered, marched expediently to the doorway. She was still trying to think of a good excuse to call him back, when Andrew scampered after him. Frowning, she rose to her feet only to have Andrew close the door sharply behind him. Completely taken aback, she sat down hard, and began thinking she might want that aspirin, after all.

"Sir?" Andrew called from the hallway, having to run to catch up with his father's longer steps. Richard turned, keeping his face composed as he looked down at Andrew's serious face.

"Yes?" he asked. Did he sound too intimidating, too harsh? Did he sound like a parent at all? He didn't know how to tell.

Andrew hesitated, then drew himself up smartly. "I would like to speak to you," Andy declared loudly. "On a subject very important to both of us."

Richard arched a surprised eyebrow. Leaning back slightly, he crossed his arms in front of him and adopted the child's grave tone. "I see. And what would this be?"

"Liz," Andrew stated immediately. "We must do something to protect Liz."

For a moment, Richard was almost too shocked to speak. But he then collected himself, looking at the little blue-suited boy in front of him with new respect.

"What do you mean?" he probed carefully.

Andrew gave his father a slightly patronizing stare. "These accidents. They can't really be accidents. Even *I* know that."

Richard pulled himself together quickly, thinking he should dismiss the boy's allegation, then realized that tactic would never have worked on him when he was six. Unconsciously, he kneeled, becoming eye level with the child. "I see. You've been giving this some thought?"

Andy nodded vigorously, and Richard found himself almost smiling.

"The morning of the picnic," Andrew reported stiffly, "Jillian and Blaine went on a walk. I thought you should know that."

In spite of himself, Richard looked at Andy with genuine surprise.

"But Blaine returned alone," Andrew rushed on, his face still somber as he relayed his findings. "He said he was thirsty, and that he never liked to walk as much as Jillian did, anyway. And he went to find Parris and Greg, but they weren't in. Mrs. Pram said they'd gone out to the stables. Mrs. Pram keeps her eye on everyone."

Andrew nodded smartly, having concluded his report, and Richard felt his chest tighten. At this moment, he could understand why Liz and Blaine thought Andrew was so much like him. That nod, that rigid stance. It was Richard as a six-year-old. And suddenly, he realized fully that Andrew's parentage truly didn't matter anymore. Even if Blaine was the child's father, Andrew would still be his nephew. Perhaps that was close enough to son, and if Richard ever did have a son, he would like him to be just like this solemn boy here.

That Andy had been this diligent touched him beyond belief. That the boy had asked so many questions, however, filled him with fear. Very carefully, he placed his hand on Andrew's shoulder, and adopted the child's serious tone.

"You did the right thing," he assured him, "in telling me these things. I'm very glad you did. But I don't want you to ask any more questions, Andrew, okay? I have something else I need you to do." Andrew leaned over expectantly, his blue eyes intent. "I want you to keep an eye on Liz. Make sure she's okay."

Andrew's eyes widened, and he nodded vigorously at this new and important charge. Richard found himself smiling, and the feeling in his chest intensified a hundredfold.

Giving in to instinct for the first time, he reached over, and hugged this precious little boy. There was a moment of hesitation, then suddenly, Andrew threw his arms around his father's neck. And it was then that Richard could smell all the little kid smells from five years ago: the scent of children's shampoo, the freshness of youth, the tinge of baby powder. And the feeling was the same, the precious burden of a child's trust weighing upon his shoulders.

It was the way it had been so long ago, when he'd rocked the crying baby to sleep at night, feeling his love like an overwhelming swell in his chest. It was the way it had been until that one night, when Alycia had stolen it all from him with her scathing words.

Except that it wasn't gone anymore. It was here in the hallway, five years later but just as precious. Baby Andy had grown up into a six-year-old boy who could talk dielectrics and compute algorithms, and Richard thought he'd never met anyone so perfect in his entire life.

Slowly, he untangled himself from Andy's grasp.

"Go take care of Liz," he whispered, and Andrew nodded once more, then abruptly scurried back to Liz's room to promptly begin his new duties. Richard watched the boy's hasty departure with another smile teasing the corners of his mouth.

He had no doubt Liz wouldn't be able to sneeze by herself for the rest of the day. He straightened and nodded to himself. That was just as well. He couldn't keep his eye on them both for the afternoon, and he didn't know of anyone he could send them to. So he would let them keep each other safe, while he disappeared briefly back into his lab.

He patted the diary in his chest pocket. He had some bait to doctor, and a trap to set. Tonight it would all come together.

If he could just keep Andy and Liz safe until then.

Chapter 14

Liz woke to the sound of a creaking floorboard. Instantly, she was on the alert, bolting upright as her heart thundered in her chest. Her head winced at the sudden movement, the pain clearing the last of her fog. She became aware of the fact that she was fully dressed and sprawled out on the library sofa. Yawning deeply, she stretched out her muscles and glanced at the grandfather clock. One-thirty.

Richard had left twenty minutes ago to put Andy to bed after their big night out. She'd been surprised by his offer to do so, but it only fit the tone of an all-round strange night. The dinner had been a reserved affair, with Richard in a polite if distant mood.

On the one hand, he seemed more relaxed around Andrew, and the two chatted a bit between themselves. On the other hand, his gaze was unreadable each time it swept over to her. He'd seemed restrained, and there were times when she'd thought his mind wandered away completely. As the hour had grown later, the movie approaching, then ending, his preoccupation had only increased. By the time they'd returned to the house, she could feel the restlessness hovering in the air around him. His eyes were darker, his face impatient. And still, when he looked at her, she knew nothing of what went on in his mind.

She sighed heavily, wanting to bridge the distance and not yet knowing how. She spared another glance for the grandfather clock. One-forty. Apparently, Andy was making him read all of *A Brief History of Time.*

The small creaking sound came again, this time farther down the hall. She froze, then told herself it was only Richard finally coming to join her. Except, of course, the man usually walked like a cat. She found herself straining her ears even as a deep tremor rippled up the back of her neck.

A log popped in the fire, and she jumped.

With a shake of her head at her own nerves, she got off the couch and went to attend to the flames.

"You." The word was a low angry whisper coming sharply from her right.

Immediately, Liz turned, fire poker in hand and her muscles tense—only to find a gun leveled at her chest. Her face paled, and the fear that gripped her stomach was complete. Slowly, surely, she dropped the heavy iron poker to the floor.

Richard scowled as he pounded down the hall toward Liz's room. He hadn't thought it would take so long to get Andy into bed, and he couldn't shake the feeling something had gone wrong. He'd already checked in with Blaine for an evening update. Blaine didn't look happy, but he'd succeeded in his mission to keep at least Greg and Parris under watch. Both men were currently drunk as skunks in Blaine's room. Jillian had retired to her bedroom earlier, Blaine had said, his look plainly stating he couldn't watch two rooms at one time.

Richard understood that, which was why he wanted to double-check the diary before he went down to the library. The time, however, made him nervous. He didn't like leaving Liz alone for so long, especially when so many things could go wrong.

He'd done his best, in the few hours he'd had this afternoon, to create something at once discreet and efficient. He wanted a trap he could spring without the person's realizing it had been sprung. Given all the people staying in the house,

Richard didn't want to risk a panicked confrontation. So, he'd settled on rigging the diary with an ink pouch, a classic trick often used in ransom payments to pollute the money and thus render it valueless. Basically, he'd concocted a normal-looking mixture of blue ink, except it was unwashable. When the diary cover opened, the ink spurted out not only over the pages, but over the perpetrator, as well.

He had hid the diary, and made sure everyone knew he was taking Andy and Liz out for the evening. He just had to trust the killer to take advantage of the situation. Richard had even moved the armoire back a bit to aid the culprit's search. In an ideal scenario, the killer would find the diary, open it and become stained with ink. Thinking Alycia had booby-trapped the book and it was now unreadable—and thus of no possible danger—the killer would return the book discreetly. The next morning, one person would appear with the story of a pen leaking on them. At his convenience, Richard would take the person aside to a safe, controlled environment. He would announce that he'd actually rigged the diary, having, of course, read its contents beforehand, which clearly revealed the perpetrator's role in Alycia's death. The person would be rattled, and Richard could trick him into a testimony for the sake of the hidden tape recorder.

Everything would be wrapped up neat and clean by afternoon. Except, of course, for the fact that the situation rested heavily on assumptions about people and their behavior. And human behavior was the hardest factor to control for.

Richard made it to Liz's room. A quick check revealed that the diary was gone. Frowning even more heavily, Richard stood. Jillian, or Mrs. Pram? He went to check on Jillian first. She wasn't in her room, however, and he was just about to leave for Mrs. Pram, when his eyes fell on a towel on the floor, now covered with blue ink.

He turned, swearing low under his breath. Without questioning the instinct, he flew down to the library.

"You will do exactly as I say," Jillian stated in clipped tones. Her blue eyes were no longer distant, but burned with a manic rage that worried Liz far more. That, and the pistol held with calm competence in the woman's hand. "You read the damn diary, didn't you?"

Numbly, Liz nodded, only realizing her mistake too late. Judging by the look of relief on Jillian's face, the fact had clearly been in doubt until Liz had confirmed it. She wanted to swear, but her brain was still reeling from the sight of the gun and the impact that all along it had been Jillian. Jillian had killed Alycia.

Jillian abruptly held up her left hand to show it was covered with blue ink. "I suppose I have you to thank for this little souvenir, then. Very clever of you. Of course, I realized then that someone else must have found the diary first. After all, Alycia had never been quite that clever."

Liz honestly had no idea what the woman was talking about, but her silence was taken for acquiescence as Jillian kept talking.

"How ironic that you should find it after I've spent five years looking for the damn thing. I always thought the renovations would make it easier to find. If only I could have dragged Blaine back to the house more often. No matter, though," Jillian said briskly, using the gun to motion Liz toward the door. "Since you destroyed the diary, you'll just have to serve in its place. I want that money, damn it. And you're going to tell me where it is, or you won't have enough teeth left to be identified even by dental records."

"I don't know what you're talking about," Liz said mechanically, her eyes never leaving the gun.

Jillian's gaze darkened, and for just one minute, her hand clenched on the pistol. "Don't try that ignorance routine with me, you little slut. I've seen the way you've been wrapping Richard and Blaine around your finger. You think you can take Alycia's place, but I was here way before you. Blaine is *mine*. That money is *mine*. So start moving. I've always heard that compared to the first murder, the second is easy."

Liz swallowed heavily, and felt the faint drumming of her own pulse in her ears. Where was Richard? But she didn't know, and the gun in Jillian's hand didn't seem keen on waiting. Slowly, she turned and forced her feet into motion even as she commanded her terrified mind to think. Money. Jillian wanted money. Liz couldn't think of hints from the diary, so she just kept walking.

And unconsciously, her feet took them to the one room she most associated with Alycia and that dark night five years ago. The one room farthest from Andy, and the room where she might hope to buy time before anyone else got hurt.

She led Jillian up to the right-hand tower.

Richard rounded the corner into the library at a near run, only to come to a screeching halt. Empty. The damn room was empty. He felt the panic grip him tightly, his blood running cold and his head drooping as a million different horrible scenarios ran through his mind.

Liz. What if Jillian had already gotten to Liz?

Then abruptly, he felt a draft from his right, a chilling, musty draft. His head came up slowly, his face already rigid with the knowledge.

The right-hand tower. Someone had opened the right-hand tower.

And then he knew just how much he stood to lose.

He strode into the library, his face set as his cheeks paled beneath his normal darkness. He opened the bar without blinking, reaching way back to pull out what he wanted. He snapped open the leather case with efficient fingers, and spared one glance at the smooth shape of the Chief's Special. He began to walk even as he clicked out the barrel and began to load.

And each stride took him closer to the right-hand tower.

"I don't remember any money," Liz was saying frantically, watching as Jillian grew angrier and angrier before her. "The diary just talked about the blackmail, I swear it."

"Don't bother," the blonde sneered, looking at Liz with open contempt. "Do you expect me to believe you? You're no better than Alycia. Well, I sat back and watched her for two years. I let her steal Blaine and I looked on while she married Richard. And then I realized I was never going to get anywhere while she was in the picture. That day, she thought she was so clever, to have figured out who I was. She thought she could stand here and laugh at me and swear she wouldn't pay another red cent. Well, I showed her who was really the smart one.

"And then I got to be patient once more. Blaine needed time, Parris needed time. The whole damn world seemed to need time to get over Alycia. But now it's *my* time. Blaine was coming around. Just a couple months more and I'd have had him down the aisle and then I'd never have to worry about money again. Until, of course, you showed up. You should have left when I put that note on your bed, you little bitch. Did you really think I'd just sit back and let Blaine go for the second time?"

Liz shook her head furiously. "I don't want Blaine," she said, then quickly reworded her answer as Jillian's eyes glittered dangerously. "I mean, Blaine doesn't want me. And really, that's fine. I hope the two of you will be happy together. I'll be the first to throw rice at your wedding."

"Too late," Jillian said coldly. "You're going to help me find the twenty thousand Alycia still owes me, and then if you're lucky, I'll kill you with the first bullet. Don't make me run through the list of alternatives."

Liz swallowed, and wondered for the thirtieth time how she was going to get out of this. Slowly, her eyes never wavering from Jillian's form, she sank to the floor.

"It's hidden under the floor," she ad-libbed. "Alycia wrote that she hid the money here." She pretended to run her hands across the stone, as if feeling for a release lever, wondering if she sounded at all convincing.

It seemed to work, because Jillian suddenly looked at the floor with renewed interest.

"How shrewd," the blonde murmured, kneeling slowly. "Bring the money to the final site, but hide it in the floor, just in case. Perhaps I didn't look hard enough the first time."

Keeping the gun trained on Liz with one hand, the blonde felt out the stones with her other hand. Liz allowed herself another deep breath. So far, so good. Maybe if she could just keep the woman talking, absorbed in finding the last of the money, she could distract Jillian's attention from the gun. At this point, it was the best plan she had.

"So you were the blackmailer," Liz began.

Jillian simply nodded, her face cold as she searched out another stone. Liz moved over a few feet, and instantly the woman stiffened. Liz hunkered back down slowly.

"What," she asked after a minute, "what did you blackmail her with? In the diary," she added quickly, "she only refers to one day she swore never to think about again."

Jillian laughed, but it wasn't a pleasant sound. "It was a freak thing, really," she said coolly as her free hand smoothed along the stones. "Six years ago I was talking to a friend of a friend of a friend, who just happened to be in the business of performing abortions and, well, he'd performed one on Alycia. When she was sixteen. It appears Alycia had a little incident with one of her father's business associates."

Liz started, and the surprised motion earned her another level glance. For emphasis, Jillian cocked the pistol. "I'm getting impatient," the blonde said pointedly.

Liz nodded, and turned back to the floor, trying to look as if she were searching for the last of the blackmail money that Alycia apparently had never handed over. Her panic kept growing, and nervously her eyes darted around the room. It was then she suddenly noticed the shadowed form of Richard standing in the doorway. Quickly, she dropped her eyes, hoping Jillian hadn't noticed her staring. She moved back a bit, drawing Jillian's attention farther from the door.

"Why—why kill Alycia if you were collecting money from her?" Liz asked nervously, licking her lips and catching Richard's stealthy approach out of the corner of her eye. He appeared to be holding a gun in one hand, but that didn't ease her nerves. If Jillian happened to glance over and notice him...

"I didn't have a choice." Jillian shrugged. "She figured out it was me, and then confronted me up here at the drop-off site. She had the gall to say she'd brought the money with her, but now that she knew it was me, she had no intention of paying. She thought she could just turn and walk away. She thought I would just let her." Jillian's face hardened, the pistol waving in her hand with the force of her anger. Immediately, Richard froze, and Liz swallowed thickly, wondering if she was going to be shot out of pure rage. Slowly, the blonde collected herself. "I cocked the gun, thinking to scare her, and that little twit turned around and rushed me. We struggled a bit, but I was always much stronger than her. I maneuvered her over to the window, and when I got the first opening, I pushed her hard. She fell like a rag doll, and Blaine became mine.''

In spite of herself, Liz shivered. Unbidden, her gaze sought out Richard, now just steps behind Jillian's kneeling form. This time, however, the blonde frowned, and turned as if to follow the line of Liz's gaze.

"The money!" Liz cried ingenuously. Jillian whirled sharply back, only to be caught off guard by Richard's crashing form. They went down with a soft thud on the stone floor, a gun skittering across the uneven surface. Not waiting, Liz scrambled over to collect the pistol.

She saw Richard's arm come back, then move forward with remarkable fury. Jillian went limp on the floor. With an almost casual gesture, Richard reached down and examined her face. He rose, and looked at the woman one last time with unconcealed fury and disgust.

"We'd better call the police," he said darkly. "She won't stay out forever."

Dimly, Liz nodded, aware that now it was over, her arms were shaking, her knees were shaking. She wanted to wilt down to the floor. She wanted to bury her head against Richard's shoulder and thank God he hadn't been harmed.

But the look he gave her was so remote, his jaw still clenched from the tension, his eyes unreadable, that she knew she couldn't do any of that.

A tiny spark of hope within her died at that moment. She assumed that he must have rigged the diary with the ink, and maybe she wanted to believe it had been to keep her safe after the two attempts on her life, but now she wasn't so sure. Richard had said love was for fools. And maybe what she had taken as growing signs of his affection, had only been concern for her welfare. Now that the matter appeared to be solved, there wasn't even any need for that much sentiment.

Slowly, she nodded her head, and got to her feet.

For one minute she swayed, the blood rushing too fast to her face. Something intense and dark moved in Richard's gaze. He took a small step as if to go to her. Then abruptly, he checked himself and turned away, cold and harsh.

What did she expect? she reminded herself even as the pain knifed through her chest. She'd given him her body, and that was all he believed in. She'd never gotten him to understand that for her, her body followed her soul. She hadn't given him a moment of passion, she'd given him her heart.

He picked up Jillian's fallen form, and headed for the stairs. Wordlessly, Jillian's gun dangling nervously from her fingertips, she followed.

Downstairs in the library Richard called the cops, sending Liz to get Blaine, Greg and Parris. He tied Jillian securely on the sofa, then stared at the low crackle of the fire while he tried to collect his thoughts.

He should be glad it was finally over, he thought. Glad to know that Blaine really hadn't killed Alycia. But then, Blaine had still slept with Alycia, and Alycia had still been a cold woman who had kept her own secrets. Why hadn't she ever told him about the abortion? Why hadn't she allowed her husband at least that small measure of faith?

Once more he felt that sinking feeling deep within him. Alycia hadn't trusted him with the truth, just as Liz hadn't trusted his innocence. She'd kept her knowledge of the diary from him because she'd thought he might be a killer.

The worst, he realized suddenly, was the fact that the truth didn't bring him any peace. After all these years, he didn't want the finite knowledge.

He merely wanted for someone to believe in him.

He heard the sound of footsteps, and raised his head to see Liz, Blaine and the weaving Greg and Parris enter the room. For one moment, his gaze fell on Liz and her pale face. Her midnight eyes met his squarely, and even from here, he could see the pleading in their depths. He tore his gaze away, and hated the tearing pain he felt in his chest.

The doorbell rang. He went to answer.

The police questioned them until 5:00 a.m. Liz started at the beginning with the note she'd found on her bed, and the shots that had been fired at the picnic, then she described the damaged saddle. Richard threw in his part, the tampering of the diary to implicate the killer, while Blaine added the few details he knew of Jillian's financial situation. She'd gotten a small inheritance from her grandparents, but had constantly worried about running through it. To a great extent, she had lived off the other members of the gang, though never overtly. Just lots of little trips and shopping excursions here and there. The still-unfound twenty thousand would have made a nice nest egg to sit on.

By the time Jillian regained consciousness, the officers were getting out the handcuffs. Blaine, looking tired and strained, couldn't even meet her eye. Parris had sobered up enough to clench and unclench the fists at his sides with brutal intensity. Greg just kept shaking his head.

Liz didn't pay them much attention, however. Mostly, she kept her eyes on Richard.

He simply stood at the fireplace through it all, his face so remote it hurt her to see it. At times, he would prowl the library like a caged beast, seeking escape from the demons that plagued him even in the light of truth. A dozen times, she'd almost gotten up to go to him. A dozen times, she'd held back.

Finally, Jillian was led away, and everyone dissolved to their own rooms for badly needed rest. The old stone house grew quiet, the dark halls finally settling down. But Liz still couldn't find any peace. She changed into her T-shirt and robe, attempting to lie down on the bed. But it didn't do any good. Her mind just kept reeling with its own painful thoughts.

She'd hurt him, she knew that and it hurt her. Richard thought she didn't believe in him. He thought she'd kept the diary from him because she'd doubted his innocence. The fact that he was half-right made it all the more horrible for her. Because looking inside her heart, knowing how she loved him, she also had to see how she'd failed him.

Then again, maybe she was simply the romantic he'd always accused her of being. Maybe he didn't even care. He'd always said he believed only in lust. Perhaps she wanted to believe she'd failed him only because it implied she had the ability to affect him at all.

Quite possibly, he was so remote now because he simply didn't want anything to do with her anymore.

Her hand rested on her bedroom door and the confusion swirled in her mind once more. Finally, she just couldn't take it. Maybe he didn't have any feelings for her, but she knew she loved him. And right now, she didn't want to stand here alone torturing herself.

She turned the knob, and ventured once more into the house.

She wasn't sure where his bedroom was. Sometimes she had been convinced that he didn't have one. He seemed to live more in the left-hand tower than anywhere else. But Andy had mentioned something about the east wing—the original servants' quarters—so she crept over there.

The first door she came to was closed, and there was no light beneath. Somehow, she couldn't picture Richard already being asleep, so she ventured on. At the end of the long hallway, she found the most likely candidate—two thick wooden doors were closed, but she could see the light burning beneath.

Raising a tentative hand, she took a deep breath and knocked.

Nothing happened. Deciding she'd been too quiet, she knocked firmer this time, sending the rapping notes pulsing down the hall. Her only reward was bruised knuckles. But she wasn't quite ready to give up, not yet.

"Richard," she called firmly, trying not to be too loud in the long dark hallway. "Richard, open up. I'm not going away until you do."

Another couple of long seconds dragged by, then abruptly, the right half of the double doors swung open.

"What do you want?" Richard demanded at once, the scowl dark and deep in his face.

He looked haggard, Liz thought immediately. The strain of the night showed in the deep grooves in his forehead and the restless burning of his blue eyes. His cheeks were shadowed by a twenty-four-hour beard, and his black hair lay in tufts from the countless times he'd run his hand through it. His clothing matched the rest of him, his dress shirt disheveled with the top two buttons undone, his tie and jacket long since discarded.

She wanted to go to him so bad, it hurt.

Instead, she forced herself to stand patiently in the doorway. "May I come in?" she asked at last.

His scowl deepened, but he didn't say no. Finally, with a curt nod, he stood aside so that she could pass. The bedroom surprised her, she realized as she glanced around with curious eyes. It was huge, as she would have expected, but other than that, there was nothing in here that spoke of Richard. The king-size bed with its adjoining nightstands looked like a hotel relic, and the bed cover was so smooth and nondescript, she wondered if he even slept there at all. But then her eyes turned to the right-hand side of the room. It was built on a raised platform, and was easily twice the size of the bedroom area. In the middle stood the dominating form of an enormous desk, where yet another computer and various piles of paper waited. A fire burned low in the fireplace behind the desk, while a deep leather chair and stool, permanently dented by use, sat not too far from the flames.

This was Richard, Liz thought with some satisfaction. And she wouldn't be surprised at all if he regularly fell asleep at the desk or chair, versus the sterile bed. Without being asked, she walked into the den area, running one hand along the fine oak wood of the desk.

"It's beautiful," she said softly.

Richard didn't bother with a reply. Then, realizing she wasn't going to simply leave, he also walked into the den area, picking up his brandy glass as he passed on his way to the fire. There, he leaned back against the stone chimney, folding his arms in front of him as he contemplated her with cold and relentless eyes.

"Six o'clock in the morning is a little early for a social call," he stated abruptly, challenging her with his gaze.

She merely nodded, not giving him any opportunity to attack her. The frustration merely fed the myriad other emotions racing through him. Unconsciously, he uncrossed his arms and began prowling the den once more.

It hurt to look at her, he thought suddenly. Her long hair was cascading down her back in wild abandon, fairly dancing with the red highlights of the fire's low flames. Even her eyes, such a dark, haunting blue, looked large and luminous in the shadowed light. He wanted to pull her into his arms and run his hands down the curves of her graceful body. He wanted to plunder her mouth with his own, to lose himself in the sigh of her surrender. He wanted to take her, to fill his sense with every feel, sound and smell of her, until there was no more room for the doubts and memories that haunted him.

Until the ghosts of his mind left him at last and there was only her.

Yet, at the same time, he wanted to push her away harshly. He wanted to scream at her to leave this room, because it hurt him to see her, and it hurt him to want her and know he shouldn't be wanting anything. He'd sworn off love, he'd sworn off the softer emotions, hadn't he?

He hated the pain Alycia had caused him, and he hated the dull throb of knowing that Liz hadn't believed in him, either. No one ever had.

Cursing quietly, he pivoted sharply and crossed to the other side of the room, putting as much distance between them as possible.

"It's late," he fairly growled, keeping his eyes pinned on the wall as he took another blazing sip of brandy. "Say your piece or leave."

"I don't know what it is I want to say," Liz said finally, and it was true. She'd come here because she wanted to make things right. She wanted to ease this aching distance that seemed to gape between them. But looking at him now, prowling the room with all the dark heat of a panther, she no longer knew what to say. He radiated restless energy and consuming demons. To even stand here was like being at the edge of an electrical storm, feeling all the crackles and sparks of a tightly restrained power.

She suddenly wondered what it would be like if it was unleashed. And the thought alone made her shiver.

But it wasn't from fear.

She licked her lips nervously, a low flush of color rising to her cheeks. Crossing her arms in front of her, she searched for her composure.

"So you know who did it now," she said at last. One hand came down, and began to idly fidget with the various objects on his desk. She found it was easier not to look at him.

"Yes," Richard said curtly, taking another sip and willing the brandy to burn all consciousness away. It didn't work. The damn woman was too near, and he could feel it in every over-wound nerve ending in his body.

"Doesn't it help at all?" she inquired, feeling the restlessness gnaw at her stomach. She found herself chewing on her lower lip, seeking some respite from the relentless ache growing deep within her.

Richard simply shrugged, his face impassive.

"What about the money?" she pressed. "We never found the twenty thousand."

"I doubt Alycia brought it," he said curtly. "Her cash had already been drained by that point."

"What about what happened with Andy in the tower? He said he'd heard someone, but no one was home."

"Most likely Jillian didn't close the door all the way and he heard the draft banging it around."

"And the third nanny, Mrs. Louis?"

"Overactive imagination combined with dreary atmosphere," he said flatly. He looked at her a moment with hard blue eyes. "Alycia's dead, Liz. And I don't believe in ghosts. It's over."

She brought up her chin a notch, forcing herself to meet his gaze squarely. "Is it, Richard?" she challenged softly. "What about you and Blaine?"

"We had a discussion." Another sip. His hand was trembling slightly, and even as he swore at the weakness, he could not make it stop.

"A discussion?" She lifted a bronze paperweight and traced a long delicate finger around its smooth curves as if to disguise the intensity of her interest.

"We came to a basic understanding," he admitted with a growl. "We'll never be the best of friends, but I suppose we'll muddle through."

Liz nodded and found herself holding her breath. "And Andy?" she asked quietly.

"He's mine," Richard said flatly. "I don't care if he is or isn't my biological son. I don't even want to know. He's mine in name, and I'm going to raise him that way." He looked away for a minute, and when he spoke next, his voice was thick even to his own ears. "I want my son back."

Liz nodded, and felt her heart constrict in her chest. Her own eyes suddenly burned with suspicious moisture.

"I think you two are perfect together," she whispered. "He idolizes you, you know. Wait until he wakes up tomorrow and hears how you caught a killer."

Richard nodded, but it wasn't really Andy's opinion that weighed heavily on his mind.

"Would you really have confronted a murderer all alone?" she asked abruptly, still seeing him creep into the tower with a gun in hand.

"I've been taking care of myself a long time," he said simply. "And I took precautions."

Liz could only nod, but the statement didn't help. Unconsciously, her hands began rubbing her arms, trying to warm herself from the chill she felt inside. If Jillian had glanced over at the wrong moment and seen Richard, she would have shot him. Liz was sure of it.

Losing two loves in one lifetime would have been too much to bear.

Richard watched her from his corner with brooding eyes. Her back was still to him, but he could see her agitation by how she moved. And once more, he felt it sink bitterly into him.

Did she trust him that little? Did she really think he wouldn't have kept her and Andy safe? His jaw tightened, and his grip on his glass threatened to nearly break the fragile vessel. He came forward, slamming his glass down on the desk as he crossed to her. Brandy sloshed over the edges to splash on his hand, but he didn't notice, his dark attention focused only on her.

He forcefully turned her around.

"Look at me," he commanded harshly. "Look at me, Liz."

But she kept her head down, unable to meet his eyes even as her heart thundered in her chest.

"Is it that hard to believe in me?" he demanded to know, his blue eyes blazing fiercely. "Alycia wouldn't trust me with the truth, and you wouldn't trust me to be innocent. Hell, you didn't even trust me to keep you and Andy safe. Now, damn it,

I want to know. Why is it so hard to believe in me? Tell me, Liz. Tell me.''

Her head came up abruptly, and all at once he was struck by the tears coursing down her cheeks and the fire in her eyes.

"Trust you?" she cried out. "Of course I trust you. And I would have told you about the damn diary, but I wanted to read it first. And I don't think you aren't capable of keeping Andy and myself safe—for crying out loud, you saved my life twice! But did you ever stop to consider, you thick-headed, stubborn brute, that I might be worried about you? That I might care if you get hurt?"

The words took the wind right out of him. He opened his mouth to say anything, anything at all, but nothing came out. He could hear the blood roaring in his ears, the thundering pounding of his heart in his chest as his entire body stiffened at her words.

She cared. *She cared!*

Once again the emotions washed through him, past demons and present faint hopes warring inside the hollowness of his heart, each seeking dominance. Until once more his jaw tightened and his eyes ached as he searched for an anchor of sanity to cling to.

He didn't stop to think anymore. His mind was beyond the fierce logic that had dominated his entire life. Instead, he leaned down, and with hungry, desperate lips, he claimed her mouth with his own.

It was not soft or tender or sweet. It was the kiss of a drowning man overwhelmed by the conflicting passions warring in his soul. It didn't seek to give, but strove to take all the freshness and sanity she could bring him. And she succumbed to it willingly, opening her mouth to the onslaught, welcoming the plundering thrusts of his tongue. She could taste the brandy on his lips, mixing with the salt of her tears, and she welcomed it all.

Because she loved this man, and she knew no other kind of love than to give everything she had, heart, body and soul. If he needed her, then she would be there for him.

She had failed him once, but in these dark predawn hours, she would not fail him again.

She pressed against him, reveling in the solid heat of his chest, the burning rasp of his beard and the seductive fire of his muscular thigh pressing against her own.

Her robe was in the way, he wanted it gone, all the clothing gone until he could run his hands unrestrained down the lush warmth of her body. Her own hands were busy, tearing at his already loosened shirt, struggling with the buttons. But it was too slow for both of them. They wanted, needed flesh against flesh, heat against heat. With a muffled moan of impatience, he raised his head long enough to forcefully pull his shirt from his body, popping buttons as he went. Next, her robe was pushed to the floor and kicked aside, her T-shirt drawn over her head to follow, while her hands sought out the clasp of his slacks.

Piece after piece their clothing was thrown aside, until there were no barriers whatsoever. And she was so beautiful, his passion-crazed mind recognized. The low shadows of the fire flickered across every gentle indent and rounded curve of her body until she glowed like warm marble, open to his touch. He could feel her hands, running across his chest, tracing the muscular outline of his biceps and the low planes of his pectorals. Every touch left a trail of fire, and he kissed her hungrily to fan the flames.

His mouth was urgent and insistent and she answered with demands of her own, pressing tightly against him. She could feel the light tickling of his chest hair against her tender breasts, and her nipples hardened immediately. Her hands crept behind his neck as she arched into him, wanting him more than she'd ever wanted anything in her life. Every fiber of her being cried out to him. She wanted his touch, she wanted his taste. She wanted the wonderful feel of him sliding deep inside her and stoking the flames still higher.

She murmured impatiently, her hands dancing across his strong back while one leg came up to hook around his waist. The position brought them closer together, until she could feel the rigid heat of him pressed against her thigh. His hands came to her breasts, kneading them as his tongue dipped into her ear and brought goose bumps to her skin. Then his head came down, and almost lazily, he drew one nipple into his mouth.

She cried out at the impact, feeling the desire rip through her like a sharp knife. Her hands came down, finding him and reveling in the heavy, sculpted feel of his rigid length. She shifted again, bringing him closer to her own heat. He responded by rubbing his pelvis against hers, feeling the moistness of her impatience.

He had to grit his teeth to keep from throwing her down on the floor and taking her immediately, plunging into her deep and strong while the fires in them both exploded into infernos. He was a man of iron control, he would not lose it all now.

His jaw clenched, he ran one hand down across her hips and the gentle sloping of her stomach. Then he dipped it suddenly between her thighs, stroking her even as he took her muffled cries against his mouth, kissing her passionately as she trembled against him.

"Please," she breathed, her heavy eyes drooping shut from the wonderful feelings his touch evoked. "I want you, Richard. I want you now."

He didn't need any other encouragement. With the savage groan of a conqueror, he raised her and then, with slow, muscle-clenching control, eased her down onto his waiting shaft.

She sighed, a deep sound as he slowly penetrated her throbbing body. And then he was inside, fused with her body as he'd already fused with her heart. She opened her eyes, her midnight gaze black with desire.

"I love you, Richard," she whispered as she raised herself slightly to slide back down his burning length. "I love the feel of you inside me, the sound of your heartbeat against my ear, the taste of your lips on mine. I love your genius, I love your control. I love everything about you. And I trust you with my life."

He groaned, his eyes closing as her words ricocheted through him. Her soft Carolina voice wove its final spell and stole the last of his control. With a wrenching turn, he carried them to the ground and thrust into her with all the fierce passion of a recluse's heart. And with every fiery stroke, he showed her all the things he was too afraid to say.

She opened to him as she would always open to him, taking each pounding thrust even as she demanded more, wanting all of him and refusing to let him hold back. And then, with one last final thrust, he felt her arch and climax under him, heard his name wrenched from her lips even as he toppled over the edge with her, burying his head against her neck while shudder after shudder consumed him.

Neither of them spoke for the longest time. Finally, Richard propped himself on his elbows, trying to take some of his weight off her. She shifted slightly for more comfort, wincing.

His face was immediately alert.

"Did I hurt you?" he asked sharply, his whole body tensing.

"No, no," she assured him. "Just a bit of carpet burn, I'm afraid." She shifted again, sighing slightly, but her face still carried a warm smile. "I knew there was a reason they made beds," she teased huskily.

"I'm sorry," he said immediately, and she could already see him retreating inside himself. She raised her hand and pressed a finger against his warm lips.

"I wouldn't have had it any other way," she told him softly. "And I meant what I said, Richard. I love you."

"I want to believe you," he said suddenly, the words torn from him. "But I hate the thought of being so weak again. Perhaps now you think you love me, but what about tomorrow, Liz? What about the day after that?"

She looked at him, wishing she had the right words and knowing there were none. At long last, she could only shrug. "I would give you a guarantee," she said softly, "but in love there are none. I know I loved Nick with all my heart and soul. And I know we married and promised each other forever, and looked ahead to a beautiful future, growing old side by side. But one afternoon, forever became simply two years, and rather than grow old together, I held him in my arms as he died. But I wouldn't trade those two years for anything, Richard. That's love."

He laughed, a hollow sound. "You're right. That's a far cry from a guarantee."

She frowned, growing impatient and frustrated. Unexpectedly, she balled her hand into a fist and hit him squarely in the chest. "What do you want from me, Richard?" she demanded angrily. "I'm lying here naked by your side telling you that I love you and that I plan on loving you for the rest of my life. And you're looking for a money-back guarantee? For crying out loud, Richard, I'm not a set of knives!"

He smiled, a strangely bitter and wistful smile. "No," he said. "You're not."

She sighed, feeling the tears begin to prickle in her eyes once more. What had she been expecting? She knew who he was, what he was about. She'd given him her love, knowing there was a good chance it wouldn't be returned. He was a badly scarred man, with a right to keep his heart locked away. Yet, somehow, she'd expected her words to evoke some deeper response, to melt the ice he'd built around his heart.

And then they would live happily ever after, right?

The tears were coming thicker now, and she knew if she didn't leave, she would only embarrass herself further. As briskly as possible, she pulled herself to her feet.

"It's been a long night," she said, the words husky. "I should be going."

She wouldn't look at him as she found her robe and shrugged it on. She waited for him to say something, for him to do something—anything. But minute lapsed into minute without him moving, and the silence cut her to the quick.

She couldn't help it anymore. The tears were streaming down her face and all at once she felt pure anger mixed with pain. She wanted to love him, and she wanted to curse him for not having the courage to love her back.

Abruptly, she turned away, heading for the door as the sobs consumed her. And she knew deep inside that once she opened these doors, she wouldn't be returning. She needed someone who was willing to love her, and if he couldn't do that, then it would be emotional suicide for her to stay and live in the shadows of a futile dream.

She clutched the doorknob, and felt the tears stream down her face all the harder.

"Alycia never cried," Richard said from behind her. "In all the time I knew her, she never cried. Not in anger, and certainly not in pain. She was the one that hurt me, and I was never sure if I affected her at all."

"I don't understand," Liz said at last, the words water-logged.

She could feel him come up behind her, and then there was the soft touch of his hands upon her shoulders. Slowly, he turned her around to look at her with intent eyes.

"I've never had the power to hurt anyone before," he said softly. "I've never made anyone cry. And when I see you like this, it fills me with the most awful feeling, and all I know is that I don't want to make you cry again. I think I love you, Liz."

If he'd been expecting cries of joy, it wasn't what he received. Instead, she balled her hand into a fist and hit him once again, the tears flowing even faster.

"I don't want your damn pity," she cried out. "I don't want you to say silly words so I'll stop crying and you'll stop feeling guilty. I want you to love me, love *me*. As in be there for me forever. As in hold me close and let me inside you. As in let's grow old together and be seventy sitting in the library debating *Wuthering Heights*. That's what I want."

He smiled, and for the first time, she saw a softening of his eyes. "I think that's what I mean, sweetheart. All along, the only love I've known is one-sided. But now, for the first time, I realize that while there are no guarantees for me, there are none for you, either. And even as I protect myself, I hurt you. As so it's much more logical if we both just give in to the madness, and love each other, because that's certainly better than hurting each other. Does that make sense?"

She looked at him with suspicious eyes. "I think so," she mumbled, sniffling. He smiled again tenderly, and wiped the tears from her cheek with his callused thumb.

"Help me, Liz," he said softly. "Teach me all about love, and help me build a new life with you and Andy and Blaine and even Mrs. Pram. And I promise you I will make each day worthwhile, and we will grow old together and debate *Wuthering Heights* at seventy in the library."

"If Heathcliff had been this smart, *Wuthering Heights* would have had a less tragic ending," Liz managed to say, and then a smile began creeping around her mouth, too. "I love you, Richard."

"I love you, too, Liz."

"Want to debate classical literature?"

"Actually, I was more interested in that earlier theory you had regarding beds."

"Beds?"

"Yes, you seemed to imply that beds were more suitable for lovemaking than the floor."

She smiled fully, her midnight eyes clear and bright. "Then, of course, there's the matter of desks."

"And couches," he observed, taking her hand.

"What about fireplaces and beaches and kitchen counters?"

"Sweetheart, we'll just have to see."

* * * * *

COMING NEXT MONTH

is proud to present

Laura Parker's new miniseries featuring handsome rogues whose lives are shrouded in mystery and destined for love. Start in September with

TIGER IN THE RAIN

Long ago, Michaela Bellegarde had fled from Guy Matherson, a brooding tiger of a man who had tasted her passion, then turned away. Now Guy was on the run from a desperate enemy. One look into his mesmerizing eyes and Michaela knew there was nothing she could ever refuse him. But would passion be enough to save them this time around?

Rogues' Gallery: Three hard-hearted men with trouble in their pasts—and the women who dare to love them.

PRIZE SURPRISE SWEEPSTAKES!

This month's prize:

BEAUTIFUL WEDGWOOD CHINA!

This month, as a special surprise, we're giving away a bone china dinner service for eight by Wedgwood**, one of England's most prestigious manufacturers!

Think how beautiful your table will look, set with lovely Wedgwood china in the casual Countryware pattern! Each five-piece place setting includes dinner plate, salad plate, soup bowl and cup and saucer.

The facing page contains two Entry Coupons (as does every book you received this shipment). Complete and return *all* the entry coupons; **the more times you enter, the better your chances of winning!**

Then keep your fingers crossed, because you'll find out by September 15, 1995 if you're the winner!

Remember: The more times you enter, the better your chances of winning!*

PRIZE SURPRISE
SWEEPSTAKES
OFFICIAL ENTRY COUPON

This entry must be received by: AUGUST 30, 1995
This month's winner will be notified by: SEPTEMBER 15, 1995

YES, I want to win the Wedgwood china service for eight! Please enter me in the drawing and let me know if I've won!

Name_____

Address _____ Apt. _____

City   State/Prov.   Zip/Postal Code

Account #_____

Return entry with invoice in reply envelope.

© 1995 HARLEQUIN ENTERPRISES LTD.   CWW KAL

PRIZE SURPRISE
SWEEPSTAKES
OFFICIAL ENTRY COUPON

This entry must be received by: AUGUST 30, 1995
This month's winner will be notified by: SEPTEMBER 15, 1995

YES, I want to win the Wedgwood china service for eight! Please enter me in the drawing and let me know if I've won!

Name_____

Address _____ Apt. _____

City   State/Prov.   Zip/Postal Code

Account #_____

Return entry with invoice in reply envelope.

© 1995 HARLEQUIN ENTERPRISES LTD.   CWW KAL

OFFICIAL RULES
PRIZE SURPRISE SWEEPSTAKES 3448
NO PURCHASE OR OBLIGATION NECESSARY

Three Harlequin Reader Service 1995 shipments will contain respectively, coupons for entry into three different prize drawings, one for a Panasonic 31" wide-screen TV, another for a 5-piece Wedgwood china service for eight and the third for a Sharp ViewCam camcorder. To enter any drawing using an Entry Coupon, simply complete and mail according to directions.

There is no obligation to continue using the Reader Service to enter and be eligible for any prize drawing. You may also enter any drawing by hand printing the words "Prize Surprise," your name and address on a 3"x5" card and the name of the prize you wish that entry to be considered for (i.e., Panasonic wide-screen TV, Wedgwood china or Sharp ViewCam). Send your 3"x5" entries via first-class mail (limit: one per envelope) to: Prize Surprise Sweepstakes 3448, c/o the prize you wish that entry to be considered for, P.O. Box 1315, Buffalo, NY 14269-1315, USA or P.O. Box 610, Fort Erie, Ontario L2A 5X3, Canada.

To be eligible for the Panasonic wide-screen TV, entries must be received by 6/30/95; for the Wedgwood china, 8/30/95; and for the Sharp ViewCam, 10/30/95.

Winners will be determined in random drawings conducted under the supervision of D.L. Blair, Inc., an independent judging organization whose decisions are final, from among all eligible entries received for that drawing. Approximate prize values are as follows: Panasonic wide-screen TV ($1,800); Wedgwood china ($840) and Sharp ViewCam ($2,000). Sweepstakes open to residents of the U.S. (except Puerto Rico) and Canada, 18 years of age or older. Employees and immediate family members of Harlequin Enterprises, Ltd., D.L. Blair, Inc., their affiliates, subsidiaries and all other agencies, entities and persons connected with the use, marketing or conduct of this sweepstakes are not eligible. Odds of winning a prize are dependent upon the number of eligible entries received for that drawing. Prize drawing and winner notification for each drawing will occur no later than 15 days after deadline for entry eligibility for that drawing. Limit: one prize to an individual, family or organization. All applicable laws and regulations apply. Sweepstakes offer void wherever prohibited by law. Any litigation within the province of Quebec respecting the conduct and awarding of the prizes in this sweepstakes must be submitted to the Regies des loteries et Courses du Quebec. In order to win a prize, residents of Canada will be required to correctly answer a time-limited arithmetical skill-testing question. Value of prizes are in U.S. currency.

Winners will be obligated to sign and return an Affidavit of Eligibility within 30 days of notification. In the event of noncompliance within this time period, prize may not be awarded. If any prize or prize notification is returned as undeliverable, that prize will not be awarded. By acceptance of a prize, winner consents to use of his/her name, photograph or other likeness for purposes of advertising, trade and promotion on behalf of Harlequin Enterprises, Ltd., without further compensation, unless prohibited by law.

For the names of prizewinners (available after 12/31/95), send a self-addressed, stamped envelope to: Prize Surprise Sweepstakes 3448 Winners, P.O. Box 4200, Blair, NE 68009.

RPZ KAL